She'd do exactly what her ex-husband wanted. *Exactly.*

He wanted his record collection but he didn't want her on his property. Well, that wasn't too hard. She pulled out the first vintage 78, a bakelite version of "Stardust." Darren had paid a bundle for it at a flea market. Jill raised her arm and whirled the record through the air. It smashed on the porch.

"Oh, dear," she murmured.

Well, there were plenty more records.

She pulled one out of the trunk and looked at it. It reminded her of all those Saturdays helping Darren look for these treasures. Then she was his love. Now she was "crazy." Well, maybe they weren't such a perfect couple, after all.

The thought added velocity to her throw as the record joined its fellow.

Some of the neighbors opened their doors and looked out curiously before retreating into their homes. Jill didn't care. Maybe it was wrong to feel satisfaction at destroying things Darren had acquired with such pride, yet as she threw the last recording, she felt triumphant.

So why, as she drove away, headed for a new life, did she feel as shattered as the records?

ABOUT THE AUTHOR

Candice Adams makes a sparkling Superromance debut with the delightful story *Perfectly Matched.* "I wanted to set a book in my neighborhood about people who are not quite young anymore and are going through changes in their lives," says Candice. The former geologist and librarian has found her true calling in writing and now has thirty-two books to her credit. "I love to read and do research," she says. But that's not as easy as it sounds for a mother of two preschool-age children!

Candice lives in Charlotte, North Carolina, with her husband, Spencer, and children Jonathan and Christopher.

Candice Adams
Perfectly Matched

Harlequin Books

TORONTO • NEW YORK • LONDON
AMSTERDAM • PARIS • SYDNEY • HAMBURG
STOCKHOLM • ATHENS • TOKYO • MILAN
MADRID • WARSAW • BUDAPEST • AUCKLAND

ISBN 0-373-70616-2

PERFECTLY MATCHED

Perfectly Matched

CHAPTER ONE

JILL WAS NO LONGER GOLDEN. She was still tall and her shoulder-length dark curls still bounced, but everyone looked at her differently. She felt different, too—lost and a little scared.

The old Jill would never have rented the cramped apartment cobbled onto the side of someone's house. Would never have moved her carefully coordinated floral-and-striped bedspread and shams and table scarves from her perfect house in Simmerville, North Carolina, to big, unknown Charlotte. And she never would have adopted the stupid dog that had stood with his paws on the interstate, certain to get hit if someone didn't pick him up. The old Jill would have played it smart and waited for someone else to rescue him.

Kneeling on the hardwood floor, she ran a utility knife through the tape and opened the box of books she had packed three days earlier. The matching volumes had looked so pretty between the brass bookends in the walnut bookcase in their library. Now that room stood empty, closed and musty, waiting for someone else to move in; but in her heart, the library and the house still belonged to her. They represented the security she had sought since childhood and had finally found during her marriage.

Tears crowded at the backs of her eyes, and Jill lifted her face toward the ceiling, intent on staving off another torrent. She had cried enough for two people. She wasn't going to cry anymore.

The sound of banging on the screen door brought her up sharply. Uh-oh, she had left the door open after she'd carried the last box in. Had she locked the screen? She was in the city now, not in safe Simmerville, and heaven only knew what could happen here, even in broad daylight.

Utility knife in hand, she walked to the door.

"That your dog, lady?"

The man standing on her tiny wooden porch gestured behind him so recklessly he almost knocked her hanging geranium down. He was bare to the waist, and his jeans rode low on his hips to reveal a sleek, sun-kissed body. She had a quick impression of blue eyes, thick brown hair and an aura of sexuality.

Then she forced herself to be realistic. The man was a half-naked stranger!

"I don't have a dog." Jill started to shut the door. She was glad she had the knife. The man didn't exactly look threatening, but he possessed a whipcordlike body that would probably be quick and dangerous.

"Then why is that leash tied to your porch?" he demanded.

Jill swung the door back open and blinked guiltily at the nylon leash strung out like a giant snake across the porch. When she'd last seen the leash, a dog certainly had been attached to one end. A big, dumb, black dog with large paws and a yen for scratching his droopy ears.

"He's gone," Jill said.

Silent relief flooded her. Now she wouldn't have to find a home for the animal or feed it or bathe it or do all the other things that went with pet ownership. Right now, it was all she could do to take care of herself.

"No, he's not gone," the man countered. "The dog you don't have is over in my yard." He pointed again toward the backyard her apartment faced. "He dug up half my tomato plants and now he's chewing up a shirt he dragged off the line. My best shirt."

"Oh!" Jill's hand flew up to her mouth. Her ex-husband, Darren, had once found that endearing. But this man only looked at her with a level, waiting expression.

He had sculpted cheekbones and casually cut brown hair that nipped at the top of his shoulders. Brown eyebrows accented blue eyes. He was not classically handsome, but he was good-looking enough to rate a second look. Perhaps even a third.

"I'm so sorry, Mr. —" As Jill waited for him to supply his name, she tried not to notice the curly brown shield of hair on his chest. He had a flat stomach and a tan that extended as far as his jeans had slid.

"E.J. Robbins."

"I'm Jill Howard. I just moved in—"

"Yeah." He backed off the porch, his footing sure and his expression sour. "Look, lady, will you come get your dog before he does more damage?"

"Well, of course."

Only it wasn't really her dog, so she didn't know how to go about disengaging it from the white shirt once she reached her neighbor's backyard.

Fido stood on the deck and whipped the shirt over his head with a gleeful vengeance. Jill had felt that same kind of abandon when she'd smashed Darren's prized collection of 78-rpm records.

She stiffened at the memory and of all that had gone before it. Switching her attention firmly back to the present, she crouched on the deck and stretched out her hand.

"Here, doggy. Give me the shirt, doggy. Nice boy."

Fido didn't even glance at her, but sank his teeth more lustily into the shirt. She heard the sound of fabric ripping and a low, delighted growl.

"Here, doggy, doggy..." She felt foolish and inept and was glad the stranger had wandered away, even if he had given a long-suffering sigh before leaving.

E.J. was back a moment later, dragging a hose. He shot a stream of water over Fido, causing the dog to yelp and release the shirt. E.J. turned off the hose, left the yard and returned, carrying the leash.

Scooping up the shirt he muttered, "Great. This is going to look terrific on my date tonight."

He turned his attention back to the dog. Jill had been right to think her neighbor would be strong and fast. Even Fido howled in surprise at the speed with which he was captured and reattached to his leash.

E.J. tied the dog to the wooden railing that rimmed the deck and then, with legs planted apart and hands on hips, he surveyed the garden. "What a mess."

Jill looked reluctantly. Leafy green plants were strewn everywhere. Roots lay exposed to the sky and a brown patch of dirt marked a spot where Fido had dug with particular determination. At home, Jill had kept flower beds of delicate impatiens bordered by a neat row of bricks, so she knew how much work and pride went into a garden.

"I'm so sorry." She stopped, at a loss for further words. It seemed she had botched everything lately.

"Maybe some of the plants can be salvaged," he finally said.

"I'll be glad to help replant them."

"You darn sure will."

That took the wind out of her sails. When Jill looked at E.J., though, he was studying her with a kinder expression. Suddenly he smiled and she saw dimples dart inward and a spark of darker blue flash in his eyes. She wondered, with total irrelevance, if he and the woman he was seeing tonight were serious about each other.

"You don't look like you're used to being yelled at, Jill Howard," he said, slipping his hands casually into his pockets.

"Yelling makes me uncomfortable," she confessed. It always had. From the time she was a four-year-old princess in the Little Miss Blumford County contest, Jill had worked for approval and success. Failure and disapproval made her anxious. She had been anxious a lot, lately.

"I'm surprised Mrs. Casey let you have a dog," E.J. declared.

Jill studied the toes of her white tennis shoes. Mrs. Casey had sent a five-page letter of dos and don'ts along with the lease. *No loud parties*. As if Jill knew anyone to party with. *No working on cars in the yard*. That wasn't a rule she was likely to violate; she barely knew the engine from the trunk. *No animals*. Well, Fido hadn't been in her plans when she'd signed the lease. But life was full of surprises, as she had recently learned.

"Fido isn't really mine," Jill explained. "I picked him up off the side of the road on the way here. I'm going to find him a home as soon as possible." The pound, though practical, was out of the question. It didn't make sense to save the animal from becoming road kill only to have someone else kill him.

"You want the shovel or the hoe?" E.J. asked.

She blinked. "What?"

"We need to get started on the garden right away."

She intended to help, of course, but not now. "Fine. But first I have to unpack and get my apartment in some sort of order. I don't even have the bed made. The dishes need to be rinsed and put away. Everything has to be dusted." She ticked off the tasks on her fingers.

"Dusted, huh?" Head tilted to the side, he mulled that over. "Wait right here."

E.J. left and returned with a hoe. Wordlessly, he lifted her hand and wrapped her fingers one by one around the smooth wooden handle. "These plants will be dead before you're finished. They're already starting to wilt. We've got to get them back into the ground while they've still got some life in them."

"I guess I could unpack afterward," Jill said slowly. His hands felt warm and firm. She hadn't experienced a lot of touching or warmth lately, and she decided she must be starved for such things if a stranger's touch appealed to her so much.

"Atta girl." E.J. led her out into the garden.

Fido sighed happily and sat on the deck, thumping his tail. Jill set to work digging. She thought about changing out of her clean white shoes, but her gardening clogs were still packed away. So were her cotton gloves.

A little dirt under her nails wouldn't kill her, she reasoned. She owed it to E.J. to help replant the garden. Besides, it would do her good to be out of her apartment and away from the boxes and boxes of memories of her marriage. Away from that one particular box that was small and square and filled with such pain.

E.J.'s voice interrupted her thoughts. "Just save the plants whose main stem isn't broken. Throw the rest on the compost heap at the back of the yard. Keep the stakes."

"Okay." She angled a look at him and saw a man not much older than her. His muscles bunched and flexed with his movements. His back was tan and smooth, she noted, and his shoulders lifted and fell as he shoveled dirt. There was a rhythmic force in the motion that was vaguely suggestive of other things.

Jill forced her attention back to the work.

Her white tennis shoes were soon dirty and she felt little drops of sweat bead on her skin. The sun grew hotter as she worked silently beside E.J.

He was anything but silent. He talked to the plants and threw occasional comments at the dog. "That's right, Fido, boy. I see you over there smirking." He hummed a few bars of Elton John's "Secret Garden." He slung dirt and came over to inspect the hole Jill had dug and advised making it deeper.

He stood beside her as she patted a small tomato plant back into the earth. "Where'd you move here from, Jill Howard?"

"Simmerville. You can call me Jill," she added crisply, and glanced up to see amusement cartwheel through his eyes.

"I've heard of it. Is it a nice place?" he asked.

"Yes." The town sat on the North Carolina Piedmont between the serene Blue Ridge Mountains and the turbulent ocean at Cape Hatteras. "Very scenic and historic. Beautiful old houses." She had spent most of her childhood there in her grandmother's elegant Greek

Revival house. After her marriage, she and Darren had lived in an exquisite old Colonial on the main street. A For Sale sign now stood in its front yard. Something caught in her throat when she thought about that.

"So what brought you to Charlotte?"

She looked at him with quick suspicion but saw only honest curiosity. His was a harmless enough question. This man didn't know anything about mortifying scenes, stunned faces or impulsive acts. He didn't know about her desperation to escape from a town where people who had once viewed her as perfect now looked at her with shock and disapproval. He didn't know anything about her burning need to get back to those precious years with Darren when, for the only time in her life, she had felt secure.

"I'm going to finish my degree in education at Queens College," she said. She had also outlined a program of self-improvement so she could make the most of her time in Charlotte.

E.J. nodded. She noticed he had nice hair and lots of it. Darren was a hospital administrator and it was important that he look well-groomed. He used lots of mousse to style his hair. It always looked good, but it felt stiff. E.J.'s hair appeared thick and clean and un-disciplined. She thought it would feel soft to touch.

"What kind of work do you do?" Jill asked, as she glanced toward his two-story white clapboard house. Not a mansion, but it was respectable. Forest green shutters and a trellis with an overgrown white clematis outside the back door added to its turn-of-the-century ambience. It was the sort of house a family man might have, but E.J. had mentioned a date. He was divorced, probably. Just like her. She wondered if his divorce had been neat and amicable, or sloppy and painful like hers.

"I inspect houses. Government job," he replied.

"If you work for the government, you must have other white shirts," she said, daring to tease. Then, afraid he might think she wouldn't pay for the damage, she added, "I'll buy you a new shirt, of course, but I won't have it in time for tonight. You said you had a date."

Jill Howard, you are shamelessly fishing for information. And why? What could this man possibly mean to you?

"Kim won't mind if I wear a blue shirt even if it is a fancy banquet. She's cool."

Jill pictured Kim as blond and laughing and confident. Kim would wear a tight red dress and have the figure to do it justice. She probably had the courage to tell people to shove off if they took her parking space, and she would never let a divorce devastate her. But then, Kim probably hadn't known a childhood of abandonment.

Why did Jill care if E.J. was dating someone? She wasn't in the market for a man. In spite of everything that had happened, she still loved Darren and believed he loved her. His feelings might have gotten muddled during those dark, turbulent days when her world spun out of control, but she knew his fundamental feelings for her hadn't changed.

There was no question in her mind that she and Darren would get back together. She had told him she would be ready when he was. With Darren she had finally found the safety and stability she had missed all her life. She didn't want to live without that again.

"All done." E.J. flinched and rubbed his knee.

Jill thought he was being overdramatic for someone who had only worked in the garden a short time.

She followed him back to the deck and untied the leash. "I'll find something stronger to keep Fido on once I get back to the house. Maybe I've got a chain or something."

E.J. nodded. Then he took the hoe and she felt those warm, rough hands against her skin again. She liked the contact. God, she was becoming pathetic.

"I really am sorry about Fido tearing up your yard," Jill said as the dog strained to drag her homeward.

"It worked out okay. Most things do."

He walked away without saying goodbye or giving her a smile or anything she could hold on to while she spent the next few hours in her small apartment, unpacking reminders of her seven-year marriage. Even a pleasant word would have been some comfort.

Yet Jill knew it was illogical to resent E.J. for dismissing her so abruptly. Her dog had dug up his yard and ruined his shirt. It wasn't his job to make her feel better about herself. He had a date to go on and a life of his own to pursue.

Jill had a life to pursue, too, but it was back in Simmerville. She was going to focus on getting her degree and acquiring big-city polish so that she would have more to offer Darren. Then she was would return home more golden than before.

SATURDAY WAS A GOOD DAY. E.J. felt almost no pain in his knee. He appreciated the good days. His mother had taught him that. "Ernie Joe," she used to say, not caring that he invariably winced at the sound of that name, "things can always get worse."

Next week they *would* get worse, he feared.

E.J. spent the morning folding laundry while he watched television. After lunch, he went out to his shop behind the house and put his racing bike up on its clamp and checked the brakes and derailer. But thoughts of next week crept into his mind, and he felt dread all out of proportion to the operation he faced. Why was he making such a big deal out of this?

And why couldn't he shake his premonition that something bad was going to happen?

Because he was an idiot and he needed to find a distraction, he told himself.

He found it by looking out the kitchen window at the next-door neighbor he'd met two days ago.

Jill Howard was prissy and pretty and something about her made him smile. Right now, she was carefully planting red geraniums at precise intervals on the left side of her short walk to balance the row of geraniums on the right. White geraniums—two, no more, no less—stood just outside her front door. The whole effect was cute and compulsive and it made him want to go over there and scatter purple and blue flowers among the perfect rows just to watch her big green eyes cloud over.

She was wearing denim shorts and some kind of print top and gloves. *Gloves?* E.J. always dug with his bare hands, letting the moist earth cling to them.

Even with gloves, though, Jill looked good. Her dark brown hair was caught back in a girlish ponytail. Her legs were long and curvy and led up to a very nice backside. He watched that backside wiggle as she moved from left to right, digging with a hand spade.

He knew she wasn't his type. He suspected she wanted a BMW, Rolex kind of guy, and that sure wasn't him. Still, she was a distraction, and these days he needed something to keep his mind occupied.

Maybe he'd mosey over and borrow a cup of sugar....

Just as E.J. reached the side yard of Mrs. Casey's house, Jill looked up. He gave an easy grin. "Need any help?"

Her smile was reserved. "No. I'm doing fine."

"I see the dog is gone."

She wasn't what you'd call prickly, but she had a "Don't touch" aura about her. He didn't let that bother him, though. Maybe it just took her a while to warm up to people.

Jill pulled off cotton gloves dotted with little flowers. She switched the spade from one hand to the other. "Yes. He's at a kennel."

E.J. chuckled. "What about the new home you were going to find him?"

"The kennel is temporary," Jill informed him curtly, and bent to straighten a geranium that wasn't perfectly aligned with the one beside it. "I'm running an ad in the paper for a good home."

"It'll never happen." E.J. liked watching her. Liked the way her voice wavered a little when she was indignant. Liked those green eyes with the dark lashes.

"Why not?" she demanded.

"'Cause nobody wants a garden-wrecking, shirt-tearing, eat-you-out-of-house-and-home big dog."

Her lips formed a pout. It was a look that belonged on the cover of one of those women's magazines where they always had models with perfect cleavage and sultry, pursed lips. He was glad he'd come over; deviling her was better therapy than puttering around the house.

"Fido has spirit," Jill said defensively. "He just needs a home with a few acres and a nice owner. I *am* going to pay for your shirt," she reiterated.

"Why don't we go to the store and pick one out?" The suggestion had come from nowhere but he liked it.

It would get him away from the house and the ridiculous fears that had grown like kudzu since his visit to the doctor. Who knows, he and Jill might even end up in the sack.

E.J. glanced at her and revised that thought. He doubted Jill could ever be casual about sex or anything else in her life. There was a tenseness in the way she held herself. Sometimes a look of panic dashed across her face, but it was always gone before he could get a handle on what she feared.

"Go to the store now?" she repeated. "Together?"

"Well, it's a thought." He hooked his thumbs over his belt. "I'm left without a good shirt because your dog ruined it. Who knows when some woman might need an escort?" He and Kim were no longer lovers, but they maintained a companionable friendship, and he had other women friends. His only requirement was that they not try to turn him into a suit-and-tie man. He wouldn't do that to please any woman.

"Make me feel guilty," she muttered.

"I'm trying." He grinned and kept his gaze fixed on her, ignoring the fact she avoided looking at him. He made her uncomfortable, and suddenly he was sorry. He honestly wanted to get to know her better.

"Look, I'll be glad to write you a check," she said, "but it's not a good idea to go with you."

She looked at him then, and he got the full impact of her solemn green eyes. "I'm not in the market for any kind of romance."

"Who said anything about romance? I'm talking about cotton, wash-and-wear, long sleeved." Boy, was she skittish. He wondered about that. She'd be a challenge to any man, but he'd never been one for tallying conquests. He liked the curve of Jill's mouth when she smiled, though, and he considered that a good enough reason to ask a woman out.

She grinned grudgingly. "I think you're a con man, E.J. Robbins. I'll bet you've got a line for every occasion."

"I'm just trying to be friendly. After all, good neighbors are hard to come by."

Her smile turned sly. "How do you know I'll be a good neighbor? I might play my stereo too loud and turn my dog loose in your garden again."

"You won't."

"How do you know?"

"You're too conscientious. It's a nice trait as long as you know how to have fun, too."

"I know how to have fun," she objected.

"Great. No better place to do it than at the mall."

"You really are a con man." But she smiled and he thought she was weakening.

E.J. motioned toward his car. "Let's go."

She looked down at her outfit. "I can't go like this."

"Why not?"

"I'm a mess."

He didn't mind cooling his heels for thirty minutes. It was worth it to see her emerge from the house wearing a swirling white skirt and a matching blouse with little pearl beads on it. She wore black sandals and carried a black straw hat. She had let her dark hair fall loose, and it teased around her face and stroked her pink cheeks. E.J. had another thought about luring her into his bed.

She glanced at him uncertainly. "Is this okay? Am I overdressed?"

"You look fine. Come on."

They went in his blue sedan. He'd bought the used government vehicle last year, and for a good price. He didn't see the point in buying a new car just to prove he could. This one ran fine. All it needed was a new paint job.

He noticed Jill looked at the car a little uncertainly but she didn't say anything.

At the mall they wandered in and out of men's shops even though E.J. knew exactly where to go for the shirt he wanted. But Jill was enjoying herself. She stopped to look in dress-store windows and dragged him into the bookstore to see if they had a mystery she'd been trying to find. They stopped at an ice-cream shop and had chocolate milk shakes, and she deliberated at a shoe store over a pair of navy spectator pumps.

"Pumps?" E.J. questioned, as the shoe salesman explained this was their bestselling style. "Why are they called 'pumps'? And why spectator?"

Both Jill and the salesman looked at him pityingly. "They just are," Jill said, and the salesman nodded.

"Well, that certainly explains that."

Jill returned to her transaction and E.J. went back to watching her. She was nice to watch. Her smile came quickly and easily, and her movements were graceful. She had a waist worth putting your hands around and soft, round breasts. Now, *there* was something worth putting your hands around....

As they left the store with the shoes, he casually draped an arm around her. She tensed.

"Sorry." He let go and moved away. He didn't want to, though. The trip to the mall had been a good diversion. He'd felt a few catches in his knee, but he hadn't thought about the hospital and the upcoming operation or about his bad memories.

She took a long breath. "I—I just want to be friends."

"Fine. No big deal."

She stopped in front of a jewelry store and turned to him, her face set in intent lines. "I'm not some high school girl who doesn't know what she wants. My future is very certain. I'm going to get my degree and go back to Simmerville."

"Why?" he asked in simple puzzlement.

The question made her edgy. She ran her fingers around the brim of the hat she carried. "Because it's the right thing for me."

"Then, why did you leave in the first place?"

She turned to look at a display of sapphire rings. "It's complicated."

"I had a feeling it might be," he said dryly. "I'll bet there's a man in there somewhere."

"I really don't want to talk about it." Jill's gaze wandered to the wedding bands and she unconsciously rubbed at her left ring finger.

"Uh-huh." So that was it. She was probably just out of a failed marriage. She might be confused or scared or bitter or all three and a whole lot more. He'd seen plenty of women fresh from divorce and it was never a good place to be. He was in no position to be very supportive, because he had too much on his own mind.

Still, he searched for a way to offer some brief cheer. "I've got an idea. Let's go to the food court and start a food fight."

She smiled and moved away from the jewelry-store window. "I'll bet you were the bane of your teachers."

"All my teachers adored me," he assured her piously.

"Ha."

He was glad he'd nudged her away from thoughts of her marriage. He took advantage of the moment to argue with her over the best recent movies and to enjoy the luscious curve of her smile.

There was no harm in wondering what it would be like to kiss her and wondering if she would withdraw again if he turned on the old Robbins charm. But indulging in a fantasy was one thing and actually getting involved with this woman was quite another. Clearly, her agenda didn't include him.

CHAPTER TWO

On Sunday, Jill attended church. After the service, she went for coffee and doughnuts in the church hall.

Although the large room was crowded, Jill remained an outsider, on the fringes of the gathering. She thought about the last time she'd gone to church in Simmerville, and felt a pang. People she had known all her life had stared at her. Whispered. Avoided eye contact.

Jill's fingers curled more firmly around her plastic coffee cup as she remembered the feeling of no longer belonging in the community that had been her home most of her life.

That church service had been the day after a lunch that remained etched in her mind. With one bold stroke, Jill had left behind a lifetime of being the dutiful, all-American girl raised by a rich and proper grandmother. She had done the unthinkable, and the whole town was surely still talking about it. She cringed at the memory.

Jill looked up as a woman with short black hair and a friendly expression stopped in front of her.

"Hi. I'm Phyllis Bonner, pastor for youth services."

"Jill Howard."

"I don't believe I've seen you here before. Are you new in town?"

"Yes."

"You'll love Charlotte. There's so much to do. What kinds of things do you enjoy?" Phyllis asked in a friendly tone.

Jill had liked cuddling up to Darren in front of the television and entertaining his business associates with perfect dinner parties. She'd liked going to the country club for dinner, playing doubles tennis with Darren and waterskiing with him in the summer. But those were all things she used to do.

"I want to go to the theater and art galleries and do some of the cultural things that weren't available where I'm from."

"That'll be nice. Are you single?" Phyllis asked.

"I'm recently divorced." Jill heard her voice go lower with suppressed tension. It still hurt that her marriage had ended.

"I understand," the minister said gently. "Why don't you come to our One-of-a-Kind group? We meet every Tuesday night at seven."

Jill shook her head. "Thanks for inviting me, but I don't think so." She neither wanted nor needed a singles group.

"If you ever decide to come, we'd love to have you. You might find support there from other divorced women."

A child tugged at Phyllis's arm and the minister excused herself. Alone again, Jill realized the room was nearly empty.

She was turning to leave when she saw it. And stopped. Over by the door a young couple stood beside a pink stroller with white eyelet trim. Jill had bought a stroller exactly like it the day she'd found out she was pregnant. The joyful, perfect, rainy-but-she-didn't-care day when everything in her life was flawless.

Now she stood motionless and watched the new mother lift the baby out of the stroller. The infant had a fuzz of black hair and a rounded little body. Miniature fists stabbed the air.

Suddenly Jill couldn't bear the sight any longer. All she had ever wanted was a home, a loving husband and children; the child across the room was a tangible reminder of everything she'd lost.

She escaped out to her car like a miner fleeing a cave-in. There she fastened her seat belt and switched on the radio. She stared out through the windshield but didn't see the roses in full, pink bloom. Instead, she looked into a time of unendurable loss.

She had been the happiest woman alive on her wedding day. Darren was steady and sensible and caring. He had a wonderful job and he offered her the refuge she had dreamed of from the day her parents left her to live with her grandmother. Darren had made her feel loved and protected.

The miscarriage had devastated her.

Darren left a couple of months later. He hadn't understood how she could grieve so long over losing the baby. It hadn't even been a person, he'd pointed out. Working in a hospital, Darren knew of women all the time who lost babies. They didn't let their grief consume them. They got over it and went on with their lives. Yet Jill didn't.

At first she was angry with him for not understanding. Then she was angry with herself. How had she watched like a distant observer as her marriage crumbled? After her parents' divorce, Jill had vowed never to let her own marriage end that way. She'd been convinced that her and Darren's love for each other would hold them together.

But there had been little love in evidence that day in the restaurant Millie Sullivan had opened in the old Collins mansion. The elegant house with marble pillars and a side veranda overlooking a courtyard of pink roses had been just the place for Jill to wear her new teal green dress and pretend that she was coping beautifully with the divorce.

Betsy was already seated when Jill arrived. Betsy had plumped out since their cheerleading days, but she was still pretty. Today, though, she frowned as she sat next to a window hung with lace curtains.

Jill waved to the elderly women from the garden club who occupied a long table beside the fireplace. Several of the women looked at her curiously as she made her way across the room and sat down. Jill wondered about that.

"Hi, Betsy, sorry I'm la—"

"Let's go somewhere else to eat." Betsy reached for her purse.

"What are you talking about? We have reservations here."

"This isn't a good idea."

Jill followed the direction of Betsy's gaze. Darren sat alone at a corner table. The sight of him in his beige jacket and brown slacks tugged at her heart.

She started to rise.

Betsy pulled her back down. "Don't."

"I can't just sit here while he's over there all by himself. I have to speak to him." This could be the beginning of a reconciliation.

Betsy sighed. "Jill, he's not alone. His date got up to go to the rest room."

The thought of Darren with another woman seared her. Jill pressed her hand over her mouth, but quickly forced herself to lower her hand to the table. Then she deliberately unfurled the pearly napkin that matched the tablecloth. She could almost hear her grandmother admonishing her to "be civilized."

"Darren has a right to date," she declared.

The words nearly stuck in her throat, but she got them out and prided herself on sounding sophisticated and accepting.

Jill *knew* better than to look at him, yet her gaze sought the corner table with an insistence she couldn't control. She watched Sylvia, a petite blonde full of aerobics-fueled energy, rejoin Darren. Sylvia sat down and leaned closer. He leaned closer, too.

Jill looked away.

"For pity's sake," Betsy muttered. "Let's get out of here."

Maybe that was the best idea, after all. Jill knew if she didn't leave, she'd be reduced to tears in front of all these people.

While Jill fumbled for her purse, Darren approached. He clamped his hands over the edge of the table and bent close to her. Hope soared.

"What the hell is the meaning of this?" he asked in a rough whisper.

Jill stared. Why was he acting this way? She could only guess he felt awkward and guilty because he was with a woman.

"I don't know what you're talking about, Darren."

"Oh, come on. You were at the dry cleaners Monday when I was there and at the grocery store Tuesday. Now you *just happen* to show up at the same restaurant where I'm having lunch with a date?"

Betsy reached out to pat Jill's hand. At the same time, she looked up at him. "Darren, I really think—"

"I'm talking to Jill, Betsy." His gaze remained pinned on Jill. "It was bad enough that you obsessed over losing a kid, but I'm not going to let you obsess over me."

So that was it. Everything seemed to come back to the child she had miscarried and the different ways they had dealt with their grief. He thought she was going to cling to him.

Jill maintained her poise. "Darren, I was dropping off a dress at the cleaners and buying cookies at the grocery store."

"Right."

Betsy's hand tightened on Jill's. "You don't have to explain to him."

Darren's expression was cold but he kept his voice low. "I intend to date and have a life, and you need to get on with your own life, Jill. You can't keep mooning over me."

Jill pushed her chair back and got to her feet. Grandmother's lessons in decorum and her own sense of propriety were swallowed by her anger.

"I've heard enough." Her voice brought tinkling ice in the drinks of restaurant patrons to a standstill. It silenced the talk at the garden-club table and it froze waitresses in midstep.

Darren looked uneasily around. "Keep your voice down."

"Why?"

Jill lifted an eyebrow toward Sally Anderson and Agatha O'Brien and the whole group of garden-club dowagers. The women looked back with a mixture of horror and wonder. There wasn't much excitement in Simmerville, and they clearly thought they were on the verge of some fast-breaking action.

They were on the verge of something, Jill thought grimly. They were about to see a different side of her. The side of her that was fed up and not going to take it anymore.

"Don't you run into people you know at the grocery store, Sally?" Jill's question was too loud to be conversational.

"Well, yes, of course." Sally looked guiltily pleased at being included.

"Do you ever see your friends at the dry cleaners, Agatha?" Jill asked.

"Yes, I do," Agatha said.

The whole room hummed with anticipation. Darren stood his ground but a deep red flush worked its way up his face. The color wasn't very becoming.

Jill gave him a tight smile. "You see, Darren, this is a small town and you might run into anyone. Why, look what happened to me today. I came here expecting a pleasant lunch and I found you here."

"Jill, you're making a spectacle of yourself."

"Maybe I am, Darren, but I don't care." She'd lost her baby and her marriage and now her self-esteem faltered on the brink of oblivion. What more could be taken from her?

"Well, I do care." He pivoted and marched back toward his table. A white-faced Sylvia rose to leave.

Jill sat down, breathing heavily but feeling a rare sense of exhilaration. Her fingers trembled as she picked up the menu. "What's the soup du jour?"

"What a performance!" Betsy exclaimed. "Bravo."

"It was rather magnificent, wasn't it?" Jill said.

The high of that confrontation carried Jill through lunch, although she hadn't a clue what she ate, and it sustained her on the drive back to her house.

By the time she returned home, she felt less sure of herself. She should have kept her anger in check and suggested that she and Darren go outside to talk. He had never acted like that before and she should have realized the stress of the divorce had clouded his judgment.

She set her purse down in her living room and glanced at the red light blinking on the answering machine. The message was from Darren.

"You made fools of both of us today. I hope you're satisfied."

He'd called back. "I want my record collection over here now. Tonight. Got that? I only left the records there for storage because I thought you were a sane person."

The next message was also from him. "I want you to stop following me. If you step foot on my property, I'll get a restraining order against you. You're crazy."

Jill turned off the recorder and stood trembling with hurt and bitterness. What about their seven years of commitment and dreams? What about the months spent planning their wedding and looking for a fairy-tale house? Yet here was Darren, running full tilt at her with dagger drawn.

Didn't he know how much he was hurting her? Didn't he know it brought back all the pain she had experienced when her parents divorced and abandoned her? She felt the same shame and failure and hurt that had overwhelmed her as a child.

There was one way to shake herself out of this and that was by doing exactly what Darren had requested. Exactly.

He wanted his records but he didn't want her on his property. Well, she'd have to figure out a way to accommodate both of those requests.

Jill went upstairs to the spare bedroom and carried down the boxes he'd left there. The vintage 78-rpm records were heavy, and it took a while to drag all five boxes to the car. But Darren had lovingly collected the records over a period of years. He deserved to have them back. He certainly did.

It was dark by the time she reached his house and parked at the curb. No lights glimmered in the house he'd rented in the new subdivision. He was tired of old things, he had told her. At first she'd thought he meant their old house and antique furniture. Now she knew he meant her.

He must still be with his date. Maybe Jill would have another message from him when she returned home. Another message that would shred her pride and deepen the anguish.

Jill flung open the trunk and pulled out a Bakelite version of "Stardust." It was one of Hoagy Carmichael's early recordings of the song, and Darren had paid a bundle for it at a flea market in Wilmington. Jill raised her arm and whirled the disc through the air. It smashed on the porch floor.

"Oh, dear," she murmured.

Well, there were plenty more records.

She picked up another and thought of Darren cranking his antique record player, then sitting down beside her to listen to the scratchy old ragtime tune. Back then, he had kissed her. Now he threatened to get a restraining order against her.

She hurled the record and listened to it shatter on the wooden porch floor. Pieces splintered and ricocheted, filling the night air with clinking noises that silenced the crickets.

The next record was one she didn't remember. Still, it reminded her of all those Saturdays spent scouring yard sales and flea markets, helping Darren look for treasures. Back then she was his love. Now she was crazy.

The pain of his words added velocity to her throw as the disc joined its fellows on the porch floor.

Some of the neighbors opened their doors and looked out curiously. Then they closed them and retreated. Curtains flicked back and Jill thought she saw lights go out as if people were hovering in the dark to get a better view.

She didn't care. The words from the answering machine played over and over in her mind.

Maybe it was wrong to feel satisfaction at destroying things Darren had acquired with such pride and pleasure. Yet, when she threw the last recording, she felt triumphant.

So, why, as she drove away, did she feel as shattered as the records?

THE CHURCH PARKING LOT was empty by the time Jill's thoughts returned to the present. Moving woodenly, like a toy with an aging battery, she put the key in the ignition and started back to the apartment.

The divorce had been ugly, but the years before had been wonderful. She and Darren had had a fulfilling, loving relationship and she missed that. She ached to have things back the way they had once been.

Days after the scene in the restaurant, Darren had called her to discuss work that needed to be done on the house to sell it. They had ended up talking—emotionally at first, but gradually more calmly—about the restaurant scene. He'd said he could strangle her for breaking his records but admitted he'd provoked her. And he apologized.

That was one of the nice things about Darren. He could admit it when he was wrong.

But he was in Simmerville and she was in Charlotte, and it was surely the greatest wrong of all that they weren't together. She had told him so in the letter she'd written. She had also said that in spite of everything, she wanted to work things out.

Jill was almost home when she realized she couldn't bear to go back to her empty apartment.

She turned the car around and found her way along the city streets to a funky area lined with old stores that had been converted into art galleries. She had planned to go to galleries and museums. Why not start today?

Jill parked on an empty side street and walked around the corner to the Center of the Earth gallery. It was closed. Two doors down she found a gallery whose door stood open. Now that she was actually here, she felt foolish.

Would they expect her to buy something? She didn't know enough about art to make a purchase. She wouldn't have the money, anyway, until the house sold. She was living on the savings she and Darren had divided.

Maybe she should just go back to her rented place—it wasn't home and she couldn't think of it as that—and put scented paper in the drawers and arrange her toiletries in the wicker cabinet in the bathroom.

"Come on in," a voice called.

Jill stepped inside and found herself facing a tall, bone-thin young woman with a waif's face and a shock of unnaturally black hair. A row of earrings marched up the lobe of her left ear. She wore a black sleeveless top, black skirt over black lace tights, and red patent-leather shoes. She didn't look more than twenty years old, but the red lipstick, heavy eye makeup and chalk white powder made it hard to be certain.

"Hi," the woman said. "We just got some new things in. Look around."

"Thanks." Jill slipped her purse up onto her shoulder. She'd felt fresh and pretty when she left for church this morning. The ivory suit matched her ivory heels perfectly. Next to this woman, though, Jill felt dowdy. She began to circle the room, looking at the pictures and stopping occasionally to glance at a price tag.

The pictures weren't the Turner-style pastorals or even the angular abstracts Jill had expected. One whole wall was devoted to big, jagged pieces of wood with metal rivets and protruding iron spikes. Dashes of bold red or blue paint had been applied at odd angles. She would never have anything like this on her walls. Not even in the tiny apartment she had rented sight unseen in her haste to get out of Simmerville.

The woman came up behind her. "Pretty weird, huh?"

"Well, it's not my style."

"We don't sell much of it." The young woman glanced toward the door, then lowered her voice. "I added a little extra paint to some of them to help jazz them up 'cause they were pretty, you know, like, grim."

"You're the artist?"

"Me! Are you kidding? I just watch the shop a couple of days a week. I don't know nothing about art except that all of this looks like crap to me."

"You're quite a saleswoman."

"Hey, I call it like I see it."

There wasn't anything wrong with that, Jill supposed. She'd never been very good at bluntness. She had learned to sugarcoat things from a grandmother who explained year after year that her parents loved her but this wasn't a good time for her to live with either of them. New jobs. New husbands. New wives. New cities. It was all so complicated. In the meantime, they wanted her to be a good girl and study hard.

Jill looked around the gallery a little while just to be polite, and then started for the door.

The woman followed her. "You going down Central Avenue?"

"I take Central a short way, yes."

"Great. Mind giving me a ride?"

"Well, I—"

"The bus doesn't run for another half hour." The woman picked up a key hanging on the wall. "It's not closing time but nobody else is going to come in. Only losers wander around art galleries on Sundays."

"Oh."

The woman colored beneath the white powder and laughed. "I didn't mean anything by that. I'm sure you just had a little extra time. I mean, nobody makes a special trip to a gallery." She gave a big, red-lipped smile. "My name's Xandralene. Actually, it's Kathy, but I'm getting it legally changed."

"I see."

"I'd appreciate a ride."

Jill hesitated. Well, she did want to meet people. This girl wasn't exactly what she had in mind, but maybe it was time she broadened her horizons a little. "Sure. My car's around the corner."

They walked together to Jill's white sedan, Xandralene chatting the whole time. She talked about the "gallery crawl," when the really "happening" people came out one Friday night a month to go gallery hopping. She talked about her plans to become a holistic healer. And she talked about the tattoo she was going to get at a tattoo parlor on Central Avenue.

"You think an alligator would look good?" Xandralene asked as she threw a monster-size purse into the back seat.

Jill pulled out into the sparse traffic and headed toward the light. "You're kidding?"

"No. I think there's something sexual about an alligator. On my butt. Men look, you know."

No, Jill wouldn't know. The only man she'd ever been with was Darren. That had been in the privacy of their bedroom, usually with the lights out and the covers shielding them. Twice a week. When had it fallen into such a predictable pattern? She had read articles in *Cosmo* and other magazines about ways to initiate new intimacies. "Ten Tips that Will Have Him Begging" and "Hot Sex for Cool Nights" had sounded promising, but Jill had found it awkward to follow through. Some of those positions sounded complicated. Interesting, though.

From out of nowhere the thought hit her that E.J. had the look of a man who might have had more experience with women. Last night, just before slipping off to sleep, Jill had thought about the hard slab of his bare chest and about those jeans riding jauntily on his hips. Something told her he would step out of the jeans without any false modesty. She thought, too, that he'd laugh a little during lovemaking and perhaps suggest some new, dangerously thrilling things.

"You ever think about getting a tattoo?" Xandra-lene asked.

The question yanked Jill back to sanity. "Good heavens, no."

"Turn here."

Jill turned, then cast a curious look at the thin black-haired woman. "Are you from Charlotte?"

"No. I'm from a hick town. I had to get away 'cause it was, like, wearing me down. Too dull." She picked at a mole on her chin.

"I'm from a small town, too, but I intend to go back," Jill said.

"Well, I suppose you can." Xandralene fished in the pocket of her skirt and came up with a piece of chewing gum. "You look real ordinary and like you'd fit right in. I didn't fit in."

Jill could see how *that* was possible. Yet something about the words struck a chord. Xandralene didn't sound wistful, exactly; just resigned to the fact she was no longer small-town material. Things would change for Jill, but right now she didn't fit in at Simmerville, either. She had created high drama in a town where people weren't likely to forget anytime soon.

Once some time had passed, though, everyone would look back more kindly because they'd realize that hadn't really been Jill at all. Just like it hadn't really been Darren who was so cold toward her. Her Darren—the real Darren—was a sweetie who might complain about overwork but who really loved to cuddle and spend time with his wife after all the long work-days and occasional weekends on the job.

"Turn right at the next light," her companion said.

"How long have you been in Charlotte?" Jill asked.

"Three years. I left the day I turned eighteen."

"I'm thirty-two," Jill confided. Thirty-two and she'd never had a tattoo. Thirty-two and she'd never had a man look at her naked and smile a slow, sensual smile that made her weak and tingly with anticipation.

"So you married?" Xandralene asked.

"No."

"You got a boyfriend?"

"No."

"Stop here."

Jill pulled into a parking lot and was suddenly reluctant to see the other woman go. "No boyfriend," she repeated.

"I wouldn't worry 'cause you're, like, pretty and everything. Even older women like you find men." She smiled and Jill saw the kindhearted girl behind the harsh makeup. "Come to the gallery crawl this Friday night and I'll introduce you to some guys."

"I'm not looking for men," Jill said. For one impulsive moment, though, she thought about a tumultuous, fevered affair with a dark, handsome man who spoke with just a hint of an accent and swept her into a frenzy of passion.

"I'll introduce you to some women, then." Xandralene grinned and jumped out of the car. She blew her bangs out of her eyes as she leaned into the back seat to retrieve her bag. "Thanks for the lift."

She was gone then, and Jill headed back to her apartment. She shouldn't have given a ride to a complete stranger, she admonished herself, simply because she felt obliged to do so. Mostly, though, she thought about what a pleasant experience it had been to talk to someone, even someone a little off center. Xandralene wasn't the type to be invited to Jill's grandmother's parties, but maybe it was time Jill expanded her personal envelope a bit. After all, she could hardly acquire sophistication and worldliness if she stayed with the same kind of people she'd known in Simmerville.

As she pulled into her driveway, she wondered if Xandralene would opt for an alligator.

Then she braked to a stop and saw Fido tied to her porch. Groaning, she got out and started toward him. The dog was on a chain now, but he had wrapped it around and around the porch pillar until he only had a foot of play left. She stood in silence, looking down at the big black mutt.

"Why did I bring you home from the kennel?" she finally asked, as she bent and offered Fido a hand to sniff.

"Because you're a softie."

The male voice had come from behind her, but Jill continued to gaze into the dog's clear brown eyes. "Ah, so you can talk. I knew you were special. You're going to make me a lot of money, and I won't have to work or worry about anyone's chewed-up garden."

"Ha. I'm going to eat myself silly and look to you to pay the bills," the voice said.

Jill turned then, and saw E.J. Straightening, she raised her eyebrows in feigned surprise. "Oh, was that you talking?"

"The dog said the part about eating himself silly." He wore a madras shirt and white duck trousers. His feet were bare, though. The man seemed to always have some part of his anatomy unfettered by clothing. His hair was a little damp, as if he was not long out of the shower. Wet mahogany brown tendrils lay close to his head, and even his eyebrows looked tamed by the water.

He grinned and moved a step closer. "I'm here to run interference for you because Mrs. Casey has been throwing a fit about our canine friend."

Jill looked guiltily down at the ground. "I was going to tell her about the dog after church." She couldn't afford the kennel indefinitely and she'd thought having the dog back would give her the incentive to be more aggressive about finding him a home.

She looked back up at E.J. "I can handle Mrs. Casey."

"Oh, yeah?" Grinning, he slouched on one hip. He looked amused and like he shortly expected to be even more amused. "I'd like to see your technique. Me, I always take her out for a beer when she gets this mad."

Of course, he was pulling her leg. Elderly women like Mrs. Casey didn't go to beer joints. Before Jill could say anything, though, the landlady marched around the side of the house. Her gray hair shook along with the rest of her pudgy frame as she headed toward them. Jill realized E.J. had been right about Mrs. Casey's anger.

"There you are, young lady." The older woman pointed an accusatory finger as she plunged toward them, her seersucker housecoat flapping around her knees. "How dare you bring a dog here! I sent you the rules. *No pets.* Now here you are with a dog chained to my porch. I'll not have it! Do you hear me?"

"Mrs. Casey, I'm not keeping him," Jill said meekly.

"Boy, you really get tough," E.J. murmured.

Jill shot him a dark look.

"Then would you mind telling me what that horse is doing in my yard?" Both of Mrs. Casey's chins quivered with indignation.

"I'm going to find him a home. I'm placing another ad first thing in the morning." Jill nodded to back up the claim and pushed aside the vision of Fido staring mournfully back at her as someone else drove him away.

"Well . . ." Mrs. Casey subsided and looked toward E.J.

He sent her a melting smile. "You're doing something different with your hair, aren't you, Grace?"

She patted her loose curls. "It's a new rinse. Gray Goddess."

E.J.'s smile softened. "You don't need a rinse to make you look like a goddess, Grace." He put his arm around her shoulder and squeezed her with affection.

As Jill watched, she wondered if she had been too quick to object to E.J.'s hand on her shoulder at the mall. Maybe it was part of his character to touch without expecting something in return.

"Oh, you." Mrs. Casey swatted him playfully, then touched her hair again. "At my age, I need all the help I can get."

E.J. turned to Jill, including her as he said, "Don't let Mrs. C. kid you. She took up ballroom dancing last year and now she's out every Saturday evening dancing the night away."

"Is that right?" Jill was glad for the momentary reprieve, even if E.J. had engineered it.

"Well, I am rather good at the tango." Grace Casey gave a pleased, self-deprecating shrug that made the seersucker housedress shimmy.

Fido barked.

"Your dog's got a great sense of timing," E.J. observed dryly.

Mrs. Casey glanced at Fido and sighed. "I'm not trying to be mean, but I simply cannot allow animals."

"Of course," Jill said.

"Fido was just coming over to my house for the night," E.J. explained, unfastening the chain.

"I *am* going to find him a home," Jill averred with less insistence than she intended.

The look E.J. shot Jill said he knew she would keep stalling and looking for excuses. It said she didn't fool him one bit. Jill shifted uneasily at the idea of him being able to read her and to communicate without words. It suggested a level of understanding between them that she didn't want.

As Mrs. Casey turned to leave, E.J. said, "We haven't been for a beer in awhile, Grace. We'll have to do that soon."

"I'd love to," the older woman said. "Your turn to buy." She disappeared around the side of the house.

It annoyed Jill that he was right about Mrs. Casey. But it was nice of him to take the dog into his yard. He was also easy to look at. Jill liked his thick hair, the blue lakes of his eyes, his trim physique. He was tanned to a butterscotch glow, probably from working in his garden.

She'd watched him out there the other day—well, she'd been standing at the sink anyway, washing her dishes—and he had spent a lot of time digging and weeding. As he bent and lifted and turned and twisted his taut body, she'd felt a ripple of pleasure like the one she got when she watched a sexy movie. She had stood at the window a long time—after all, one couldn't get dishes clean unless one washed them thoroughly—and she'd wondered again about him and Kim, or him and any other woman. What would it be like to indulge in kisses or lingering caresses with E.J.?

His grin turned devilish. "I know what you're thinking."

Embarrassment stabbed her. Was she that transparent? Fast on the heels of that question came irritation for allowing herself such cheap thrills. She had no business indulging in such fantasies when she didn't intend to get involved with this man or any other.

She turned the statement back on him. "What am I thinking?"

"You're wondering how to repay me for pulling your cookies out of the fire with Fido. I'll tell you how—"

"If you expect me to feel grateful because you interfered, I don't. I would have taken care of things."

Jill prided herself on being good at handling people. She had cheered friends when they were down and pacified Darren when his work overwhelmed him. And she had done it in a calm, quiet style that everyone said was so like her grandmother.

"Aha. You interrupted me, Jill. To show your gratitude, I'm going to let you take me out for an ice-cream cone. Chocolate in a sugar cone."

Fido had strained to the very end of his chain and managed to reach the massive trunk of the oak tree in the yard. Then he lifted a leg. Jill looked back at E.J.

She was annoyed, and it had nothing to do with the dog or E.J. or Mrs. Casey. It had to do with being out of control and the desire to have her life back the way it had once been. It had to do with being thrust into unknown territory and invited to singles events when she really wasn't single at all. It had to do with missing the safety she had felt in her marriage.

She wanted her life back. She wanted people to look at her with the old admiration. She wanted to push back the universe to the time before she lost the baby and Darren left. And she wanted to spin the universe forward to the time when she and Darren would be together again.

"I'm afraid you'll have to get your own ice-cream cone," she said crisply. "I have things I need to do in the house."

"Still fighting the dust?" he asked with an expression of exaggerated concern.

She leveled a look at him. "You don't give up, do you?"

"Well, you said I have a line for every occasion and I want to live up to that."

Jill sniffed. Fido tramped back, panting up at them as if he'd just run a marathon.

"Some women actually like me." E.J.'s smile gave emphasis to his twin dimples.

"I'm sure you have a raft of friends." She meant to sound tart but somehow he undermined her reserve by including her in his invitation to laugh with him at the world.

Fido licked at E.J.'s big toe and E.J. jumped back in surprise.

"Thanks a lot, fella. How would you like it if I licked your toes?"

Fido cocked his head as if considering the question.

Jill considered it, too. Hadn't that been one of the ten tips? Starting at the toes and working upward to the first interesting junction?

"Something wrong?" E.J. asked.

Jill started. "No, why?"

"You looked kind of strange."

"Nothing's wrong. Thanks for taking Fido."

"I think we've been dismissed, boy," E.J. confided to the dog.

Jill smiled in spite of herself. It was hard not to be swayed by someone who conversed with dogs. But she wasn't going to buy E.J. ice cream. And she did have things to do. Still, she wished her last vision before she turned and went up her steps hadn't been E.J.'s bare, tongue-wet toes.

CHAPTER THREE

LATE FRIDAY MORNING, E.J. pulled himself out from the crawl space of a ramshackle rental house and marked several items on his clipboard. Even though the place was falling apart, he suspected the elderly tenant was paying good rent. He went in through the back door and nodded to Isaac Walter, who rose from behind a battered kitchen table.

"Mind if I go up into the attic, sir?"

"No. The openin' is through the closet. Ye may have to set a few things outer the way to get up there."

E.J. suspected the old man's rural Southern cadence had survived decades of city life.

The tenant was right about the closet. E.J. ended up lugging a dozen boxes aside and shoving clothes to the end of the rod in order to clear a space to climb up. He braced himself for the moment of heaving himself up into the opening and putting weight on his right knee. He landed in the attic and felt the familiar pain reverberate through his leg. The doctor had explained the situation in complicated medical terms, but it all boiled down to a bum knee. E.J. couldn't let his problems get in the way of doing his job.

He looked around the attic. As he'd suspected, there was no insulation. The electrical wiring was clearly overloaded. The house didn't even meet minimum code requirements and was a damn fire hazard. E.J. thought of the old man living below and scowled to himself.

He intended to see that this mess got fixed. He didn't care if he had to oversee repairs from his hospital bed. Lazy landlords bothered him. When children or old people were involved, they bothered him twice as much.

E.J. finished his inspection of the attic and made his way back to the opening. He looked down and saw Isaac waiting below.

"You must get cold in the winter," E.J. said.

"Yep. I have ter run my stove all the time and keep the oven door open for heat."

E.J. dropped to the floor and froze as a wave of pain shot through him. The pain was usually just steady enough to remind him not to do stupid things like jumping out of attics and putting too much weight on his bad knee. Sometimes, though, he forgot.

"Somethin' wrong?" Isaac asked.

"No, I'm fine." E.J. bit his lip and finished filling out the form. After assuring Isaac that someone would fix the many problems, he left.

He sat in his car a moment and waited for the pain to subside to a dull burn. When it did, he started the engine and drove through the neighborhood of sagging bungalows. This had been an up-and-coming area when he was a kid. Now it was sliding recklessly downhill. The house on the corner with the rickety porch and the fancy car out front was probably a drug house. The rest of the buildings were in various stages of disrepair. Here and there, efforts had been made to achieve brightness with red flowers and bright blue shutters. Mostly, though, the houses had peeling paint and looked generally unkempt.

It was hardly a neighborhood in which to raise children. That was one of the reasons E.J. took his job so seriously. He wanted people to have decent places to live. He wanted little kids to grow up in houses that were safe. Better housing meant better neighborhoods.

E.J. turned on the radio and let his thoughts drift with the oldies music as he headed toward the interstate where he was to meet Charlie for lunch.

E.J. and Charlie had gone to grade school together. The two later attended rival high schools where they competed against each other in track. Disagreement lingered over who had *really* won that photo finish in their senior year.

Charlie was waiting inside the restaurant when E.J. arrived. His hairline had receded and his stomach appeared to be entering its sixth month of pregnancy. When pretty women walked by, Charlie made a point of sucking it in to the four-month size.

"Hey, fella," E.J. said.

By way of greeting, Charlie swept a hand around at the hanging ferns and new brass trim and maroon wallpaper. "What the hell has happened to this place? Where are the Formica tables and the chairs that didn't set level?"

"Progress," E.J. informed him.

"Humph."

They were seated at a small table near the back and given menus with maroon covers.

"Wife's got me on a diet." Charlie patted his gut. "Says I'm fat. I tell her they're love handles." He raked a look over E.J. "How come you stay so skinny, Robbins?"

He shrugged. "My job keeps me in shape. I jog. And bicycle, of course." E.J. regretted that he'd have to be off his bike until the thing with his knee was over.

"That long bike trip you've been talking about is coming up, isn't it?" Charlie raised his hand to flag a waitress. She darted by without seeing him.

E.J. shook his head regretfully. "That's on hold for right now. I've got to have an operation on my knee."

"What's that about?"

E.J. closed the menu. "The doctor says it might be an old track injury. I figure it's from that time you stuck your foot out and tripped me when I was about to break the school record for the hundred meter."

"In your dreams, bubba. You landed flat on your ass when you fell over your own big feet." Charlie turned suddenly sober. "This isn't anything serious, is it? I mean, I figure it's some little surgery so you can run faster when you chase chicks."

E.J. smirked. "They chase me."

"So you say, but you're still single," Charlie said dryly. He looked around. "What's a guy got to do to get a bite to eat around here?"

"They're busy, Charlie. They'll get to us."

A waitress finally appeared, took their orders without writing anything down, and dashed off.

"Fat chance she'll remember," Charlie grumbled.

They talked about sports and their jobs until the waitress returned with their meals.

"Did you remember my fries?" Charlie demanded. "Oh, there they are. What about the coleslaw? Got it, too. Well, good."

She left.

E.J. chuckled. "You sound disappointed that she got the order right." He was glad for Charlie's idiosyncrasies and glad for a chance to laugh at something. The last few nights, he'd lain awake with a gnawing sense of foreboding. And with those bad memories. He remembered the bleeps of the machines and the soft noises of nurses' shoes. He remembered Lisa's face. He shut the memory out.

Buttered roll aloft in his hand, Charlie asked, "How's the woman situation?"

"I'm not dating anyone," E.J. said.

"Why not? Good-looking stud like you ought to be beating them off with a stick."

E.J. winked at Charlie. "I think you're cute, too."

Charlie glared and muttered.

"You don't need to worry that I'm lonely," E.J. continued. "I have a lot of women friends. When an interesting woman happens along, I'll ask her out."

Charlie waved the roll more vigorously. "Who wants 'interesting'? Find somebody sweet and pretty who agrees with everything you say."

E.J. laughed. "Is that what your wife does?"

"Lord, no. That's why I'm trying to steer you right." Charlie attempted to flag the waitress for the bill but she kept going.

"In that case, my new neighbor sounds just like the person you have in mind," E.J. said. "She's a small-town honey." Had he been waiting for an opportunity to bring Jill into the conversation? He had certainly noticed her a lot lately, coming and going from her house and walking Fido.

"Pretty?" Charlie asked with a lift of his eyebrows.

"Yeah. Dark hair and a big smile. You don't see the smile too often, but the eyes are nice. Green." Real green, like a football field or a garden at summer's end. It would be a great color to paint his bicycle. Jill's body was nice, too. She wasn't so fragile a guy had to worry about cracking a rib if he gave her a good hug, but she was certainly feminine.

"Yo, E.J. You drifted away from me. Thinking about the little honey?"

E.J. laughed. "There's nothing there. She's not my type."

"What's your type?"

"Someone spontaneous who'll drop everything and go hiking. Someone not too concerned with appearance and what people think. Anyway, I'm not looking for a woman while I'm facing surgery."

Charlie thumbed through a handful of change, trying to decide on the tip. "You don't have to put your life on hold, bubba. You're just going in for a simple operation."

"I know." That unreasonable doubt surfaced again. Lightning didn't strike twice, E.J. told himself.

"Want my advice?" Charlie didn't wait for an affirmative. "You need a woman to take your mind off this thing. Ask the lady next door out, buy her a cheap dinner and take her home and neck with her in front of the TV."

E.J. rose and laid a tip on the table. "I'll mention your suggestion to Jill and see what she says."

He had already thought about "necking" with Jill, but had quickly resolved it would never happen. He'd been single long enough to be good at getting the lay of the land. Jill Howard wasn't going to be laying on *his* land. She'd pick a doctor or lawyer or some other "successful," uptight guy.

"What are your plans for the weekend?" Charlie asked, as they paid their checks.

"Go home and eat nacho chips and get stupid in front of the television," E.J. said. And rest his sore knee.

"Have fun."

Yet that evening when E.J. got out of his car, he saw Jill sitting on her porch stoop. The wind caught at her hair. She sat with her elbow on her knee and her chin on the back of her hand. She looked like a woman whose dog had just died. Well, in her case, that would probably cheer her up, he amended with heartless humor at Fido's expense.

Her gauzy beige dress reminded him of curtains his aunt used to have. Soft, fluttery curtains that blew in the breeze.

Television forgotten, he approached her. "Going out?" he asked in a friendly tone.

She sighed. "I'm not sure."

"Oh?" Did that mean someone had stood her up? It wasn't his business, but he hung around looking curious and waiting to see what she'd say.

"Somebody mentioned that the art galleries stay open late tonight."

"Oh, yeah, the gallery crawl."

"I'd love to go, but—" Jill lifted a braceleted wrist and let it fall back to her side in a jingle of silver charms. "The truth is, I want to go but I don't like being out alone after dark in the city."

"I don't have any plans." He wouldn't get to rest his leg, but he could take a couple of pain pills. "I could go with you."

He saw uncertainty war with longing on her face. "Would you mind?" she asked tentatively.

"No."

She broke into a smile. The smile pushed her cheeks up into soft pink circles beneath the green-on-green eyes. Her smile radiated straight across to him and zapped him.

Knee. What knee? he wondered.

Her perfume smelled like the air after a good rain—fresh and sweet. He moved a step closer and inhaled deeper.

Jill was on her feet in a swirl of beige lace. They'd always fascinated him as a child—those lacy, touch-me-not curtains.

The prospect of a night out with Jill put E.J. in a good mood as they left together.

THEY STARTED THE GALLERY crawl at a downtown office building. The lobby was lined with large murals of men and women working in factories. Jill glanced around with interest as trendy, attractive people milled about, looking at the artwork and at each other. Jazz pulsated from a combo in the corner.

"E.J.!"

A woman in a handwoven black shift enveloped him in a long hug. An extremely long hug that involved a lot of rubbing of E.J.'s back. Jill kept her smile as the woman turned to her, but she noted with mean satisfaction that the woman's mascara had gummed together and left little black marks beneath her eyes. Jill didn't believe for a moment the woman was a natural redhead. *Meow.*

"Jill, this is Morgena." E.J. stepped a little closer to Jill, and she was absurdly appreciative of the gesture. It was as if he meant to reassure her Morgena wasn't going to whisk him away.

"Nice to meet you." Jill shook hands with the woman and then fell back beside E.J. After all, they were a couple—of sorts—for tonight. There was no reason they couldn't enjoy each other's company. Strictly on a platonic basis, of course.

"Having a good time?" Morgena echoed the beat of the music with her foot and scanned the room.

"Yeah," E.J. said.

"I don't usually see you at these things." Morgena waved to someone.

"Jill wanted to come." E.J. smiled at Jill.

He made it sound as if they'd been sitting around the living room with their shoes off while they gazed into each other's eyes, and they had decided to do the gallery crawl before going back to finish a cozy evening together.

"I'm interested in art," Jill said, and then wondered why she'd made such an inane comment.

"What do you think of this stuff?" Morgena waved a hand up at the walls.

Jill blinked. She didn't think anything of it. The pictures looked vaguely familiar—like something she might have seen somewhere before—but she didn't know enough to offer criticism or compliments. "It's interesting."

Morgena must have clued in. "You know what it is, don't you?"

"Of course, Jill knows it's WPA-style murals," E.J. said. "Who could mistake those brawny men and strong women and that workingman's theme?"

"Not my style," Morgena said. "I don't know why artists want to re-create bad paintings from the Depression. The government just gave those people jobs in the first place to keep them off the dole."

"That's exactly what Jill was saying," E.J. murmured.

Morgena spied another target and was off.

Jill turned to E.J. "I might buy you chocolate ice cream for running interference on that one. I don't like looking stupid."

E.J. chucked her under the chin. "Good girl. I knew you'd come to see I have some value."

A female voice resonated behind them. "E.J.! Sweetie."

Jill groaned. "How many women do you know?"

"Legions. All art experts. All natural redheads bent on embarrassing you." He turned toward a tiny woman in blue silk. "Esther. How the heck have you been? This is Jill. I board dogs for her."

"You do?" Esther looked taken aback, then shrewdly hopeful. "I'm going on vacation next month. Would you keep my terrier?"

"You couldn't afford my rates." He glanced soulfully at Jill. "We have a very special arrangement."

Jill couldn't control a gurgle of laughter.

Esther swept them both with a curious, undecided look, chatted briefly, then moved on.

"Are you always like this?" Jill asked.

"Only when I'm trying to impress a gorgeous woman."

His expression suggested he just might mean those words. His eyes were two blue dots of interest and his smile was thoughtful, verging on gentle.

Jill looked away. Enough of the eye contact. "So what's next?" she asked brightly.

"We forge on in search of food."

Over the next hour, E.J. proved a good companion. He ushered her in and out of buildings, his hand firm on her elbow. He introduced her to people and made quips about the paintings. He handed her stuffed mushrooms over the heads of others crowding around the refreshment tables. He would have gotten her fresh strawberries dipped in chocolate but someone snatched the last berries right out from under him.

E.J. and Jill exchanged a look of commiseration over such rotten luck. She was careful not to let the look last too long, even in fun. The line between friendship and attraction could become blurred. She didn't want to give the appearance of leading him on.

E.J. and Jill walked and stood and chatted. Sometimes he suggested sitting, and they'd find a place in the corner where he stretched his leg out and gently rubbed his knee.

After they'd toured all the downtown galleries, they headed to Davidson Street, where Jill had gone the Sunday before. As he parked the car, E.J. explained that the tiny stretch of old buildings had been mom-and-pop groceries and tiny dime stores in the 1920s. The character of the buildings had been preserved in their worn wooden floors and pressed-tin ceilings.

In the second shop, Jill ran into Xandralene. The young woman stood near a statue that looked half pig, half Loch Ness monster. Xandralene wore a dress as white as her powdered face. The dress fell to the tops of high-top black tennis shoes. She was explaining the sculpture to a clean-cut man in a double-breasted suit.

"It's about, like, freedom and the right to be what you, um, choose," Xandralene said.

The man circled the statue. "Hmm."

E.J. circled behind him. "Looks to me like the artist got drunk and botched the job and decided to try to pass it off on some poor schmuck anyway," he observed to no one in particular.

"It's about dignity and the need to search for inner options," Xandralene continued earnestly. She looked up and saw Jill. "Hi!"

E.J. wheeled toward Jill. "You two know each other?"

"Yes." Jill didn't explain they had met by the chanciest of circumstances. It felt good to see someone *she* knew. And someone interesting, at that.

The man walked away and Xandralene's smile faded. "They're giving me a commission on anything I sell tonight, but nobody's buying."

"Well, people are mostly here to see and be seen," E.J. consoled, as he stuck out his hand. "E.J. Robbins."

"I'm Xandralene. Wanna buy a sculpture?"

"Hell, no. Couldn't afford it and don't want it."

Jill wondered if E.J. was this easy and unpretentious in all situations. Darren had always wanted to impress. Jill didn't think E.J. worried about impressing anyone but himself.

"You should see the exhibit coming up next week." Xandralene twirled a spiral earring. "It looks like vomit on canvas."

"I'll have to be sure to get back over here for that," E.J. said.

Xandralene turned back to Jill. "I was hoping you'd come tonight. I'm, like, lookin' for a place to crash. My roommate has gotten weird on me and I gotta get out of there."

E.J. came up behind Jill and whispered into her ear. "Does that mean her roommate has started wearing underwear?"

Jill jabbed him in the ribs and tried to squash the fluttery feeling she got when his breath teased her ear. She must indeed be lonesome if a small, unimportant thing like that made her feel good. She might have to take the minister up on her offer to attend the One-of-a-Kind group.

"I'll give you my phone number." Xandralene wrote on a crushed piece of paper she fished out of her pocket.

"If they do wear underwear, it's probably interesting," E.J. whispered. "What do you think?"

"I think it's none of my business." A giggle undermined Jill's attempt at severity. It was an evening for fun and teasing, and that made it hard to be annoyed with him.

"Mine's white cotton," he volunteered. "Just in case you were wondering."

"Here." Xandralene handed Jill her phone number. "Call me if you hear of anything. I'm desperate. I'm hoping I could, like, house-sit or something, 'cause I don't have much money for rent." She looked around forlornly. "I might if someone would buy some of this crap, but people are so picky."

"Aren't they?" E.J. said sympathetically, and side-stepped another jab from Jill.

Xandralene laughed. Then Jill laughed, too, and suddenly she felt relaxed and unconcerned. They were just a trio of happy people out on a Friday night who didn't have to worry about going back to an empty apartment or thinking about that solitary little box tucked in the back of the closet. Tonight was for free wine and chocolate strawberries if you could get them, and meeting new people and forgetting bad incidents involving Bakelite records.

A woman approached. She wore a flowing blue dress and a cloche with real flowers bobbing on the brim.

"Let me handle this." E.J. smiled brilliantly at the woman. "Great art, huh?"

She tilted her head to examine it in more detail.

Xandralene looked hopeful.

"It's about power and struggle and the ability to create your own destiny," E.J. said. "Real feminist stuff."

The woman looked at him with slow amusement. "I think it's junk, and I happen to be an art critic."

"Well, you should know." He slipped an arm around Jill's waist. "Come on, dear. We don't want to waste our time on inferior art. Any free food next door?" he asked over his shoulder.

"Two doors down," the woman said.

"Thanks." He herded Jill out the door and down to a gallery that was a mad collection of blond fifties furniture, avant-garde T-shirts and some reasonably good art. At least, Jill thought it was good.

"I kind of like it," she said hesitantly. A painting of two children standing hand in hand appealed to her. She had always hoped to have two children of her own.

"Buy something," E.J. said, encouraging her. "It would be a memento to take back to Simmerville."

"I'm not sure the people there would appreciate it." Jill cast him a sidelong look and confided, "Some of the home folk call it Simpleville."

"Heretics."

"Yeah, I guess so." She grew serious again because she didn't want him to get the wrong impression. "It really is a great town, with tulips in the spring and a nice celebration with the high school band in the fall, but the town is small. We don't have any art galleries."

"So how come you want to go back there?" he asked.

Jill might as well say it outright. "My former husband lives there. I think we'll get back together eventually."

"Why?" E.J. asked, as he pulled her to a red-and-gray vinyl couch and sat down. His hand went automatically to his knee.

"Why?" she echoed. "Well, because it's the right thing to do." She stopped short of telling him it wasn't just her husband she wanted back. She wanted her old life where everything had been known and familiar. She wanted the friends. The house. The security.

"Who asked for the divorce?" E.J. asked.

Jill knew he was trying to make eye contact, but she pretended an interest in an awful picture of a sunflower. "He did."

E.J. didn't say anything. He just massaged his knee and looked at her until she couldn't hide behind a phony interest in the sunflower any longer. She turned to meet his gaze.

"What's that look supposed to mean?" she asked defensively.

"I didn't say anything."

"You're thinking something."

"Yes, I am." He straightened on the sofa. "I'm thinking that marriages are complicated and only the two people in them can decide what's best for them."

"Oh."

It was spoken like a man who knew marriage from the inside. Jill was grateful he hadn't made her defend Darren or her own actions or hopes. Some of her friends had told her she was crazy to want Darren back after all that had happened between them. How could she apply logic to emotions? How could she reason with sentiment? And how could she ever explain that being abandoned by her parents had left a hole in her life that marriage to Darren had filled?

E.J. rose. "Come on, you're starting to look too thoughtful."

Outside, Jill felt the cool night air seep through her light dress. She rubbed her hands up and down her arms.

E.J. put a warm arm around her and she left it there. He had plenty of women friends. There was no reason she couldn't be one of them. She had told him about Darren, so he knew exactly where he stood.

"Xandralene is an interesting character," he said.

"Yeah." Jill couldn't resist asking, "Do you think alligators are sexy?"

E.J. swung her to a stop beneath a streetlight. As he faced her, she smelled wine and the suggestion of sandalwood cologne. "You're attracted to alligators?"

She pursed her lips and thought it over. "No, I guess not."

"Good." He spun her around and they resumed walking. His hand remained draped over her shoulders.

No, she wasn't attracted to alligators. And until now, she'd never even thought about being attracted to men—with the exception of Darren. Yet with E.J. a close presence beside her, her thoughts free-associated. She thought of a big bed with lots of fluffy comforters and soft blankets. Of him. Her. No clothes. His body hard and lightly fuzzed with chest hair. Hers warm and moist. Searching hands. Soft caresses. Hard kisses. Pressing deeper into the comforter. Deeper into each other—

Whoa, girl!

Jill's thoughts thudded back to reality. She wasn't going to experiment with sex just because an opportunity might present itself.

"Jill, this is my car."

"Oh." She laughed self-consciously and jerked to a halt.

"If you're not ready to go home, we can walk some more, but this area gets seedy a couple of blocks from here."

"No, I'm ready to leave." She gave him an over-bright smile.

As they started back, E.J. told her more about his job and mentioned an operation but brushed aside her questions. Instead, he turned the conversation to his writing. He said he wrote short stories.

"I'm impressed," Jill murmured as he drove toward downtown, where lights gleamed on the side of a building that looked like an old-fashioned domed radio. "Where have you published?"

"Nowhere." He shrugged. "So far, all I have is rejections, but I'm still trying."

"What are your short stories about?" Jill turned to look at him.

"One is about a tree house my father and I built when I was ten. He wanted to build it his way and I wanted it mine, and we didn't speak for a week afterward." E.J. laughed, then was serious again. "Another is about a woman whose house I inspected. She saved every single newspaper. Her whole house was piled to the ceiling with them, and there were only narrow paths to walk along. She couldn't throw anything away because she'd been in Poland during the Nazi occupation and anything burnable had value there. She wore two or three sweaters all the time, and she talked a lot about the terrible cold of that first winter.''

"How strange that she couldn't get over it," Jill said.

"I thought so at first. Then I found out her baby froze to death.''

"That's awful." Jill covered her mouth with her hand. "Awful," she repeated, but the words had expanded to cover not only the poor demented Polish woman, but all women whose children had died or disappeared or been snatched away. Jill also thought about babies not yet born.

She thought about the little pink stroller at the church and the little box at home in her closet. She thought about carrying her pain alone because friends had been reluctant to discuss the miscarriage. Her mother had counseled her long distance from Paris to visit a nice spa and buy new clothes. Darren had seen no reason to talk about a life that no longer existed.

Suddenly Jill was crying. Harsh, searing sobs pulled at her chest. Grief she had thought fully buried rose like fog in a haunted cemetery—swirling and threatening and seeping into her soul.

Her baby. The child she had helped create. How could she pretend that child had never existed?

She tried to stifle her sobs. Jill Howard didn't lose control and break down in front of someone she hardly knew, but the tears were beyond her power to stanch.

She scarcely noticed when E.J. pulled over and stopped. She heard his seat belt unsnapping, then she felt him pull her against him. He was solid and real, and he offered comfort against the fog—and she'd had precious little of comfort.

After a moment's hesitation, she curled into his embrace and they sat that way for a long time. Even after the storm of tears gentled and her breathing resumed its normal pattern, Jill remained with her damp cheek meshed against his smooth cotton shirt, inhaling his sandalwood scent.

"It's been bad, hasn't it?" E.J. asked, his voice low and husky.

Jill nodded.

He found a box of tissues in the back seat and handed her a fistful. She dabbed at her eyes and cheeks and didn't even feel too self-conscious to blow her nose.

They didn't talk the rest of the way home. He didn't ask it of her, and she lacked the strength to muster an apology for falling apart. Nor did she have the energy to try to cover the whole incident with mindless chatter. Instead she sat quietly beside him and enjoyed the luxury of being human and knowing the world wouldn't fall apart because she was.

CHAPTER FOUR

WEDNESDAY MORNING, Mrs. Casey hurried into the big warehouse full of mounds of clothing and waved to a woman who stood near the front with a clipboard.

"Good morning, Maria," Mrs. Casey said cheerfully. "I'm here."

The harried woman pointed toward a pile of clothes near the back. "You can work in the back this morning, Mrs. Casey. With Ted."

Mrs. Casey joined a skin-and-bones man who stood beside a heap of clothing piled higher than his head.

She smiled at him. "Hi, Ted. I'm Grace Casey."

He blinked as if trying to clear his vision.

She pulled a moth-eaten sweater off the top of the pile and tossed it into a bin marked Discards.

"Honestly, it's a disgrace what some people donate to charity," she said. "I wouldn't give something that was worn-out. I'd throw it away. Wouldn't you?"

"Say what?" Ted blinked at her again.

"It's nice of you to volunteer to work here," she continued, as she whisked three pairs of men's slacks from the pile. "Not many young men do."

"Yeah, well . . ."

Ted wasn't much of a talker, but anyone kind enough to volunteer was a sweet person in Grace's book.

"I didn't start doing volunteer work until my husband died. He was a good man but he kept me busy doing the books for the rental property. And he liked his meals on time and cooked just so, so there wasn't extra time for this sort of thing."

"Yeah."

"Ted, those our ladies' slacks you just put in the Infant's bin."

He dragged them back out and looked at them uncertainly.

Oh, dear. Was it possible the poor man couldn't read? "Here's the Ladies' bin." She pointed. "This is the Men's, and here's Children's and— Ted, are you listening?"

"Yeah, sure." He shifted restlessly and looked toward the door.

"It's important. People are depending on us, you know." She softened her words with a smile. "I hate to lecture you, but we really must do this right."

He dug into the pile again.

"Do you have family in Charlotte, Ted?"

"No."

"I don't, either, now that my husband is dead. He had a niece but she moved to Florida and doesn't write much. I'd like to hear from her. It gets lonely sometimes."

Ted didn't say anything.

Grace shut up. She didn't want him to think she was some pathetic old woman who had no family or friends and nothing to do with her time. She had a full life, what with her crafts class on Thursday mornings and dance classes two evenings a week. And every few weeks, she and E.J. went out for a beer.

Now, there was a nice young man. She worried that he might be lonely, but whenever she brought home girls from her church to meet him, he hadn't seemed interested. Maybe he wasn't over his wife yet.

"I got family in Georgia. A couple of brothers."

She beamed at Ted, pleased that he was talking to her. "How nice for you. Do you get down to visit them very often?"

"Henry ain't allowed visitors right now."

How odd. She didn't pursue the subject. Instead, she asked, "Where do you live in Charlotte?"

"I got me a room near downtown."

Grace lowered her voice and leaned toward him, looking directly into his red-rimmed eyes. "You be careful. There are some bad neighborhoods around downtown. You could get knocked over the head by a bully."

He shifted his eyes away. "Yes, ma'am."

"You can call me Grace." She pulled out a child's pink snowsuit. "Isn't that precious?"

Ted looked at the snowsuit with the flowers appliquéd on the front and shrugged.

Well, he was a man, so he couldn't be expected to appreciate such things. Her new renter, Jill, would. Jill was a nice person and Grace felt bad about not letting her keep the dog. But she had to have rules. To soften the blow, she had baked Jill a Mississippi Mud cake last night. She was going to take it over to her as soon as she got home today.

Mrs. Casey looked up and saw Ted stuffing a ragged pair of jeans in the Boys' bin.

"Don't put those in there! The knees are torn out and the color is all faded."

She retrieved the jeans and threw them into the Discards bin. "Just because these children are poor doesn't mean we give them rags. If someone had taken the time to patch the knees, they might have been usable.''

"The knees are supposed to be tore out, lady. And they're acid washed." Ted looked at her belligerently.

"Oh. I'm sorry." She laughed self-consciously. "I'm not much up on young people's trends."

A young man with headphones in his ears, baggy pants, and a plaid flannel shirt strolled by. "How you like community service, man?"

"Get lost," Ted said.

Grinning, the other man left, keeping jerky time to the music from his radio.

Grace's thoughts remained on the ragged jeans. "I'm sorry if I appeared bossy, Ted. I don't mean to be. I'm by myself so much that I get used to doing things a certain way and think I'm always right. I do apologize."

"Ain't no big deal."

"I'm trying to get out more," she explained. "I'm taking dance lessons. It's good exercise and I meet new people. And the instructors are so sweet." Especially Rick. He knew how to explain a dance step and how to make her feel graceful even when she made a mistake.

She'd looked around at the dance studio for some nice young woman to introduce to E.J. She worried about him now that he was having this operation on his knee. The right woman could look after him and cheer him up. If would have to be someone fun loving and easygoing.

"It's ten o'clock," Ted announced. "I can go now."

Grace switched her attention back to her companion. He was so thin. She wondered how long it had been since he'd had a decent meal. If he were her son, she'd make sure he was better cared for.

"It was nice working with you, Ted. Do be careful and don't go out at night downtown."

"Uh, yeah."

After he left, Grace uncovered a men's sweater that looked brand-new. She thought it would look nice on Rick. Maybe she would ask about buying the sweater when she left today. Rick had come up to her twice at the end of the dance lessons to talk. Last night he'd walked her to her car. She bet he would appreciate a nice sweater.

She knew it was sneaky, but she could ask him to walk out to her car again with her to get the sweater.

ON SATURDAY MORNING Jill talked to her mother, who was between planes at Dallas airport.

"How are you doing, dear?"

"Fine. I went out last night." Jill still felt excited about that, which proved how much she'd been cooped up lately. During her separation, she hadn't felt like getting out much. Although she had concentrated on volunteer work during her marriage, she had taken a job as a teacher's aide after Darren left. It had helped occupy her, but the nights were still long and depressing.

"Good for you," her mother said. "I'm glad you're getting over Darren. I was worried for a while."

"I still think about him."

"Of course you do, darling. I think about each of my former husbands now and again."

Jill shook her head. Her mother had been divorced five times. To her, men were as disposal as tissues, and she didn't understand Jill's dependence on Darren, just as she had never understood a younger Jill's need for her parents.

"The important thing is that you've moved away from Simmerville and from your grandmother. I love her dearly but she has positively antiquated views of the world. You need to start fresh. What are you doing for yourself? A facial? A mud bath?"

"I'm going back to school to get my teaching degree. Classes start soon."

"No, no, darling, what are you doing for yourself?"

"I got a new perm yesterday." Jill touched her hair. She had gone in for her usual permanent but at the last minute had opted for something fuller and softer. It looked a little more daring.

"Good for you. Uh-oh, they're announcing my flight."

Her mother was gone in a flurry of kissing sounds and promises to be in touch soon. After she hung up, Mrs. Casey appeared at her door.

"I brought you some Mississippi Mud cake," her landlady said. She looked sheepish, as if she still felt uncomfortable because she hadn't let Jill keep Fido. "Thank you. Won't you come in?"

"No, I'm only going to stay a minute."

As Mrs. Casey chatted about her dance class, Jill stood in the doorway holding the foil-wrapped cake.

It was a glorious day to be outside. Sunshine dappled the lawn. Children rode by on bicycles, leaving behind the innocence of their laughter. The aroma of roses stole over a white picket fence from the yard behind Mrs. Casey's.

Out of the corner of her eye, Jill saw E.J. step out his back door wearing khaki trousers and a white sleeveless T-shirt. He went into a welcoming crouch as Fido bounded toward him. The moment was so spontaneous and compelling. The men in Jill's life had been reserved and she wasn't used to such open affection, even with an animal. She tried to focus on Mrs. Casey's words.

"I hope you enjoy the cake. I'll be glad to write out the recipe for you."

"It smells wonderful."

Mrs. Casey turned to go and spied E.J. "Come get some cake. I'm sure Jill will share with you. Won't you, dear?"

"Of course."

There wasn't really any way Jill could escape into the house. The memory of Friday night with E.J. made her feel awkward today, but Jill remained in the doorway as he started toward them. He stopped to say a few words to Mrs. Casey, then approached.

"Fido said to tell you he's hungry," E.J. said as he walked up the sidewalk. "Actually, he said, 'Woof,' but lucky for you I can translate."

E.J. reached her porch and stood only a few feet away. His hair was in casual disarray. He looked carefree and vibrant and very male.

Jill squared her shoulders. "The directions say to feed only twice a day."

"Why don't you step next door and explain that to Fido? Tell him about nutritional content and the dangers of obesity. Mention the latest studies on canine well-being." E.J.'s blue eyes twinkled.

Jill pursed her lips. "You can't expect a dog to know what's best for him."

"No, I guess not. Heck, most people don't know what's best for them. Look at you, you took in a dog you don't want. Now you're stuck with him."

"I'm not stuck with him. I ran an ad in the paper," she told him.

He shook his head slowly, patiently. "Jill, Jill, no sane person will answer that ad. You'll get a call from some pervert who'll ask a couple of questions about the dog and then make a shocking suggestion. Shocking," he repeated, and his voice played over the word in a way that tugged at her midsection.

E.J. dropped down onto her porch steps as nonchalantly as if he'd been invited. He turned sideways and put his back against the post.

"The only other call," he continued, "will be from a woman with a whiny voice. She wants a dog for her daughter. But the dog must be spayed, have its shots, and come with a year's supply of food. If her daughter doesn't like the dog, you have to take it back."

"Do you have a better idea?" Jill asked tartly.

He flashed a rogue's smile. "Of course."

She tried not to like the smile. "What?"

E.J. patted the step beside him and pulled his legs up against his chest. "Sit down. You're making me nervous standing over me."

Jill sat because it was easier than arguing. "What's your idea?"

"We'll go around the neighborhood posting signs and take Fido with us. Then we'll stop and ask daddies who are working in their yards if they need a dog. Their kids will flock around and badger their father into letting them have one."

"You seem sure of yourself. Have you done this before?"

"As a matter of fact, I've placed two possums, a weasel and a warthog using this very technique."

"Uh-huh." The wind drifted through her hair and the scent of roses ebbed and waned. She found she liked sitting here talking nonsense with him.

"Putting up signs is your best shot." E.J. pushed himself up from the steps. "We might as well get started."

If he was offering to help, she wasn't going to refuse. Jill stood and brushed off her slacks. "I'll have to buy some poster board to make signs. And—"

"Naw. Just cut up packing boxes and use them."

She hesitated. She was saving the boxes to repack in when she moved back to Simmerville. They were lying flat and ready underneath her bed. She couldn't give them up.

"I need the boxes," she said.

He shrugged. "I've got some cardboard at the house from my yard sale. I'll go get it."

An hour later, Jill and E.J left behind a clutter of felt-tip pens and cardboard shreds on her kitchen table and carried two dozen signs out the door.

E.J. stopped at his house to pick up a hammer and nails and to get Fido. The dog pranced along beside them, straining at the leash and panting excitedly as they started down the sidewalk. As they walked, Jill glanced around at the older houses and big trees. She'd read that the neighborhood was called Elizabeth and had been created seventy years ago when the trolley line freed people to live away from downtown Charlotte. The bungalows and little Victorians were dwarfed by oaks and pines that had been saplings when the houses were built. An occasional quadraplex or duplex gave diversity to the neighborhood.

"Have you lived here long?" Jill asked, as they waited for Fido to sniff a caterpillar.

"Six years. My wife and I moved here right after we got married."

My wife. Jill hesitated, but he had brought the subject up and she *was* curious. "You're not married any longer?" she asked cautiously.

"No. Lisa died."

Jill hadn't expected that. She had assumed he was divorced, and now she felt uncertain. "I'm sorry. I didn't know. It must be hard to stay in the same house." She flushed hotly. What in the world was she saying? Where was her tact?

"Lisa didn't want to live in this area," E.J. said matter-of-factly. "She wanted to be out in the new suburbs. A lot of her friends from college lived there."

Jill sensed something left unsaid. Did talking about his wife make him sad? It was logical that it would. She cast about for a way to change the subject and latched on to the word *college.*

"Where did you go to college?" she asked.

"I didn't."

"Oh." Everyone in her crowd from high school had. Jill had quit at the end of her junior year because Darren had graduated and gotten a job. She hadn't wanted to stay behind in Durham, and he hadn't wanted her to.

E.J. stopped at a street corner and handed her the leash. "Let's put a sign here."

"I'm going back to school to finish my degree," Jill continued. "It's never too late, you know." She would feel better about herself once she completed her degree.

He looked at her sideways, then nodded as if some belief had been confirmed. "I figured you were the ambitious type." He didn't make it sound like a compliment.

"There's nothing wrong with that," she said briskly.

"No, but that's not my thing. I don't have to be vice president of some company to feel successful."

In a nearby yard a man clipped hedges and children threw a ball back and forth. Ignoring the opportunity to show them Fido, Jill snapped, "People don't get ahead unless they have goals and ambitions."

E.J. looked at her curiously. "What do you consider 'getting ahead'?"

It was a ridiculous question, but she tried to answer it seriously. "Moving up to a better job is certainly one sign."

"You mean a job that pays more money?"

"Of course."

He patted Fido's back. "Why does a person need more money?"

Jill sensed a trap. Watching him warily, she began to walk again. "To realize dreams like a vacation or a beach house or a nicer car." She rushed to add, "Success isn't only about material things, though. There's a lot of satisfaction in getting ahead in a career."

Darren enjoyed the challenges of his job and the satisfaction of each new step forward. She had shared the joy with him, feeling like a partner even though she had worked behind the scenes. Nevertheless, she had begun to feel that she needed to have more to offer, and that was one of the reasons she intended to use her time in Charlotte to make herself a more worldly, interesting person.

"Know what I think?" E.J. cupped a hand around her waist and steered her away from a telephone pole in her path. Without missing a beat, he continued. "I think if more people were content with what they have, fewer people would die of heart attacks and stress."

She searched for a response, but her thoughts fragmented when his hand stayed on her waist. *Get a grip, Jill.* She was too old and too practical to react like a moonstruck teenager every time someone touched her. Granted, her only reactions so far had been to E.J., but that was because he was the only man she'd spent any time with since Darren.

"Let's drop this discussion," she said. "We need to concentrate on finding a home for Fido."

"You're right."

Over the next twenty minutes, they maintained a general, stilted conversation as they tacked up signs. Oblivious to any undercurrents between the humans, Fido pranced about and lunged at squirrels.

"This is the last poster," E.J. finally said.

Thank goodness. She was uncomfortable being with E.J. after their discussion. Not that it had been a real argument, but they definitely looked at the world differently.

"We might as well go back," Jill said.

Suddenly he grabbed her forearm.

The force of his grip startled her. "What's wrong?" she asked in alarm.

He relaxed his hold. "Just a catch in my knee."

"Are you okay now?"

"Yeah."

His hand slid off her arm and he began to walk, but he moved at a slower pace. She thought about the time in his garden when he'd clutched at his knee and how he had favored it when they had gone on the gallery crawl.

"You should see a doctor," Jill said.

He laughed mirthlessly. "I have. I'm scheduled for surgery this week."

She stopped on the sidewalk beneath a mimosa fuzzy with pink flowers. "Why didn't you tell me? Why did you let me drag you to the gallery crawl and out to put up signs today if you don't feel well?"

"You didn't drag me. I was glad to get out of the house. It keeps me from thinking about the operation."

"But your leg hurts."

"Not all the time." He smiled. "Come on. I'm not going to get any better if we just stand here. I'm not at death's door."

"You still should have told me about the operation," she insisted.

"Jill, quit making such a big deal out of it."

It *was* a big deal. If his knee problems were serious enough to warrant surgery, then he must be in true discomfort. "When do you go into the hospital?" she asked.

"The fifteenth."

That was less than a week away. Guilt assailed her again and she softened her tone. "If you want me to do anything, I'll be glad to."

He reached over and chucked her under the chin. "Let's not worry about me. Let's get you back home so you don't miss any phone calls from perverts."

Jill let it go because she knew he was trying to lighten the atmosphere between them. But she was concerned. And she felt terrible about giving him a lecture on ambition. What he needed right now was a supportive friend. She could at least be that, after all he'd done for her.

IT WAS MIDNIGHT by the time Darren returned home from his date. He loosened his tie and sank into a leather love seat in a den with decorator sofas and indirect lighting.

He had expected to have a good time with Wendy, a bubbly blonde who worked in the records department of a nearby hospital. They had gone to dinner, a movie, and then for coffee. Over cheesecake and cappuccino he'd made a joke about the decor of the restaurant being "early pretentious."

Blinking solemnly, she'd asked, "Is that a new style?"

Wendy might be cute but she sure wasn't Stephen Hawking. Jill had always understood his jokes, her eyes shimmering when she laughed.

Darren pulled off his tie and let it spill from his fingers onto the Oriental carpet. He'd been thinking about Jill a lot lately. Frankly, the more he dated, the better she looked.

He'd been mad as fire at her for breaking his records. But Joe in Radiology had pointed out that Darren hadn't been very nice to Jill at the restaurant. He'd thought for a while that she was following him. Now he saw he'd been paranoid during those early days of the divorce. Maybe he'd been so intent on proving he was free of her that he hadn't wanted reminders of their past together.

Darren still had the letter she'd written saying she would be willing to work things out if he ever decided he wanted to. He'd thought she might contact him again, but he hadn't heard from her since she'd moved to Charlotte. Part of him worried about her. She had never lived in a city before, and he didn't like the thought of her alone up there, lost and adrift.

If only Jill had been able to get past the miscarriage. That was when their marriage had foundered. She had mourned too much. He had tried to talk with her, but she always became tearful and defensive. If only she could have seen that he wanted to help her.

Oh, hell, the marriage was over. There was no point in rehashing history.

Still, he thought about her more than he'd expected to, and more than he wanted to.

THE DAY AFTER JILL AND E.J. put up signs about Fido, Jill got a phone call.

"I'm calling concerning your ad about a dog," a man said.

Jill smiled into the receiver. "Yes?"

"Tell me about the dog."

Jill described Fido, emphasizing his friendly personality and neglecting to mention a tendency to chew, gnaw, ingest or otherwise destroy anything not nailed down.

"Sounds good. Can I come see him?" the man asked.

"Of course. When?"

"You gonna be there in an hour?"

"Yes." Jill gave him directions.

"See you then," he said.

As she hurried out the door toward E.J.'s backyard, Jill reviewed ways to show off Fido at his doggy best. She would comb his coat and spray a whiff of perfume on him. Would a bow on his head be overdoing it? she wondered. Yes, she supposed it would.

Jill stopped short at the gate.

"Oh, no," she breathed.

Fido had overturned a watering can and created a mudhole to wallow in. Dried mud hung from his tail like dark icicles, and his face was a brown mess. He saw her and barked gleefully.

She looked toward E.J.'s door, then back at Fido. She hated to bother E.J.—partly because of his knee and partly because she was still a little uncertain where they stood after their conversation yesterday—but there was no way around asking him if she could give Fido a bath. No one was going to adopt him looking like *this*.

Taking a deep breath, she marched up to his door and knocked.

E.J. opened the door, holding a submarine sandwich in one hand and a TV schedule in the other. He wore a gray sweatshirt with a torn neck and jeans that looked too old to survive another washing. She looked down at her own pink blouse and crisp new jeans. She had always taken care with her appearance, and realized she never dressed as casually as E.J. did.

"What's up?" he asked.

"A man is coming in an hour to see Fido, and he's an absolute disaster. Look at him." Jill waved wildly toward the cavorting mud-coated dog. "No one is going to take him looking like this. I didn't even get the man's name and phone number, so I can't call him back. If I'd known that—"

"Calm down," E.J. interjected. "The hose is at the front of the house. Bring it back here and I'll get a tub."

She hesitated. "I can't ask you to help me. You aren't up to it. Just tell me where the tub is."

"Jill, you don't have time to stand around arguing. Now go get the hose while I change clothes."

"But I—"

"Go."

Jill obeyed. She returned with the hose just as E.J. stepped out of the house wearing a pair of cutoff jeans and nothing else. Had he said "change"? "Undress" would have been more like it. Jill stared at the lean, tanned body and the well-defined arms. His blasé expression suggested he didn't know he had a body that could sell calendars. At least to the type of women who bought such things. Jill never had. She had always thought them tasteless, but there really wasn't anything wrong with fantasizing, she suddenly realized.

"Don't just stand there," he said, and headed toward a shed in the backyard. "Bring Fido into the yard and I'll get the tub."

"Yes, sir."

E.J. grinned. "Do you like it when I'm masterful?"

She hadn't ever felt he was flirting before. She wasn't sure he was now, but there was a teasing quality in his blue eyes that she didn't want to examine. She looked away.

Fido followed her to the appointed spot and sniffed at the sides of the tub with interest. E.J. placed the running hose in the tub, then swooped down on the dog and set him in it.

Fido howled.

"Poor boy. The water's too cold," Jill protested. "Is there any way to warm it?"

"No. Put this soap on him and lather it good," E.J. shouted over barks of protest.

Jill tried, but it wasn't easy to apply soap and lather it while Fido fought to climb out of the tub. E.J. clung to the dog's collar as Jill leaned in closer to rub the soap into a foam.

Fido twisted sharply away and almost succeeded in escaping. E.J. hauled him back.

Jill rubbed Fido's neck.

"Hurry up," E.J. shouted. "He's losing patience."

Jill suppressed a retort. E.J. *was* helping her, even if she didn't appreciate him yelling directions at her.

Fido's next attempted leap sent water streaming down her face and plastered her hair to her skin.

"Keep washing," E.J. said.

Jill turned to him in exasperation. "I am." She pushed aside her wet hair with the back of her forearm. "I can't help it if he's uncooperative."

"You missed a spot behind his ear."

"Of all the—" She looked over to see E.J. laughing at her.

This time there was more than playful teasing. She saw plain old sensuality in his cocky smile.

Jill looked away, dumped more soap on her hands, and bent toward Fido with grim purpose. At the same time, the dog leapt from the tub, and Jill's hands slipped to E.J.'s bare chest. Her palms felt wiry curls and the warm, wet texture of his flesh. His heart pulsated beneath her fingers.

Something elemental overwhelmed her. Calendars... Fantasies... Suddenly she wanted to let her fingers massage his chest and glide over his naked torso. She wanted to let her mind take her on a forbidden journey.

She glanced at E.J. again. His smile had vanished. He was regarding her with heat in his blue eyes. It was the look of a man who had been to the center of a secret maze and knew how to take her there.

She couldn't bring herself to break eye contact. Sexual tension throbbed in the air. She imagined him pulling her closer and fitting his mouth against hers in a kiss devoid of inhibition. A kiss hot with possibility. What if he peeled away his wet cutoffs and spread his big hands over her body?

The thought excited and horrified her.

Jill Howard, get a grip on yourself. You're supposed to be washing a dog, not indulging in some inappropriate fantasy. But she stayed where she was.

E.J. lifted a hand to touch her wet hair. "I haven't ever kissed you, have I?" he asked.

"N-no." She was as breathless as a Channel swimmer. This wasn't really happening. His damp hands weren't really clamped possessively around her forearms, and she didn't really want to act on raw impulse.

But it felt real.

Then E.J. bent toward her. Jill was certain that when he kissed her, she would remember it for a long time.

She closed her eyes and waited, holding her breath until his mouth settled over hers. She couldn't remember ever anticipating a kiss with such urgency.

But the next touch she felt was the slap of a wet tail. She opened her eyes as Fido jumped. Jill wrenched away.

"Fido, you dumb mutt!" E.J. yelled. "Find your own girl."

That was enough to pull Jill the rest of the way back to sanity.

Flustered, she babbled in disconnected fragments. "The man will be here any minute, and— Need to get him clean— Fido, I mean—"

She felt E.J.'s gaze on her even though she refused to look up at him. She was too embarrassed, too rattled. E.J. retrieved Fido from where he was trying to hide amid the tomato plants.

Once the dog was back in the tub, Jill lathered him with a vengeance. Fido apparently sensed he was outnumbered, and Jill finished without getting too much wetter than she already was. The tricky part was avoiding eye contact with E.J.

She had just patted the dog dry with an old towel when she heard a car pull into the driveway. She was relieved, but then looked down at her wet clothes. "Do you have something I can throw on quickly?"

"Yeah. Be back in a sec."

Was E.J. as regretful as she about their little scene? Jill wondered as he went in the back door. He didn't seem to be. Men were less apt to be bothered by such things, even spur-of-the-moment kisses.

He returned with his neckless sweatshirt. "This okay?"

Not having much choice, Jill pulled it on. She smelled the faint male muskiness of E.J.

Just then a man came around the back of the house.

He was balding and smiled jovially. "Hey there, folks. Hear you've got a dog looking for a home?"

"We do," Jill replied with tinny brightness.

Fido barked.

"Here, boy." The man held out a dog biscuit, and Fido bounded over for the treat. "I'm Harvey Lance. I called a while ago."

Jill and E.J. introduced themselves and Harvey produced another dog biscuit. Fido looked adoringly up at him. E.J. launched into friendly conversation. Everyone seemed happy.

Except Jill.

She didn't like Harvey Lance.

"Got a nice bit of acreage on the edge of town," Harvey was saying.

"Great." E.J. gave a smile big enough to sell encyclopedias. "Isn't that wonderful, Jill? Fido would have a place to run."

She nodded but she still felt troubled. "Why do you want a dog, Mr. Lance?" she asked.

"Please, it's Harvey. The missus and I have had a couple of break-ins, and I figured a dog would be good protection. Cheaper than a security system, too." He laughed.

Somehow that bothered her. That and the biscuits and something about Harvey she couldn't put her finger on.

"Fido is a terrific guard dog," E.J. said. "Isn't he, Jill?"

"Well, I'm really not sure—"

"'Course he is," E.J. interrupted, and shot her a quizzical look.

"I can train him if he isn't a guard dog now," Harvey offered.

Train him? How? Jill looked at the stranger with new skepticism. "You won't beat him, will you?"

Harvey laughed heartily. Too heartily, she thought.

"Jill, of course Harvey won't hit Fido. Look, he even thought to bring biscuits." E.J. smiled at the other man. "I think Fido is just the dog you're looking for."

"He is big," Harvey agreed. "And I like that."

"Big dogs are the best guard dogs," E.J. said.

"Damned straight." Harvey scratched Fido's ears.

"I'm afraid he's too friendly to be a guard dog," Jill said. When neither man looked at her, she spoke louder. "I've thought it over and I want to keep him."

Both men turned to stare at her.

"Come again, little lady?"

"I'm going to keep Fido."

Harvey looked at E.J. "This your dog or hers?"

"Hers."

"I'm going to keep him," Jill repeated, and nodded to back up her claim.

"I wish you'd told me that before I drove all the way over here." Harvey wasn't smiling anymore.

"Wait a minute, Harvey." E.J. moved toward the back door. "Jill, could I talk to you inside?"

"Not now, E.J."

Harvey glared at Jill. "I can't figure why someone would run an ad if they weren't serious."

Jill moved closer to Fido, feeling suddenly protective toward the big, dumb mutt who'd caused her nothing but trouble.

E.J. sighed. "I guess that's that. Sorry it was a waste of your time, Harvey."

Harvey turned and left without another word. Jill exhaled her relief.

"Would you care to tell me what that was all about?" E.J. inquired.

She looked past him to the unkempt white clematis blooming on the trellis beside the back door. "I didn't like him."

"Why?"

"What kind of person brings treats for a dog?"

"A nice person?" E.J. suggested.

"Don't be ridiculous. It was an underhanded thing to do. Harvey was trying to gain Fido's trust in a dishonest way." Jill knew she sounded insane. "Oh, it's too complicated," she ended impatiently.

"Jill, you can't keep the dog and you can't afford to board him. This was a time to be practical and place him."

Did he have to be so darn logical? "I didn't want to give a dog to someone cruel." She wrapped her hands across her stomach and felt the oversize sweatshirt dip off one shoulder. She tugged it back up.

"Cruel? Oh, I see. You were concerned because he was dragging a blood-splattered ax. Or was it the AK-47 that worried you?"

"Very funny. Don't you ever have a gut feeling about something?"

She expected a retort but got only silence. She looked at him then and saw his expression had turned tense. The lines beside his mouth formed deep brackets. Even though he hadn't moved, he had somehow retreated. She saw it in the distant look in his eyes, and Jill felt something like regret that he had left her behind.

"Yeah," he finally said. "I know about gut feelings."

She guessed he knew all too well. For a moment, she wished they were close enough that she could offer him comfort or encouragement or whatever it was he needed. But they weren't that close, and they were never going to be. The wisest action was for her to leave.

CHAPTER FIVE

THE FIRST SATURDAY NIGHT of every month was poker night.

Floods might hit, hurricanes threaten, disasters loom. E.J.'s operation might creep closer. But on poker night the peanuts and pretzels would be in their wooden bowls and the beer and soft drinks in the refrigerator.

Tonight was E.J.'s turn to host.

Charlie arrived first. "I sure hope you got some good eats. The wife is trying to starve me with this danged low-fat diet. You ever eat green beans and spinach three days running?"

"Never have." E.J. led the way into a den furnished with worn plaids and wooden venetian blinds. He scooped up a pile of magazines from a chair and dumped them onto the floor. It was an imperfect housekeeping system, but he kept the place livable if not immaculate.

"It's rough, let me tell you," Charlie said.

The front door opened and a moment later Roger breezed into the room. His hair was moussed, his shirt open to below his chest and his smile orthodontically perfect. "Hey, hey, hey. Time to play." He did a little gyration with his hips.

E.J. suffered Roger only because he had founded the poker group.

"I need a drink," E.J. said, heading for the kitchen.

Charlie followed. "Make that two."

Roger tagged along.

"How's the real estate business?" E.J. asked as he handed Charlie a beer. He wanted a beer, too, but he'd taken pain medication for his knee and didn't want to mix the two.

"Business is great!" Roger said. "You thinking of putting your house on the market?"

"No," E.J. answered flatly.

Roger ran his palm over the hair on his chest and surveyed the room. "I could get you a good price. The kitchen was remodeled last year, wasn't it? People like this pickled-pine stuff, and white appliances are back in style. Let me know when you want to list."

"I'm not selling," E.J. said. Right now, it was where he wanted to be. He wasn't tied here, though. Someday he might decide to live on a houseboat and then he'd up and sell. He liked having options.

"You've got three bedrooms upstairs on a center hall, don't you?" Roger peeked out the kitchen door. "Formal dining room. Nice long living room. I could get you good money."

"He's not selling," Charlie grumbled, and headed into the den. "I thought you were a newscaster, anyway."

"I'm still the weekend anchor." Roger blazed a smile around the room as if cameras might be rolling. "This is just a sideline."

Charlie sat down at the round table in the corner and disappeared into his beer.

The front door opened again.

"Dave's here," Roger announced.

A slight, balding man joined them.

"Dave, Dave, you're all the rave." Roger beamed again.

"Margo sent brownies." Dave set a plate in the center of the table and Charlie reached for them.

E.J. blocked his hand. "Not so fast. Are they low fat, Dave?"

"Gee, I don't know. I don't think so."

Charlie knocked E.J.'s hand aside and grabbed a brownie. "You don't know what it's like," he said between mouthfuls. "It's not natural to give up fat. The body craves it. It's a drive that just can't be ignored."

Roger smirked. "I know all about drives, but *mine* isn't for food."

The others ignored him.

Dave lit a cigar. E.J. didn't usually like to be around smoke, but the poker games were different. Here they all chomped on cigars and muttered out of the side of their mouths like James Cagney. It was a small rebellion against civilization, particularly the female domestication that had been imposed on Charlie and Dave.

E.J. began shuffling the cards.

"I'm a guy of taste, right?" Roger asked rhetorically as E.J. began to deal. "So how come I end up with dates that are losers? The last chick walked out on me."

"You!" Charlie picked up his cards. "What is the matter with women?"

"You've been out of the dating game so long you don't know what it's like." Roger rubbed the hair on his chest again. "I tell you, women today are unreasonable."

"Why did she walk out on you?" E.J. kept a stone face at the sight of five worthless cards.

"Who knows? I left the table for a minute and when I came back she was gone. Go figure."

"Left the table?" E.J. echoed.

"Yeah." Roger chuckled. "I slipped away to get the phone number of the sexy broad who waited on us. You should have seen her. This woman really filled out a T-shirt. When I say jiggle, I mean—"

"You tried to pick up another woman while you were on a date?" Dave asked.

"You didn't see her. Long blond hair. Big blue eyes. And legs! Did I mention her legs?"

"I hope you called your date the next day and apologized," E.J. said.

"Why should I? She's the one who walked out."

E.J. folded his hand as the bidding got heavy between Charlie and Dave. He turned to Roger. "You know what your problem is? You don't treat women with respect."

"What are you saying? I took her to a nice restaurant and told her she could order anything she wanted. I was stuck with the bill and didn't even get a chance to collect on the debt later that night, if you know what I mean."

"You're sick, Roger," Charlie mumbled around his cigar. "Raise you five, Dave. If I had a sister, I wouldn't let her go out with you."

Roger shot him a pitying look. "Charlie, you've forgotten what you were like in the old days. All men are out for what they can get. That's how it is."

"Excuse me," E.J. said, "I disagree. I'm certainly not a monk, but I don't want to jump into bed with every woman I meet. In fact, I want to know the woman and actually *like* her before anything major happens."

"No offense, E.J., but you're not in my league. I've seen you with a couple of pretty ordinary-looking women. I stick to babes, but you go out with women and waste time talking to them. Me, I get right to the action. If they're not hot to trot, I dump 'em."

"Let me add something to what I said earlier, Roger." Charlie leaned forward to rake in the pot. "I wouldn't let my sister or my *goldfish* go out with you."

"Your problem is you don't like women," E.J. said, picking up his hand.

"What are you talking about?" Roger looked at him in astonishment. "I *love* women."

"They're sex objects to you. Me," E.J. continued virtuously, "I enjoy women as people."

"Of course I enjoy them as people. I've been married three times, haven't I?"

E.J. suppressed a laugh. "You've got to be in love with a woman for a marriage to last."

Roger shook his head so emphatically, the moussed hair actually moved. "Marriages are based on great sex and a woman who knows when to keep her trap shut."

"Are we going to play?" Dave asked plaintively.

"Dave must have a great hand if he's revving to play. I fold." Charlie laid down his cards.

Roger and E.J. both put down their cards.

"I'll start the bidding at twenty," Dave announced.

"We're all out."

"Pick up those damn cards and play. This is my first good hand all night."

"Sorry, Dave."

From outside came the sound of barking.

"Do you have a dog?" Charlie asked, curiously.

"Not exactly. My neighbor has one that stays in my yard."

"Tell him to keep the mutt in his own yard," Roger said. "You're too much of a pushover. It's probably some old geezer with a mangy dog that'll get fleas all over your yard."

"Actually, my neighbor is a woman," E.J. said.

"That's even worse. I'll bet it's some old lady who puts a pink collar on the dog and talks to it like it's a baby."

E.J. rubbed at his knee and wondered if a sip of beer might help ease the throbbing that pushed past the medication. "I wouldn't call her old." He thought about Jill's fresh skin and floating cloud of dark hair. He didn't always understand her, but he did like to look at her.

The game continued, with Roger winning. E.J. didn't mind losing, but he hated Roger's gloating. Dave played with steady determination and Charlie followed his usual erratic style. It wasn't a game that would have made for excitement in Vegas, but E.J. enjoyed the unpredictability of the cards, the bluffing, the whining, and the occasional wins.

At ten o'clock, Dave announced he needed to get home and left.

Ten minutes later, Fido barked excitedly and someone knocked. E.J. opened the kitchen door to find Jill outside in the dark.

"I'm sorry to bother you," Jill murmured, "but I fell asleep and forgot to feed Fido. I've brought the food over but I can't find his dish. I was hoping you had a plastic bowl I could use."

She did indeed look as if she'd been asleep. Her hair was in wispy disarray and her tan shorts and black top were rumpled. He looked down at her feet and saw house shoes with little roses embroidered on them. He looked back into her face. Her right cheek was pink, as if she had slept on it. He half wanted to touch it and see if it was warm.

"Well, hell-lo."

E.J. turned. Roger stood behind him, staring at Jill. "I'm Roger Richardson. I don't believe we've met, but you might have seen me on television. Station WMMM." He flashed a white smile. "'Weekend Edition.'"

"I'm Jill," she said with absent politeness, and turned back to E.J.

Roger crowded in closer. "Your name is really Jill? That's my sister's name. What a coincidence."

"Your sister's name is Susan," E.J. muttered. Jill could probably see right through the jerk, but just the same, he didn't like Roger sniffing around her.

"I'll see if I can find something to feed Fido in." E.J. knelt on the floor and searched in the cabinet for a whipped-topping bowl. A crescendo of pain screamed its way up his leg. The medication was definitely wearing off.

"Don't leave Jill standing out there in the dark, E.J.," Roger chided. "Where are your manners? Come on in, hon."

"No, thanks," Jill demurred. "I'll just feed the dog and run."

E.J. stumbled to his feet. "How about this?" he asked, ignoring his throbbing knee and Roger's annoying presence.

She nodded. "That'll be fine."

E.J. watched as she went outside and placed food in Fido's dish. There was no moon and the streetlight must be out. It was black as pitch. "I'll watch to make sure you get safely back to your house," he offered.

"E.J., you're making Jill feel unwelcome. Come on in, hon." Roger stood in the doorway, motioning to her.

"I don't want to interrupt," Jill said.

E.J. noticed she looked wistful, as if she would welcome the chance for company. He supposed she was lonely in a city where she really didn't know anyone. It occurred to him it had taken guts for her to move here from a small town.

"Hon, it's just a little poker game, not some stag party. Not," Roger added virtuously, "that I would know what a stag party is like."

E.J. rolled his eyes. This guy really did lay it on thick. A smart woman would see through that. Jill was a smart woman, but he also sensed that she was vulnerable right now. Even smart women made dumb choices.

"Do you play poker, Jill?" Roger asked.

"Well, I—"

"We'll teach you. You can take Dave's place."

Jill hesitated and looked toward E.J.

E.J. saw the interest on her face. She wanted to stay. What was more, in spite of Roger, he wanted her to stay. He wanted to get a whiff of her scented powder over the nasty cigar smell. He wanted to watch her new dark curls dance as she swung her head from side to side. He wanted to be with her.

E.J. shrugged. "Why not? I'll loan you a few shekles."

Jill came into the den and sat down at the table.

Roger scooted his chair closer to hers and spoke in an overly kind voice. "Now these are the cards. See them?"

"Of course, she sees them," Charlie snapped.

Roger launched into an explanation of straights and flushes and royal flushes. He talked to her as if she were the village idiot, but Jill listened meekly and nodded each time Roger asked, "Do you understand, hon?"

E.J. should have been able to laugh at Roger's heavy-handed tactics but he was annoyed because Roger was sitting close to her and smelling the powdery fragrance. Hell, if E.J. didn't know better, he'd think he was jealous. But that would imply his feelings for Jill were deeper than they were.

Sure, he liked her, but she wasn't right for him. She might be living in a little apartment now, but he knew she had come from something better; and she'd made it clear she wanted to go back there. E.J. suspected her ex-husband was a successful businessman. The suit route wasn't for E.J. Their personalities were different, too. He was relaxed; she was orderly.

"Now, four of the same kind of card," Roger continued. "By that I mean four tens or four jacks or—"

"She knows what you mean," Charlie shouted. "Let's get on with it."

"I'm ready," Jill said.

Her hair looked freer today. Since she'd moved to Charlotte, she'd done one of those mysterious body-wave things to her hair and the effect was to shape the curls softly. Very softly. He wondered what they would feel like to touch.

"Is this a good hand?" Jill asked. She laid down a terrible bunch of cards for inspection.

"No, sugar," Roger said patiently. "No matching cards and no cards with faces like the king and queen are bad signs."

"Oh." She cast her eyes down. "I'm sorry."

"That's okay."

"We'll start over." Roger smiled at Jill.

She smiled back, but E.J. was gratified to see it wasn't a warm smile. In fact, she looked wary of Roger. E.J. was glad she had taste. Maybe she didn't, though. Maybe her former husband had been a jerk, too, and that was why he had let her go. E.J. had sensed a lot of pain when he'd held her the other night. Only a fool would let a woman like Jill suffer like that.

Charlie dealt again.

This time E.J. had a good hand. He flipped money into the pot. Charlie threw in some. Jill carefully counted out coins and placed them in the center. Her hand looked delicate and manicured next to all those hairy male hands.

Get your mind back on the game, Robbins, he chided himself. Jill was here to play a few hands of poker. Just because Roger might try to make more out of it, didn't mean that E.J. should.

The bluffing began.

"I hope you can afford to lose money tonight, people, because my ship has definitely come in." Charlie threw more coins onto the heap and sat back with a sigh.

With Charlie, those words could be a lie or the absolute truth.

Jill hesitantly added her own coins.

"Hon, you don't have to do that," Roger said gently. "You might want to play a few hands safe until you get the feel of the game."

Jill smiled at him. It was a warm smile, and E.J. felt himself bristling at the exchange.

"It's okay, Roger," she murmured.

E.J. sent his own coins crashing onto the pile. "I'm in." It would be dumb to be jealous of a jerk like Roger.

The bidding went higher. Roger nudged closer to Jill to tell her she could borrow from him if she needed to. He also told her he dabbled in real estate and had just sold a house for a handsome commission. Very handsome. He was going to buy some new clothes with part of the money. Paul Simon suits, of course, and Julian Alexander shirts.

Did that impress her? E.J. wondered.

"Yes sirree, this is my night!" Charlie upped the ante.

E.J. looked at his hand and folded.

It came down to Jill and Charlie. E.J. could see Jill was enjoying the play even though she was probably overestimating her hand. He had never seen that reckless light in her eyes before. He had never seen her be reckless at all. He wondered at the possibilities of that.

Roger patted her on the shoulder. "I'm here if you need me."

E.J. wanted to hit him.

"Okay, Jill. I'll bite. What've you got?" Charlie threw down his hand to reveal a full house.

Jill's face fell. She put down three of a kind.

"Tough break." Roger squeezed her shoulder.

E.J. wanted to rip Roger's hand off her. He knew he was overreacting. This wasn't some cheap game of strip poker where the winner gets the girl. E.J. rubbed at his aching knee and decided he was making a big deal out of everything because he didn't feel so great.

He got up and took a pain pill, figuring that would make him rational again.

Jill played more cautiously for a hand, but soon she turned reckless again. Coins piled up on the table in a shiny metal heap. She borrowed money from Roger and upped the stakes.

E.J. watched her with a mixture of concern and fascination. Her face glowed with anticipation and her eyes shone like green jewels. He'd already noticed that she was attractive. He'd even recognized her subtle sensuality. He just hadn't felt the lure quite so strongly before.

E.J. and Roger folded again, leaving Jill up against Charlie.

After some heavy bidding, Charlie laid down his hand triumphantly. "Full house."

"Straight flush." Her eyes positively danced. E.J. had never seen her look so radiant.

"You win, hon!" Roger pulled her into a deep hug.

E.J. experienced hot resentment. Then Jill slipped out of Roger's embrace and winked at E.J. He stared at her and the moment of aggression faded. She was too smart to fall for Roger. E.J. felt relieved.

"Ever play poker before, Jill?" Charlie asked grumpily as he picked up his cigar.

"Well . . ."

Roger gave her a suspicious look. "Did you already know how to play?"

"Yes," she admitted, and smiled without remorse.

E.J. laughed. He was suddenly in a very good humor. "I think we've been hustled."

"Looks like it." Charlie rose and picked brownie crumbs off himself. "Can't have any evidence on me. I wouldn't want the little woman to think I've cheated on her. Gotta go."

"I'm leaving, too." Roger shot another cold look at Jill, then followed Charlie out the door.

E.J. looked over to see Jill sitting across the table counting her winnings. A sweet, satisfied smile curved her mouth upward. Her lips were soft and glistening.

"It's not nice to gloat," he said.

She smiled up at him. "I guess I'll take my winnings home."

"Not so fast. The winner always helps clean up."

So it was a lie. It was all he could think of on the spur-of-the-moment to keep her there. It was important that she stay. She had a new vitality he hadn't seen in her before. He wanted to explore this impishness. On top of that, he didn't want to be left alone with the smell of cheap cigars and the thought of his operation coming all too soon.

Now he didn't have to contend with Roger or any feelings of being left out. He had her to himself and he intended to enjoy that.

"What do you want me to do?" Jill stood with her hair tumbled and her lips trembling upward with victory. His thoughts veered away from cleaning the kitchen. What did he want her to do? *Oh, Jill, you don't know what a dangerous question that is.*

He cleared his throat. "Why don't you start by bringing the glasses into the kitchen? I'll wipe the table."

Jill went into the den, humming "Only the Strong Survive." She returned to the kitchen and began loading dirty glasses into the dishwasher.

E.J. slung his dish towel over his shoulder, leaned back against the counter and watched her. "I guess you know I let you win."

"You most certainly did not." Still bent over the dishwasher, she turned to look up at him. "I won because I'm good."

"And because you took advantage of poor, innocent Roger by pretending ignorance." He pushed away from the counter and moved toward her.

"I'm only sorry it was Charlie's money I took instead of Roger's," Jill said.

"What a heartless woman you are." He stopped directly in front of her.

"I'm finished loading the dishwasher. What other jobs does the winner have to do?"

He put a hand on her waist and pulled her to him. "Kiss the host," he breathed, just before his mouth descended on hers. She went rigid and he knew her mind was preaching resistance. But the rigidity vanished almost immediately. He kissed her more firmly, and while she didn't respond, she didn't retreat, either. Instead, she stood like a sparrow in the rain, tentative but curious.

E.J. wanted more. He wanted her lips to invite and entice and even to entreat. He wanted her to sway closer against him and he wanted to feel her lose that ladylike control. He wanted to hear her moan with longing.

Hold on, fellow. This is a simple kiss and you want the world to shake for her. That was pretty unrealistic. Or was it, when his own world was starting to tilt off center? He was losing himself in this woman, in the lavender smell and the honey taste of her. His rising desire pushed the thought of his aching knee far to the back of his mind.

He pulled a micrometer away and felt her breath fan his face. "Kiss me back, Jill." Then his mouth reclaimed hers with a hard passion that left no room for indifference.

He felt a tremor of shock run through her. Then her lips opened beneath his like the petals of a flower. He slipped the tip of his tongue inside, and her hidden softness excited him further. Cautioning himself against the rough need surging up inside him, he clamped her against him until he felt every feminine curve.

Suddenly she wrenched away. "What do you want from me?" she asked in a trembling half whisper.

He looked into her flustered, accusatory face and hesitated. He wanted to carry her up to his bedroom and strip her clothes away. He wanted to lose himself in sex with her. A deeper, guiltier thought surfaced through the waters of his desire—he wanted her to help him forget what lay ahead for him.

E.J. had told Roger he didn't use women. Yet, in a way, he wanted to use Jill to help him forget his own troubles.

Releasing her, he stepped back. "I'm sorry. I guess I lost my head."

She bit her lip and looked away. "Everything I told you before still stands. I'm not in the market for a man."

That was what she said. He had to wonder if a woman in love with another man would have responded to him as she had. But he nodded as gravely as if he believed her.

She took a shaky breath. "I'm glad we understand each other. Sometimes people make too much of an incident."

"Yeah." Did she know he wanted to touch her one more time before she left? Did she know he wanted to see if his body felt again that lick of fire at the contact of his skin against hers?

Jill turned away and started for the back door. The little tan shorts hugged tightly to her shapely bottom. The black top was even more rumpled from their embrace.

E.J. stood where he was. He should offer to walk her home, but that would put them alone in the dark together, making it so easy for him to reach for her again and descend into another kiss. That wouldn't do anybody any good.

Instead he watched her from the doorway as she made her way across the yard. Then he tossed the dish towel onto a chair and started up the stairs to his room.

He could clean up the mess in the morning. Right now, he was going to bed. The only relief he seemed to get these days was when he was asleep. He had a feeling that tonight, though, his sleep was going to be punctuated by some pretty explicit dreams.

JILL SHIFTED RESTLESSLY on her single bed in the bedroom with crisp white walls and new slate blue curtains that matched the bedspread.

She had joined the poker game at E.J.'s house because she was lonely. She should have left when Charlie and Roger did.

She thumped the pillow and turned again. What had possessed her to kiss E.J. with such fierce need? E.J.'s kisses were harder and more demanding than Darren's. E.J. had insisted that she participate, and she had felt a woman's reaction to a man's aroused body.

Physical response was one thing, but her confused emotions disturbed her more. She liked E.J. He had offered her comfort when she was upset, neighborly help in putting up signs, and they had shared laughter. But there were emotional boundaries she could not cross.

Even if she didn't still feel committed to another man, she wasn't ready. She was too vulnerable, too unsure of herself.

The sound of the phone ringing jarred her. Who would call at this hour?

She answered in the kitchen.

"It's Darren."

Guilt dampened her joy. She had kissed another man only a short time ago. "H-hi."

"You okay? You sound different."

She heard a concern in his voice that had been missing for a long time.

"You woke me up, but it's all right," she assured him.

"Oh, yeah, it's after eleven. I hadn't realized how late it was. I can call back tomorrow."

"No. I'm already up." She held tighter to the phone, not wanting to break the contact. "Is something wrong?"

"No. I called to let you know we have an offer on the house. I tried you earlier but didn't get an answer."

She heard the question in his voice. "I was out. Is it a good offer?"

"It's five thousand less than we're asking. The realtor thinks if we hold out, we can do better."

"I see."

"We may not get as much as we want, but we can probably get closer to our asking price," he said.

She thought about the cozy years spent in that house. Safe in her own little cocoon, it hadn't mattered as much that her mother might or might not come to see her at Christmas. It hadn't hurt as much that her father phoned so seldom she didn't always recognize his voice. She and Darren had made their own little world in that house. Now it was up for sale to the highest bidder.

"I think we should reject the offer," he said.

She gave silent thanks that the house would belong to them a little longer, at least in name.

"Is that okay with you?" he asked.

"Yes."

"I'll tell the realtor." He hesitated. "How are things going for you?"

She heard the concern again. "They're okay."

She wanted to ask about his life but couldn't bear to hear the answers. He was surely dating and she didn't want to know. He might even be seriously involved with a woman. She shut down on that thought.

"You can call me, you know, if you ever want to talk, Jill. We may not be married anymore, but I'm still here if you need me. I know that wasn't always true, but I'd like to feel that you can count on me now."

She was so touched that tears clotted her throat.

He must have known she couldn't speak, because he said very quietly, "I'll let you go back to bed. Sorry I woke you."

After the goodbyes, she crept back to bed. Now she was awake for different reasons. She had left the door open with Darren, and he'd pushed it open another inch. Something was building between them—something that could take them back to the good life they'd shared before.

Knowing that helped put her kisses with E.J. in perspective. She now saw that she must have responded out of loneliness. Darren was the man she really wanted.

CHAPTER SIX

TOMORROW. E.J. awoke on Monday morning knowing the operation was tomorrow.

If it were a date, he would call and cancel. If it were a meeting with a landlord, he'd reschedule. In short, he'd wimp out if he could.

But he couldn't. The operation had to take place. He was in too much constant pain not to do something.

Sitting on the edge of the bed, he shoved a hand through his hair. Quit acting like a frightened kid, he told himself. The feeling that something was going to go wrong was just nerves.

Just nerves.

He got up and pulled a pair of underwear from the maple bureau. Then he went into the bathroom, determined to remain positive.

There were a lot of positives, he told himself as he pulled off his underwear and stepped into the shower. After the operation he would have his life back. He could bike again, slide into home for the softball team, even dance if his date insisted. He could take Fido for runs if Jill didn't get rid of the dog.

Jill.

He turned off the shower and let the last rivulets of water trail down his legs. Her kisses told him she didn't have a lot of experience with men, yet her innocence was more enticing to him than being with a woman who knew all the right moves. With a little persuasion, E.J. thought he could nudge Jill out of her defenses and into his fantasies.

Get real, he told himself, and stepped out of the shower. He didn't need complications in his life. He didn't need a woman whose untutored kisses made him want to protect her and ravish her, all at the same time.

For the next few weeks he was going to need a nurse, not a lover. Even in the best of times, Jill wasn't his type. She had made it clear she valued ambition and perfection and the things money could buy. He wasn't into that.

The case was closed.

He grabbed a towel and began drying. He flinched when a jolt of pain stabbed up his leg.

He had taken off work today because he figured he would be too restless to concentrate.

As the day wore on, he realized how right he'd been. He spent the morning pacing, trying to ignore the ache, and looking for a safe direction for his thoughts. Once or twice he thought of wandering over to see Jill, but he stopped himself each time. By lunchtime, he'd tried to interest himself in half a dozen projects. He'd turned the television on and off, on and off, and he'd left his lunch untouched on the kitchen table.

The sound of mail dropping through his door slot was a welcome diversion. He picked up the pile of letters and sorted through advertisements, credit card applications, and bills. At the bottom he found an envelope he'd been waiting for.

He had mailed off a short story to a magazine two months ago. E.J. held the letter and let hope build. What if someone had bought something he'd written? He could finally call himself a real writer. Even though he'd never been a whiz at English and he was no scholar, he liked capturing in words stories that made him happy or sad or even annoyed.

He tore the letter open and read.

Dear Mr. Robbins,
Thank you for your recent submission. Unfortunately, the story does not meet our needs. While it was an interesting study of a man interacting with his girlfriend, the story was not compelling enough and it lacked texture. We wish you the best of luck in placing it elsewhere.

Sincerely,
Laurie Lowenstein

"They weren't interacting," E.J. grumbled aloud. "They were arguing." He jammed the letter back into the envelope. "Dumb editors."

He moved to the kitchen, sat down at the table and forced himself to take two bites of his sandwich. Then he shoved the plate aside.

Texture. What in the hell did that mean?

He returned to the living room, picked up the letter and dialed the number on the masthead. He was just irritable enough and bored enough to call.

The receptionist put him through.

"This is Laurie Lowenstein."

"Hi. My name is E.J. Robbins. I sent you a short story called 'Jake and Julie.' It was about—"

"Oh, yes, I remember."

"Well, I thought it was pretty good. I didn't understand the comments in your letter." Kim had read it and liked it, too. He wondered how Jill would react to the mating dance described in the story.

"What didn't you understand, Mr. Robbins?" Laurie Lowenstein asked.

"You said something about *texture*. What is that, anyway?"

"*Texture* is the use of certain words to weave a story with a particular feel."

"Uh-huh." Her condescending words and his throbbing knee made him testy. "I don't know about New York, but where I come from, burlap bags and Grandmother's chenille bedspread have texture. Stories don't."

She gave one of those little huffs that sounded as if she were losing patience. "Mr. Robbins, if you wish to revise your story and resubmit, you are welcome to do so."

"I guess I could scratch the words on bark and mail that to you. That would add texture." He knew this wasn't smart. Any writer who wanted to sell wouldn't get on the phone and argue with an editor. But he couldn't stop himself.

"I'm afraid this conversation isn't benefiting either one of us."

"You're right there." Indignant, he hung up.

"Revise and resubmit," he muttered. "Third-rate magazine, anyway."

He knew he'd acted dumb even as he stomped back into the kitchen and sat down at the table. It wasn't fair that he couldn't sell anything when he read worse stuff than his in magazines all the time.

He was still sitting there, brooding and trying not to think about tomorrow, when someone knocked on the door.

It was Jill.

She looked good in a sleeveless blue blouse and slim-fitting white slacks. Her smile seemed tinted with reserve.

After their kisses the other night, he figured she felt awkward. He didn't. He'd learned a long time ago not to waste time regretting things that couldn't be changed. The trick was to do things differently in the future. He and Jill both knew they wouldn't be kissing each other in the future.

"Am I interrupting you?" she asked.

"No." On closer inspection, he detected an extra sparkle in those green eyes and a deeper shade of pink on her cheeks. She looked real pretty. He wished he had put that glow there.

"I noticed you didn't go to work today, and I wanted to make sure you were okay," she said.

"I'm fine."

"I also wanted to tell you what happened Saturday night," she said.

E.J. knew darned well what had happened. They had kissed and opened up a passageway into desire. Even though he had resolved that was in the past, he couldn't look at her flushed cheeks and sparkling eyes without feeling wonder. And wanting.

"Darren called me," she said breathlessly.

E.J. remained silent, betraying no trace of resentment. Was he supposed to be thrilled? Was telling him about Darren's call Jill's way of letting him know that kissing him, E.J., hadn't meant anything?

"We've had an offer on the house, but I don't think that was the only reason he called," she continued. The sparkle became even more pronounced, like light gleaming on green crystal.

"Oh, yeah?" It annoyed him that she showed this much excitement about her former husband. E.J. wasn't jealous, but male pride balked at hearing such enthusiasm for another man.

"I think Darren used the offer as an excuse to call because he wanted to talk to me." Jill touched the soft tips of her hair.

"It must have been late when he called," E.J. muttered. "You didn't leave here until after eleven."

She smiled forgivingly. "Darren lost track of time. That isn't like him at all."

She acted like it was wonderful that he'd suddenly become inconsiderate.

His knee hurt and he gave up all pretense of being polite. "I need to sit down. Come in if you want."

She followed him to the square oak table in the corner of the kitchen. She sat and folded her hands neatly on the table in front of her. "I guess Darren's call has given me hope."

"For what?"

She frowned at him. "That we can get back together, of course."

"I still don't see why you want to!" he snapped. *Careful, fellow. It's nothing to you what she decides about a reconciliation.*

"Darren and I had a good life together. I was—" Jill paused, then continued more slowly "—alone a lot as a child. My material needs were met, but I grew up feeling that I wasn't special to anyone. I didn't have a real bond with anyone until Darren."

E.J. was through pussyfooting around. If Jill was going to kiss him like she had Saturday night, she wasn't going to show up a couple of days later singing the praises of another man. "Sounds like you've got some screwy idea Darren is the only guy who can make you feel loved.''

"He may be. We were so *right* together in every way." Jill leaned toward him intently. "People give up on love too easily, these days. I don't. I have an old-fashioned sense of 'forever.'''

"And some guy inconsiderate enough to call you in the middle of the night is right for you?''

"Darren isn't inconsiderate," she retorted. "He's a hospital administrator with a very responsible job. He just happened to lose track of time.''

"He left you," E.J. said bluntly. "That doesn't say a whole lot for his dependability. Or about his 'old-fashioned sense of forever.'''

He saw pink anger rise up in her cheeks.

"You have no right to judge Darren like that. You don't even know him.''

"Did it ever occur to you that you might not know him so well yourself, Jill?" E.J. didn't know why he was pressing this. It wasn't like him to try to force advice on people. Somehow, though, he couldn't back down.

She rose in one swift movement and crossed to the door.

He didn't say anything to stop her. He knew he should apologize for being a schmuck, but he just sat where he was.

Jill closed the door firmly behind her.

"Good one, E.J." He sprawled back in the chair and looked up at the ceiling. The day was certainly going well. He had ticked off an editor and insulted Jill.

Why in the world had he said those things to her? If she wanted her fool ex-husband back, that was her business.

As E.J. rubbed a hand across his brow, he knew he had goaded her because he was worried about tomorrow.

Why else would he attack her choices?

JILL MARCHED HOME FROM E.J.'s house determined not to let him ruin her day. She had wallpapering to do and she had to buy notebooks and pens for her class. But she spent the next twenty minutes in the bathroom grimly trying to match the floral pattern before she realized she had applied the stupid strip upside down.

Darn E.J. It was his fault. She couldn't stop stewing about what he'd said. Did he think because they'd kissed that he had some kind of rights to her? Well, he didn't. He had no reason to say those things about Darren.

Jill yanked down the soggy paper, threw it into the wastebasket and went into her bedroom. This was not a good time to wallpaper. She'd weed through her closet instead. Now that she had a new hairstyle, maybe it was time to get rid of some of those prints and pastels. She was beginning to think the style was too girlish. She had noticed women at the mall in smart suits with short skirts, or sleek dresses. It was time she found a more interesting and contemporary look herself.

After all, she wanted to return to Simmerville in style.

Jill sorted through her closet for the next couple of hours. She ended up with three bags of clothes to donate to a charity organization. She put the bags by the door and went back to wallpapering.

Thoughts of E.J. still buzzed in her head and she swatted at them like flies. Like flies, she could banish them temporarily but they always came back.

The most unwelcome thought was the memory of the kiss she and E.J. had shared on Saturday night. She had spent Sunday concentrating on Darren's call and dismissing that kiss. Today, though, after seeing E.J. again, it was impossible to put it out of her mind. Was it only the result of physical hunger? It must have been, because she couldn't picture a future with E.J., while the vision of a future with Darren was very clear. So clear that it sustained her.

Late in the afternoon the phone rang. She climbed down from the chair in the bathroom and picked up the receiver in the kitchen.

"I'm so glad I caught you!" a woman said.

Jill frowned. "Who is this?"

"Xandralene. Listen, I'm working for Alternative Edibles and—"

"I thought you worked at the art gallery."

"Not full time," Xandralene said impatiently. "This is a catering business and one of the servers didn't show up. Actually, it was Callie, and I got her the job and swore she was dependable even though she— Never mind all that. Callie didn't show up and now Tony is mad at me, so you have got to get down here right away."

Jill rubbed at the dried wallpaper paste on her palm. "I don't know anything about catering."

"I'll teach you."

"I'm not sure," she said indecisively. What else did she have to do?

"You've got to come." Xandralene's voice became a plaintive wail.

"Oh, all right," Jill said. Why not? It would get her out of the house and away from all these pesky thoughts.

"Thank-you-thank-you-thank-you. Here's how to get here. Drive down Seventh Street until you get to Tryon."

Jill took down the directions Xandralene rattled off. "Got it," she said, and laid the pen aside.

"Hurry."

"What should I wear?" Jill asked.

"Don't worry about that. I've got Callie's things here. You can wear them."

Jill changed her clothes quickly because her blue blouse and white slacks had paste on them. Then she brushed her hair, grabbed her keys and drove downtown as twilight thickened into darkness.

Here and there she still saw glimpses of Charlotte's old downtown in the weathered brick buildings with turn-of-the-century charm. But most of the downtown structures were tall and new, glittering with lights and architecturally smart. Jill found a place in the hotel parking garage and took the elevator to the fifteenth floor. She hurried into Ballroom C and discovered a room filled with men in expensive suits and women in designer wear.

Jill looked around uncertainly.

Xandralene raced up to her. "What took you so long? Come on."

Jill followed. It would have been impossible to lose Xandralene in those yellow bell-bottoms, black midi top and silver earrings dangling to her shoulders.

Xandralene rushed through a swinging door and Jill went after her into a large kitchen where punkish men and women bustled about. Juxtaposed against their blue hair and Mohawk cuts, Jill noted they had sweet, young faces.

"No time to waste." Xandralene pushed Jill into a big closet. "Put these on."

The door slammed in Jill's face. She nudged aside a mop and pail and stared at leggings imprinted with Deadhead skulls and a black lace top.

She banged on the door.

Xandralene opened it. "What?" she asked frantically.

"I'm not wearing these," Jill said.

"Why not?"

"They're not me."

The younger woman threw a worried look over her shoulder. "I *promised* Tony I'd get someone to fill in for Callie. You have to help."

"I will help, but not in these. Why can't I wear my slacks and blouse?"

Xandralene looked at the brown slacks and the crisp white blouse and shook her head sorrowfully. "You're dressed like Sandra Dee."

Jill tried not to be affronted. "Based on the clothes I saw outside, I think I might blend better than you."

"You don't understand. Those people are, like, young professional types, and they want to feel hip because they're being served by grunges and New Age hippies. You'll have fun." Xandralene stepped into the closet. "Here, let me help you with your hair."

"What's wrong with my hair? I just got a permanent," Jill said.

"It's nice, but it's a little tame for the look we want. Let's try this."

Jill allowed Xandralene to have her way. It wasn't worth an argument. Anyway, she had come as a favor, so she might as well go all the way.

Xandralene created a ponytail on the right side of Jill's head. "Now, put the clothes on. And this lipstick. *Please.*"

"What the heck." Jill closed the door and tugged on the leggings. Then she pulled on the crop top.

She ran the bright red lipstick across her mouth and peered at herself in a long, cracked mirror on the back of the door. Was that her? She looked like a vamp. The lipstick was too vivid, but she didn't have any way to smudge it. Besides, it made her feel a little bit camouflaged.

She stepped out of the closet.

Xandralene stared at her. "I didn't know your body was, like, *that* good. You look sexy."

Jill saw one of the male workers looking her over, too. She bit her lip uncertainly. She wasn't used to thinking of herself as sexy.

The younger woman thrust a tray at her. "Let's get out there and circulate."

Jill's resolution faltered, but she followed her through the swing door.

Xandralene stopped beside a circle of people. "Care for an appetizer?" she asked in a bored voice.

A blond man looked dubiously at the offering. "What is it?"

"Organically grown, no-preservatives-added, whole-wheat vegetarian canapés."

He reached for one. "This I gotta try."

Jill remained by Xandralene as the man sampled the canapé. Xandralene turned toward her and whispered, "You've got to circulate. Tony's watching."

Reluctantly Jill struck out on her own. She circled the room twice before she worked up the nerve to stop beside three women.

Jill cleared her throat and fought back the impulse to pull down on the crop top so that it covered the exposed part of her midriff. "Would you like an appetizer?" she croaked.

The women took one without even interrupting their conversation or looking at Jill.

That wasn't so hard.

Jill targeted a man near the punch bowl and worked her way over to him. "Care for an appetizer, sir?"

"That depends. Have you tried them yet?" He combed her with interested male eyes.

"No, I haven't."

"Well, then, you can't recommend them, can you?" He picked one up and brought it to her mouth. "Here, taste."

She did.

"Is it good?" he asked.

"No."

He laughed. "Then I think I'll pass."

Jill ducked away, aware that his gaze remained on her. Well, there was a flirt in every crowd.

She soon discovered there was more than one flirt in this crowd. Several men developed sudden, persistent interests in organically grown, no-preservatives-added, whole-wheat vegetarian canapés. They signaled her with crooked fingers, and she felt the heat of their glances as she moved around the room.

What was more, she was beginning to like the feeling. As the evening wore on, she grew bolder. She assailed clumps of people and boldly offered her wares. She smiled when people thanked her and she winked back at a man who winked at her.

Her mother would have been proud. Not that Jill wanted to become like her mother, but her life until now had consisted of being the good granddaughter and the perky cheerleader and the dutiful wife. She had never served food in a suggestive outfit, and she'd never felt so many men look at her with such direct, scintillating interest.

Eventually the crowd began to dwindle. A man named Larry made a last stab at getting her phone number as Jill whisked empty plates back to the kitchen. He didn't get it. Jill was only going to take this flirtation stuff so far.

An hour later, the kitchen was clean and the others in the catering group were starting to leave.

"I really appreciated you, like, doing this," Xandra-lene said. "I'll bring your check to you later this week."

"Fine. I'll wash Callie's clothes and give them back to you then." Jill went into the closet and got her own things. She carried them out the door with her. There was no point in changing when she'd go straight home and change into her nightgown.

Who was going to see what she wore on her way back to her apartment? And what did it matter if they did?

She had come to Charlotte to have new experiences. Granted, she had intended to enrich her life with museum tours and by reading the classics, but this had broadened her horizons in a different way.

Jill was home in her own driveway a short time later. She parked her car and started toward the house.

"Jill."

The voice was low and masculine and unwelcomely welcome. She knew who it was even before she looked. With a rush of anticipation, she stopped and turned.

"Hello, E.J.," she said.

"I've been waiting for you to get home. I walked and fed Fido, and I wanted to apologize for—" He stared at her. "Where in the world did you get that getup?"

In the pool of yellow light spilling from her front porch, Jill looked down at herself. She wasn't even embarrassed anymore. "It's my uniform. I worked for a catering company."

"I didn't know you had a job."

"Just for tonight. I was helping out a friend."

"That's some uniform. Yes, indeed. Some uniform." He grazed her with an appreciative look like the one she'd seen on other men tonight. None of them had sparked a reaction, though. Yet now, something quick and hot ran over her, and her breathing took up a faster cadence.

She was reacting like a high school girl, she chided herself.

Then she saw how drawn E.J. looked and remembered that his surgery was tomorrow. Here she was, preening in the glow of his approval, when E.J. had far more serious things on his mind. She suddenly felt selfish and foolish.

"Are you okay?" she asked. "About tomorrow, I mean?"

"I'm a little stressed."

"Want to come in for coffee?" she suggested quietly.

He hesitated. "Thanks, but I'd better get back home. It's late and we both need to go to bed. I just wanted to apologize for the things I said to you today."

She nodded.

"I guess I was feeling mean and I took it out on you."

"I accept your apology."

There was nothing more to say, yet they both lingered. Then, awkwardly, she murmured words of parting and went into her empty apartment.

As she peeled out of the leggings and folded them neatly on top of the laundry hamper that matched her draperies, she wondered why she and E.J. never had normal encounters like other neighbors did. There always seemed to be undercurrents in motion between them.

She found him attractive, but she was here to finish her degree and work toward her reunion with Darren.

MRS. CASEY STOOD in the circle and watched the dance instructors, Rick and Marva, execute the step. Then Rick crossed the room to the tape machine, pushed the Play button, and the beat of the cha-cha filled the room. At the Avanti Dance Studio the dancers changed partners every few minutes. Grace was dancing with a bald-headed man at the moment. His hands were sweaty and he moved woodenly.

She smiled encouragingly. "You're doing well."

"You think so? Wife wants me to learn. Me, I think I got two left feet."

"Nonsense."

Grace was relieved when the dancers rotated again. Instead of the young curly-headed man who was next in line, Rick stepped in.

"Mind if I dance with you?" he asked with that gorgeous smile. He wasn't classically handsome, but he had strong, square shoulders, blond hair and an engaging way of looking at her.

"Of course not, Rick."

He held her perfectly. Not too tightly. Not too loosely. He led with a fine balance of body and hand movements, and she fell right into step beside him.

Rick leaned closer to her. "I wish everyone picked this up as fast as you do."

"Oh, go on." She felt herself blushing. Rick had that effect on her. He was younger than she, but instead of making her feel old, he made her feel younger.

"I mean it and you know it, Grace. I still haven't thanked you properly for that nice sweater. I want to take you out for coffee."

Her heart fluttered. "You don't have to do that," she demurred, even though she wanted to very much.

"I want to. Besides," he added mysteriously, "I have something to discuss with you."

The tape ended but Rick didn't release her. To the room at large, he announced, "Next, we're going to work on a new sequence."

He led Grace to the center of the circle of couples.

"Grace and I will demonstrate this next step sequence."

When she started to object, he applied a reassuring pressure on her hand. "It'll be fine," he whispered. "We'll take this very slowly. First the man moves forward into this position." He demonstrated.

They walked through the rest of the steps with Rick explaining along the way. Grace was thrilled that she followed accurately. When they were through, he smiled at her. Legs shaking, she returned to take her place in the circle.

She reviewed her moment of glory again and again as the session continued. This was one of the many ways the dance lessons gave her pleasure.

Her deceased husband had been a good man but his heritage had emphasized frugality and hard work. He and Grace had spent their married lives saving and investing and never having much fun. He had died three years ago. Grace didn't want to appear disrespectful of his memory, but she was only fifty-nine, and she wanted to enjoy herself in the years she had left.

The dance classes were an inspiration. She had been driving by the studio one day and had seen the sign.

The music stopped and everyone changed partners again. Grace smiled at an older man and they began to dance.

"You're going to put Marva out of a job," the man teased.

"Go on. I don't think she has anything to worry about."

"I heard she'll be leaving soon anyway. She's moving to California."

Grace missed a step completely. "Will Rick go, too?"

"I doubt it. They just work together. They aren't married or anything."

She felt profound relief.

"Rick's a little too slick, don't you think?"

Grace blinked indignantly. "No, I don't think so at all."

The man shrugged and they finished their dance in silence.

A short time later, the session ended. As Grace was heading out the door, Rick caught up with her.

"What's your rush?" he asked in that teasing way of his.

"I was going home."

"Let's go get that cup of coffee."

She almost forgot to breathe. "That would be lovely."

They left together in his little black car. It sat very low to the ground and riding in it made Grace feel giddy. She didn't care if they stopped for coffee or not. She would be content just to ride around in this car with Rick.

She patted her hair and wished she had a mirror so she could see if it looked all right. "I hear Marva is leaving," she ventured.

"Yeah. The owner is interviewing other women to replace her." Rick stopped for a light and turned to her. "Would you mind filling in until we hire a replacement?"

Grace sat mute. Marva was a tiny thing with strong dancer's legs and good timing. It was rumored she had once auditioned for a performance with Baryshnikov. It was a small part and she didn't get it, but she *had* auditioned.

"I can't replace Marva," she argued. "She's a real dancer."

"She's too showy," Rick said with a dismissive wave. "And don't sell yourself short, Grace. You have a lot of natural talent."

"What about that nice girl who always stands on the right side of the room? She's been taking lessons longer than I have. She's better than I am." Grace didn't know why she was suggesting someone else when she wanted to help. She wanted to be Rick's partner, but she was afraid of looking too pushy.

He shot her a dazzling smile and drove through the intersection. "I like you better."

Goose bumps erupted up and down her arms. Rick saw through the few extra pounds and the gray hair. He knew that she was kind and full of fun at heart.

Rick pulled into a parking lot at the corner of Seventh and Pecan. Together they entered an old building that had been updated inside with new tile floors and a long dessert counter.

"Cappuccino?" he suggested.

"Yes." Grace had never tasted it before, but she was feeling light-headed and adventurous.

"Let's talk about when we can get together and practice, because you are going to help me out, aren't you?"

"Oh, yes."

"Good girl. I knew I could count on you."

CHAPTER SEVEN

DARREN PEELED THE sweatband off his wrist as he and Joe started off the racquetball court.

"What about Diane?" Joe asked. "She seems nice."

"They all seem nice at first," Darren said. "But after a few dates, the demands start."

The two men headed toward the snack-bar area of the upscale health club.

There Joe bought a can of juice from a vending machine and popped the top. "What kind of demands?"

"Commitment. They want a guarantee the relationship will last." It had been fun at first, but lately, dating was becoming more and more of a hassle. Darren didn't know why women weren't content to date and see where things led. They all wanted to talk the subject to death.

Joe took a long swallow of juice. "Not all women are like that."

Darren shot him a cynical look. "Oh, yeah? Did I mention half of them want father figures for their kids? I like kids but I'm not looking to be a daddy. If the right woman happened to have a child, I guess I'd deal with it, but it would be simpler if it were just me and the woman to start with."

"Yeah, I can see that," Joe agreed as they both watched a woman in a hot pink bodysuit sling a towel over her shoulder and stop for water at the fountain.

"Sometimes I wonder if it's worth it," Darren said. "Sometimes I wonder if..." His voice trailed away.

"What?" Joe pressed.

"Forget it."

"Jill?"

Darren sighed. "Everything fell apart at the end, but lately I've been remembering how good things were at the beginning. Crazy, isn't it? We're divorced and that part of my life is over." But when he talked to her the other night, her voice had sounded so good to him.

Joe rolled the empty juice can between his palms. "Lots of people get back with their exes."

Darren had never thought he'd be one of them. Still, he found himself reminiscing aloud. "I was in college when I met Jill. She was studying to be a teacher. We were so young and excited about finding each other. Jeez, we were on the phone half a dozen times a day. I don't know when all that stopped."

Joe shrugged. "Everybody loses the rosy glow as the years go by."

"You and Amy are still happy."

"Yeah, but we've got kids. That makes a difference."

Darren didn't say anything. He and Jill would have been parents today if things had gone differently. Losing the baby had hurt her a lot. Maybe he hadn't realized how much. He supposed he could have been more understanding.

It was too late to change that, but it wouldn't hurt to call her every once in a while just to make sure she was okay.

E.J. LAY ON THE STEEL gurney and looked up at the masked faces above him. Everyone went about the business of preparing for the operation with crisp efficiency.

A nurse looked down at E.J. and the corners of her eyes crinkled in a smile. "Everything's going fine, Mr. Robbins."

What did she mean? They hadn't even started yet. Buzzards of doubt circled in his head. He looked from face to face for reassurance. Above the masks, everyone looked so businesslike. And *he* was the business.

"What if something goes wrong?" he asked.

"You'll be fine," the nurse said in a soothing voice.

"Tell me the worst thing that can happen." It was a heck of a time to be asking, but he hadn't had the nerve to ask in the doctor's office. Or maybe he hadn't wanted to hear the answer then.

"Don't worry about a thing, Mr. Robbins. You're in capable hands." She smiled again.

E.J. couldn't let go of the question. "Tell me the very worst thing. I mean, could I lose my leg? Amputation?"

The nurse maintained her calm. "Everyone's nervous about going into surgery. Relax, Mr. Robbins."

He sagged back onto the gurney. They wouldn't tell him the worst. Perhaps it was just as well. In a minute he'd be floating in never-never land and when he came to it would be over. It was too late for second thoughts.

E.J. took a deep breath and willed his muscles to relax on the bed of steel. But the bad feeling didn't go away. The sense that his life was about to be altered beyond his control stayed with him as they put the mask over his nose.

Just as he began to float, he thought about Lisa and his heartbeat accelerated. He thought about how quickly things could change, hopes get distorted, and dreams become lost.

He fell further into the blanket of dense fog and his thoughts lost coherence. But the feeling of deep dread remained.

JILL STARTED CLASSES on Wednesday. She was the first person in the classroom. She sat in the front row and placed her new books on the desk in front of her. She could have purchased used books, but she wanted something clean and unmarked.

Gradually the room filled with young women in preppy clothes and men in slacks and neat shirts. When most of the seats were occupied, a dark-haired older man walked in. He looked around without smiling.

"I'm Lindall Davis," he announced in a pompous voice. "This is Education 425. Anyone who was looking for an easy class can leave now."

He waited.

Everyone looked around uncertainly, but no one got up.

"All right. You know who I am. Let's find out who you are."

He pointed to Jill.

"Tell me your name and why you're taking the class."

"I'm Jill Howard." She wet her lips. She wasn't used to speaking in public and he wasn't making it any easier. "I started college several years ago but never finished. I want to complete my degree and become a teacher."

He pointed to the next person and Jill relaxed. Even if it wasn't going to be an easy class, she was still grateful to be here. She had never given up the dream of being a teacher.

"Why do you think a degree is important?" Lindall Davis asked the student behind Jill.

"Well, you've got to have it to teach. Besides, people respect you more if you're a college grad."

Would Darren have looked at her differently if she'd had a degree? Jill wondered. She didn't regret quitting college to marry him, but sometimes she had looked back wistfully and wished she had finished school. She thought about the conversation she'd had with E.J. about going back to college. He'd made it plain that such things weren't important to him.

What *was* important? she wondered. She knew that he wrote stories but she didn't know why. His house wasn't dirty but orderliness wasn't the priority it was with her. She also knew he dated and that he had a normal male libido, so women must be important to him.

"Why do you want to be a teacher?" Lindall Davis asked another woman, and Jill brought her attention back to the class.

"I love children and I think I'd enjoy working with them."

Jill loved children, too. If she never had any of her own, she would like to nurture other people's children. As much as she had enjoyed helping Darren's career by entertaining important people and by volunteering at the hospital, it wasn't the same as having her own goal. Jill's mother had told her, "You've got to do your own thing, darling."

"This class is about papers and tests and knowing the information," the professor said in a sneering voice. "Love of children isn't going to be graded."

This guy was a turkey. Jill decided she was going to love children whether it was graded or not.

"And I'm not going to play nursemaid to anyone," he added as he pulled out his lecture notes.

The word "nursemaid" took Jill's thoughts back to E.J. She had visited him in the hospital last night. She'd been surprised by the number of flowers and balloons and cards. Most were from women, Jill couldn't help noticing. E.J. had seemed listless. With the operation over, she had expected him to be more cheerful, or at least, relieved.

How could she cheer him? He had done so much for her, she wanted to give something back to him.

"The first thing I'm going to talk about . . ."

Jill made herself take notes. There would be time to worry about E.J. when he got home from the hospital this afternoon. At the moment she needed to concentrate on her class. She had always been a good student, and it was even more important than ever to excel. Her self-esteem was on the line.

CHARLIE PARKED HIS TRUCK in E.J.'s driveway and came around to open the passenger door. E.J. stuck his cane out. He worked with slow determination. First a leg out the door, then a foot on the ground, and finally he pulled his whole body out of the truck. He hurt all over. Looking at the distance between himself and the backyard, he wondered if he could make it.

"Need a hand?" Charlie asked.

E.J. leaned against the truck door. "No, give me a minute."

It took a lot longer than a minute for E.J. to maneuver the cane and his awkward leg around the truck door.

Once on solid ground, he started slowly toward the house.

Mrs. Casey appeared from nowhere and rushed up to him. She wrung her hands in agitation. "Should you be walking?"

"Yes, the doctor says to as long as I don't overdo it."

"But you're just out of the hospital." She looked to Charlie for confirmation. "Isn't he?"

E.J. didn't have the energy to argue. He kept walking doggedly.

Mrs. Casey fluttered about. "What do you need me to do?"

"Open the back door," Charlie said. "He can't make it up these steep steps at the front."

The threesome made their way around to the back. Charlie held an exuberant Fido while E.J. limped into the house.

Then Charlie came in and pulled out a chair. E.J. sank into it and slowly stretched his leg out in front of him.

"I'm fine now," he said. "You two go on."

"I can't just leave you," Charlie said.

"Of course you can. I'll call if I need anything."

"I'll sit with you," Mrs. Casey insisted.

E.J. shook his head. "Grace, I'm going to bed. There's nothing for either of you to do." He smiled weakly at her. "You go on home and practice your rumba."

"We're working on the waltz now."

Charlie loomed over him. "I'll leave, but call if you need me or I'll beat the crap out of you."

"You're a sweetheart, Charlie."

Once the house was empty, E.J. took a pain pill, then aimed himself toward the living room. It took five minutes to drag himself to the sofa.

There he stretched out carefully and closed his eyes. The medication took the edge off the pain and it felt good just to relax and be alone.

He'd had lots of visitors at the hospital, and nurses and doctors had darted in and out constantly. There had been no time to be alone and think.

Now the surgery was over and he was home. He'd been foolish to think anything would go wrong, and he was foolish to continue worrying. Yet he couldn't let go of his fears.

Even though fatigue and the medicine made him drowsy, he fought going to sleep. He dreaded the bad dreams that had plagued him in the hospital.

But he felt his eyes growing heavier. He had gotten rid of Grace and Charlie, but he didn't really want to be alone. He wanted someone who would offer special comfort. He wanted someone to brush his hair off his brow and stroke the back of a hand across his cheek. He wanted someone whose presence brought the content-ment of intimacy, the healing balm of shared laughter, and the wonder of what could happen between them.

He thought of snuggling against such a person and finding warmth from the cold steel of his thoughts.

He drifted into a layer of half sleep where he knew he was dreaming but didn't want to wake up. He was thinking about a woman. Or more specifically, his body was responding to thoughts of a woman.

Fuzzy, incomplete sensations floated over him, drawing him off the shallow shelf of the ocean and into stronger currents and deeper waters. Fragments of thoughts carried him on gentle waves. He thought of silky, touch-me hair and of skin pale in places unexposed to the sun. He thought of his hands moving over that skin and of hearing a woman's low, provocative moan.

His body stiffened into a peak of desire and his clothes rubbed against that tender, private place. He wanted to discard the clothing so that nothing remained between him and the woman. He struggled to rise, but he moved through a thick syrup and couldn't command all the forces it took to act. He tried to see the woman's face. From far in the distance, she spoke his name. The wispiness of her voice aroused an ancient male need to possess and explore and to relieve the hard ache.

"E.J."

Yes, she was saying his name. He wondered if anyone had ever died from wanting so badly.

"E.J. Are you all right?"

He woke with a start to find Jill looking down at him.

"How did you get in here?" he demanded with a harshness that covered his embarrassment.

She blinked. "You left the back door open. I didn't mean to wake you, but you must have been having a bad dream. You were thrashing and moaning. Does your knee hurt?" she asked.

"No," he snapped.

She fell back a step and he realized he had hurt her feelings.

E.J. sighed. "I'm sorry. I don't mean to yell at you."

"It's okay. I know you're having a hard time."

He almost choked on the truth of *that*.

"Do you need anything?" Jill asked.

Yes. He needed her. On this sofa. Naked. Now. Forget the fact that his surgery made any performance infeasible. He would love to try. But the gentleman in him beat back the wild man and he managed a bland smile.

"No. I'm fine," he said.

"If you're hungry, someone left a loaf of home-made bread on the front porch, and I brought a quiche," Jill said. "Do you want me to fix you a plate?"

"No. I don't have much appetite."

"I understand." A smile teased at her mouth. He shifted his gaze very deliberately from the curve of that smile.

"You're going to have to muster one tomorrow," she said. "Mrs. Casey is cooking like crazy for you. She plans to bring you a meal."

He pushed himself up on his elbow. "She's not making onion casserole, is she?"

"Yes."

He fell back in dismay. "Arrrgh."

"Be nice."

"You've never tasted it. You don't know. I'll have heartburn for days."

"I'll bring antacids for you." Jill picked up a pillow from a chair and brought it to him. "Let me slip this behind you. It'll make you more comfortable."

He leaned forward while she placed the pillow behind him, then watched her move to the other end of the sofa, where she bent to untie his shoes.

"I'm sure you'll feel better without these," she said. She turned back toward him, her body moving in a graceful arc. "What else do you need?"

Her skin was almost translucent in the fading evening light.

This was the presence he had longed for earlier. Now that she was here, he wondered why he should ignore all the little things about her that he liked.

"Sit and talk to me." He motioned toward a chair.

She sat and folded her hands primly in her lap. She looked so serious that he wanted to muss her hair and smear her lipstick and tease her into frivolity. She needed to learn to be more playful. He could help her learn. He wondered if she'd ever been with a man who'd made a sweet game of lovemaking.

"What do you want to talk about?" she asked.

He repressed his desires and suggested, "Tell me all the dirt and scandal about Simmerville."

"There isn't any. Well," she corrected, "not much since my mother grew up and moved away. She was rather daring."

This was interesting news. "What did she do?" E.J. asked.

"She ran around with older men when she was in high school. Mother is still attracted to older men. She's been married to half a dozen of them."

Jill smiled, but he heard the pain beneath her words.

"Your parents aren't together?" he asked.

"No. My father is a career diplomat with his eye always on an ambassadorship. I don't hear from him much. He's very methodical and organized. My mother is—let's just say, she's not."

E.J. felt sympathy for the little girl caught between those two unlikely marriage partners.

"That doesn't sound like it would work very well." He knew he was probing into an area that must be painful, but he wanted to know more about what had made this pretty, compulsive, contradictory woman the person she was.

"It didn't. They got divorced when I was six." She folded her hands even more rigidly together, as if that memory brought its own brand of pain.

E.J. couldn't let it go. "Where is your mother now?"

"At the moment she's in Brussels. Her husbands are always wealthy and like to travel. That's good because Mother still has wanderlust. Tell me about your parents," she said, and he knew she didn't want to talk about her own family anymore.

He didn't push further. "My mother is a housewife. She put on the best puppet shows you ever saw. Dad was a bricklayer. He could yodel louder than anybody."

He wondered if she felt the rich affection for her parents he felt for his. He wondered, too, if preserving her own marriage was so important because of the traumas of her childhood.

"Where are your parents now?" she asked.

"They live in Florida. They come to visit two or three times a year." He grinned. "When they come next time, I'll have my dad yodel for you."

"I'd like that."

The heck of it was, she sounded like she really meant it. He wondered if anyone had ever played chasing games with a younger Jill or tickled her until she shrieked with helpless glee. He wondered who had been gently maternal and roughhouse tender with the girl who had become this woman. E.J. suspected no one had, and the thought made him angry.

He wanted to help her see the world from another side, but then he wondered if she would let him. Maybe she was perfectly happy with her life the way it was. Who was he to say he could make it better?

She glanced at the clock. "It's getting late."

He knew one thing, though; he wasn't ready to let her go. "Could you stay here tonight?" he asked. "I don't want to be alone."

Half a dozen people had offered to be with him his first night home from the surgery. He'd said he didn't need anyone. But right now, he needed her to stay.

"Yes, I can stay."

That was all he needed to hear.

CHAPTER EIGHT

E.J. WAS ON THE PHONE the next morning when Jill came downstairs. He looked pale, and that twisted at her heart.

"Yeah, I know you've got a heavy caseload," E.J. grumbled into the receiver. "But do me this one favor. Go see him today."

He looked toward her. His expression was grim.

"No, you can't call him," he continued into the mouthpiece. "Isaac doesn't have a telephone."

He pushed his fingers through his hair in that way that was becoming so pleasantly familiar to her. She wanted to settle onto the sofa beside him and pat his arm and tease him into that deep laugh she was coming to like so well. But she sat in a chair across from him and waited. She didn't like to see him agitated and she didn't like his color.

"Day after tomorrow is too late," E.J. muttered. "You've got to get over there today. If you can't go, then find somebody who can."

While the person on the other end of the line responded, Jill watched E.J. shake his head impatiently.

"Just because I'm on sick leave doesn't mean I can abandon him. He needs our help."

In the ensuing silence, he scowled. Jill wanted to hang up the phone and fix him a cup of something hot and soothing. He didn't need this worry.

"Yeah, sure. I'll talk to you later." E.J. hung up and announced, "They're not going to check on Isaac."

Jill ran her fingertips over the arm of the overstuffed chair but kept her gaze on him as he moved laboriously toward the sofa. She wanted to jump up and help him, but she sensed he didn't want that, even though she'd seen a grimace of pain shoot across his face.

"I'm sure you're not expected to worry about work while you're home recovering."

He laughed mirthlessly and lowered himself onto the black sofa. "If I don't, no one else will."

"Surely this can wait until you're well enough to go back to your job."

"Isaac may not even have working plumbing. That can't wait.

She leaned forward, intent on making him understand. "E.J., you had an operation two days ago. You can let someone else handle this."

He gave a ragged sigh. "No one will."

"Then it can wait. Your job right now is to take care of yourself."

Jill hadn't expected E.J. to be so persistent. She hadn't realized he took his job this seriously. Darren was conscientious but he was an executive. He got paid big money to worry. E.J.'s dedication was an unexpected and admirable trait, but Jill couldn't let him jeopardize his recovery by trying to do too much too soon.

His fingers went back through his hair. "I can't let Isaac down. He doesn't have any family or anyone else to help him out. He's depending on me."

"You can't drive," Jill stated. That should put an end to the discussion.

"No." E.J. regarded her consideringly.

Jill didn't like that look.

Stroking a one-day growth of stubble, he mused, "If you could drive me over there, I could—"

"Absolutely not!"

He sank back against the cushions. After a moment, he said, "I don't want to keep you from whatever you should be doing. I'm sure you have plenty of things to do other than sit with me. Besides, I'm sleepy." He yawned.

He didn't look sleepy to her. He looked frustrated and cunning. She didn't budge.

"I don't trust you," she said. "I have a feeling that as soon as I leave, you're going to call a cab and go over there."

He didn't deny it.

"Promise me you won't leave."

"Jill, I have to see about him. I'm not some nine-to-five bureaucrat who forgets about people when I'm not on the clock."

"Stubborn," she muttered. But she couldn't help wondering how many other people would be so concerned about a client. Not many. It was hard to fault a man for being so caring.

She took a long breath. "I could go for you."

"Don't you have a class?"

"It doesn't meet today. My paper is due tomorrow but I can work on it this afternoon." Granted, she had intended to devote the whole morning to it, but this was important.

"I'd be indebted," E.J. said.

Then he smiled and the room seemed to dance with the energy of that smile. Jill hadn't realized how much she had missed that full-blown, confident, pleased-with-the-world smile. It helped bring color back into his cheeks and erase some of the lines of pain. Jill realized she was watching him far too intently.

Briskly, she moved to a nearby desk and picked up a blank sheet of paper. "Tell me where Isaac lives."

E.J. drew a map.

"It's not a bad neighborhood, so you're safe. All you have to do is find out if the landlord has fixed the bathroom. The rest of the stuff can wait till I go back to work."

Nodding, she took the map. Their fingers brushed. His skin felt cool, his fingertips rough.

"Thanks, Jill. I owe you one."

"No, you don't. I owed you a favor," she said lightly. But this wasn't about obligation; she felt a growing respect for E.J. and a desire to help him.

He didn't say anything.

Moments later, she was in her car and on the way. She didn't have any trouble finding the frame house with the bare patches in the yard and the peeling paint.

The man who opened the door to her knock looked as beaten and weathered as the house itself. She guessed Isaac to be in his sixties.

"Yes, ma'am. Kin I help you?"

"My name is Jill Howard. I'm a friend of E.J. Robbins. He wanted me to check on you and make sure everything is okay with the work the landlord should be doing."

He stared at her from beneath white, beetled brows. "I've been dealin' with the gov'nment since they took my river-bottom land in the forties to put in their dam. I ain't never had one of 'em come back to see how I was a doin'."

"I'll tell E.J. you appreciate it. He wanted me to find out if the work that was ordered is being done."

"Come along in and see for yousef."

She stepped into a clean room with worn, sagging furniture. A fan in the open window circulated warm air.

"Then they have done some work?" she asked hopefully.

"A plumber contracted to the city come and took out some parts but he ain't come back to replace them. I can't use the bathroom. Beggin' your pardon, ma'am, for speakin' so bluntly. I have to go down to the gas station on the corner."

"How long has it been like this?" she asked.

"Since day before yesterday. I'd fix it myself if I could, but I ain't got the tools. Such things as that are expensive."

"I'm sure they are."

"I got lawn tools, though. I do yard work," he announced.

"Is that what you've always done?" she asked. It was seasonal work, and jobs would be scarce in the winter.

"No, ma'am. I farmed till they took the farm. Then I worked in the tobacco fields. After the wife and babe died, seemed like I had to get away from South Carolina. I come here and got work in a hardware store, but it closed a couple of years ago. Now I do yard work."

She listened in silence, struck by the tragedy layered into his few brief sentences. Here was a man who had worked hard all his life, yet he lived in poverty. And alone. Jill felt guilty, now, for balking at E.J.'s insistence that someone check on Isaac.

"We'll get someone back out here to finish this work," she told him. Jill didn't know how she was going to accomplish that, but she was ready to track down the plumber herself and drag him back here by the scuff of his neck. How dare he go off and leave Isaac in these straits?

"Thank you kindly, ma'am."

"Are there any other problems?"

"None that can't wait. The bathroom is the important thing."

"Yes."

She turned to go.

"You kin to E.J.?" he asked.

"No, just a friend."

"Is he gettin' along okay?"

"He's doing fine."

"Good. Maybe I can bring him some collard greens from my garden."

She smiled. "He'd like that."

"Take care of him."

"I will."

Jill left Isaac's aware there was a lot more to E.J. than she'd realized. She wondered what other qualities she had overlooked. She was beginning to wonder what other feelings she might have for him besides a desire to help a good man.

E.J. WAS WORKING ON A short story when Jill returned. She tossed her purse onto a chair and burst into a torrent of words.

"It's a good thing I went over there," she said indignantly.

He put down his pen and watched her sweep up and down his living room like a trial lawyer pacing in front of the jury. Her cheeks were berry red and her eyes snapped green anger.

"How dare that plumber go off without finishing the job," she huffed.

"Jill—"

"The very idea!"

"Did Isaac say if—"

"We ought to call the action line on the television station and splatter that plumber's name all over the news and ruin his business. What's the idiot's name you play poker with? Roger. He could get this on television where it belongs."

E.J. tried again. "The important thing is—"

"It's disgraceful. Isaac is all alone in the world and it's not right to treat him that way."

E.J. gave up trying to interrupt. He eased back on the couch and watched her pace. He didn't remember seeing those black slacks before, but they looked good on her. The black cotton snugged against her hips and derriere, and her pink blouse was tucked in to emphasize her slender waist. Her hair billowed with her frequent turns, and he caught the scent of jasmine cologne every time her circuit brought her near him.

She finally halted in front of him and demanded, "What are we going to do?"

E.J. couldn't hold back a smile. He'd practically had to beg her to see about Isaac, but now they were allies. "Call the plumber," he said.

She nodded emphatically. "You're darned right I will. Where's the phone book?"

"No, I'm going to call the plumber," he clarified. "I know you've got other things to do."

That brought her up short. She planted her hands on her hips and stared down at him, her eyes blinking in confusion. "I thought you wanted my help."

"I did and you've done a wonderful job. But I can't monopolize your time. You said you have a paper to write."

"Yes," she mumbled.

"Then you'd better go work on it. I can ride herd on the plumber now that I know he hasn't done the job. You take care of your own affairs."

Her expression turned petulant. Her eyes snapped with resentment and her lower lip inched out. He knew it was chauvinistic to think she was cute when she was mad, but the truth was, she was darned near gorgeous. Her hair was a dark flurry and her skin glowed a delicate pink. Her shoulders were rolled back in a way that emphasized her chest very well. If he weren't so restricted, he'd be tempted to turn that energy into a more useful passion.

"You mean after all I've done, you're just tossing me aside?" she asked in a voice that wavered indignantly.

"I can handle it from here."

She sniffed. "That's gratitude."

"I do appreciate it," he said.

"And I want to know the outcome with Isaac." Jill snatched up her purse and swung away from him.

He watched her disappear through the doorway. Fido barked and E.J. smiled at the thought of Jill sailing past the dog with her head lifted high in anger.

He relaxed against the pillows. Maybe convalescing wouldn't be so bad with Jill to keep his mind off his troubles. He had liked seeing the militant sparkle in her eyes and listening to her voice ride the scale from self-righteous indignation to gentle concern for Isaac.

Jill could easily take his mind off the pain in his knee and his fear of the future.

Reason poked through his cardboard illusions: *Hello, E.J. There's no future in getting mixed up with a woman who is bent on reconciling with her ex.*

"I think the ex sounds like a jerk," E.J. told the unwanted voice. Who asked this idiot conscience, anyway?

Darren has a good education and a good job and he does things right. Jill thinks he's perfect, and she aims to have him back.

She did want him back, but E.J. thought he understood why. She'd been abandoned by her parents and she had never felt anyone cared for her until she met Darren. E.J. fought back his dislike of the man.

Maybe Darren had loved her at one time, E.J. considered. Maybe he still did. Jill didn't have to be deluding herself that they might get back together. They really might. Where would that leave the next-door neighbor if they did?

Out in the cold.

Even if Darren *didn't* want Jill back—and he must be a full-scale idiot not to—a smart man stayed away from a woman stuck on someone else. Right?

E.J. had other things to keep him busy. The answering machine had been picking up calls all morning. He could call back and chat with one of those people. He also needed to call the plumber and tell him if he didn't fix Isaac's problem within the hour, he could forget about getting a city project again. For good measure, E.J. might hint that a third party was on the verge of contacting a local TV station.

That would cover that problem.

He heard the back door opening. Was it Jill returning?

Mrs. Casey tiptoed into the living room carrying a plate covered with aluminum foil.

"Yoo-hoo."

"In here." He tried not to be disappointed that it wasn't Jill.

"I brought you over a little something for lunch. It's already warm. You can eat it now."

"Thanks, Grace." He took the plate she handed him and pulled the television tray over in front of him. *Please don't let it be onion casserole,* he prayed.

"Mind if I sit down?" she asked.

"Please do." It was onion casserole.

"I wanted to let you know if you see a man at my house over the next few days, don't be concerned," Grace said.

"Why Grace, you shock me."

"He won't be *living* there. He's just going to come occasionally. We're working on some dance steps."

"You giving private lessons?" He forced himself to eat a forkful.

"No, silly. I'm going to help teach the class." She beamed.

"Congratulations."

Mrs. Casey smoothed the lap of her skirt and smiled. "I was surprised when Rick asked me, but he insisted I was the right person for the job."

"Rick is the guy who will be coming over to your house?" E.J. asked and made himself eat another mouthful. He wondered how many he had to eat to be polite, because he wasn't going to take one single bite more.

"Yes." Grace dropped her voice and confided, "Yesterday when I was sorting clothes at the center, I found the most wonderful green dress. Well, it wasn't really green. It was more of an aqua. That very pale, delicate shade. I'm sure you know what I mean."

"Yes." He didn't have a clue.

"Anyway, I bought the dress and I'm going to wear it to the first session I help teach. I want to look especially nice," she explained.

"You always look nice, Grace."

"You're sweet to say so. You should take lessons when your knee is better. You could meet some nice girls."

"How come you don't try to fix me up with Jill?" he asked.

"Jill? She doesn't seem your type. She's more serious than you are and sometimes she seems kind of sad." Mrs. Casey scooted to the edge of the chair and lowered her voice. "Don't *ever* tell her I said this, but she strikes me as one of those girls whose family has money. She probably had a coming-out party and expects the finer things in life. Are you interested in her?" She looked suddenly guilty, as if she feared she had put her foot in her mouth.

"We're just friends."

"I think it's wise." She rose. "I'd better go. The television repairman is coming this afternoon and you know they always come the minute you step out. I'll look in on you later, and you call if you need me."

"I will."

"And finish that casserole. You need to build up your strength."

"I will."

He shoved the dish aside as soon as she left. Then he called the plumber and laid down the law. He dozed afterward and didn't wake up until Madeline stopped by with a cheesecake. Later in the day, some guys from work brought him a book of dirty jokes and spent the whole visit leafing through the book and guffawing.

Jill came that night.

She smelled of a perfume he recognized from the expensive counters of the department stores. She wore a blue jacket with shiny black buttons and a short black skirt. Her hair was stylishly twisted and caught at the back.

"I can only stay a minute," she said. She sounded businesslike, and he figured she was still annoyed with him about this morning.

"Are you going out?" he asked.

"Yes. There's a guest lecturer at the college who sounded interesting."

"Is that part of your class?"

"No, but while I'm in Charlotte, I think it's important I take advantage of every opportunity to improve myself."

Improve herself? Did she feel she had to impress this dweeb who had been stupid enough to divorce her? Sometimes E.J. couldn't figure out what went on in Jill's head. But the suit looked good and showed enough long, curved leg to make any man feel randy—even a man who couldn't act on his impulses.

"I want to make sure you're okay before I go."

He remembered how feisty she had looked when she left that morning. Now she looked dignified and stiff, like the rich girl. Mrs. Casey had suggested she was. Which one was the real Jill?

"Anybody here?" a male voice boomed from the kitchen.

E.J. suppressed a curse. Not Roger.

He strode into the room. "Hey-hey-hey, what'd you say?"

Jill's mouth formed the weakest smile E.J. had ever seen. "Hi, Roger. I was just leaving."

"Leaving?" He blocked her path. "You can't do that. The party is just starting. I brought a six-pack. Now don't feel you have to chip in to pay for it. Hey, you're all dressed up. Hot date?"

"No, Roger." Jill brushed past him and left through the back door.

Roger turned to E.J. "She's good-looking but too uptight. How's the foot, fella?"

"It's my knee."

"Whatever."

"The operation was only two days ago. I can't tell any difference yet."

Roger roamed the room, picking up objects and looking on the bottoms to see if the prices were still on them. "I knew a guy once who went into the hospital for a kidney operation and they took out the wrong kidney. Ha, ha, ha. Wow, you only paid seven bucks for this lamp?"

"Put it down before you break it."

Roger did and plopped down across from him. "This guy with the kidney? It was a mess."

"Spare me the details," E.J. said.

"The guy never got over it. Know what I mean?"

"Roger, did you come to cheer me up or just to be a pain in the rear?"

"You sure are touchy." A slow grin wrapped itself around Roger's face. "You're not letting that little thing next door get under your skin, are you?"

"Her name is Jill."

"Jill, Jill, give me a thrill."

"Shut up, Roger."

"Well, what's wrong with having a little fun with what's available?"

E.J. had gone out with a lot of women and had fun and enjoyed their company without ever worrying whether it was going to become serious. Somehow, though, he couldn't see himself dating Jill casually. If they were to get together, it would have to be something much more, and he didn't think either of them was in a position to make that choice right now.

Roger rose. "Lighten up. It isn't like you had some botched surgery and aren't going to get better. You'll be good as new and playing your same crummy softball game next spring."

E.J. digested Roger's words. Without knowing it, Roger had put his finger right on the problem. E.J. didn't think he *was* going to be as good as new.

He had a feeling the bottom was about to fall out.

JILL SPENT THE NEXT FEW days alternating with Mrs. Casey and Charlie and half a dozen other people who checked on E.J. He was clearly chafing under the confinement and she wanted to help cheer him. She enjoyed seeing him, too, but he was in darker spirits these days and there was no flirtatious edge to their conversation. Each time she saw him, there seemed to be something—something hard to define—that passed between them, but it was quickly veiled.

She didn't want to explore too closely what that emotion was.

Darren had called her just the other day. She felt optimistic about the call, so she didn't let things get too chummy with E.J. Still, helping keep his spirits up was the least she could do.

Fido was still in his backyard, too. Sighing, she pushed aside the take-home test she was working on at the kitchen table.

She was still running an ad to place Fido and had received a couple of responses. But one person didn't show up and the other was a fussy woman who needed a poodle instead of a real dog like Fido. Ads were expensive but Jill intended to place a larger one before she was tempted to do something drastic.

She tried to return to working on the test, but she was relieved when Xandralene arrived. The younger woman wore a black top, a huge gold cross and red stretch pants. Jill had gone shopping the night before and bought a slim-fitting purple-and-white outfit that had seemed trendy in the store. Next to Xandralene's, though, it looked matronly.

Jill offered tea, but Xandralene shook her head and sat quietly on the sofa. Too quietly, Jill thought.

Jill sat across from her in the apricot wing chair that matched the sofa and the print in the curtains.

Xandralene put a red nail into her mouth and chewed on it.

"Is something wrong?" Jill asked.

"Sorta."

"Do you want to talk about it?"

She sighed. "I lost my catering job. Tony fired me and hired Callie. They're dating now. Anyway, Callie was my roommate but Tony moved in, so there isn't much place for me. Without the money I made at the catering job, I can't afford the rent, so I had to move out."

"Where are you living?"

"I spent last night at the bus station."

"Oh, no!"

Xandralene shrugged. "It wasn't too bad. I had to get up and move around every once in a while 'cause, like, weird people would sit down next to me."

"You must call your family and tell them you need help," Jill said.

"That's, like, not possible. My mom is dead and my dad remarried a woman with a bunch of kids. Besides, he's about to lose his house and he doesn't have any money, either."

"Oh."

"I hoped your landlady might have someplace I could stay. I could clean her house for her or do something else to pay for the rent."

"This is the only unit she owns now."

"Oh. Well, thanks, anyway." Xandralene rose and managed a red-lipped smile. "I've got some more friends I can check with."

Jill doubted Xandralene would have come to her if she'd had other options. This apartment was small and would be cramped for two people, but she thought about Xandralene, so vulnerable beneath all that heavy makeup and the trashy clothes, sleeping in a bus station.

"You can stay here," Jill said.

Xandralene hesitated. "I don't want to put you on the spot."

"I wouldn't offer if I didn't mean it."

Jill saw the relief in Xandralene's eyes and knew she'd made the right decision.

"I'll help out however I can," Xandralene offered.

Jill smiled. "You can walk Fido and weed E.J.'s garden. He's been over there stewing about the pokeweeds for the past three days."

"The what?"

"Pokeweeds."

"Oh, those."

"Where are your things?" Jill asked.

"I left them in a locker at the bus station. I'll take the bus down and pick them up."

"I'll have an extra key made on my way home from class," Jill said. "I should be back by five."

"So, um, great."

Xandralene smiled and Jill smiled back at her. This certainly wasn't something she would have done in Simmerville, but now she didn't have to justify her actions to anyone but herself. It felt right to help Xandralene, even though she knew Darren would have been concerned about her taking in such an odd person. But Xandralene was odd in a nice way. Darren sometimes couldn't see past people's clothes and cars to the real person. It was one of his few faults.

After her visitor left, Jill returned to the take-home test. She finished it an hour later. She had another hour before she had to leave for class. That gave her time to feed Fido and ask E.J. if he needed anything from the store.

She went next door and found E.J. sitting at the kitchen table with a checkbook and bills in front of him. He looked grumpy.

"I can only stay a minute," she said. "I thought you might need something."

"Yeah, I need to get well." The lines around his mouth were getting deeper, and he wasn't smiling much these days. Jill found that she missed his smile.

"You will," she said. "It takes time."

"I'm sick of watching game shows and soaps."

"I know you are." The stress of being cooped up was definitely getting to him. Someone who had been active and athletic was bound to chafe at confinement.

Jill had intended to pop in and out, but she couldn't leave him in this frame of mind. She crossed to the table and sat down.

"Are you in pain?" she asked.

"Not too much."

"Then what?"

"Nothing."

She had a sudden clear knowledge that something more than cabin fever was eating E.J. She didn't usually pry, but this was important.

"Tell me what's really bothering you," she said.

He was mute.

"And don't say nothing, because I know there *is* something," Jill pressed.

"Yes, there is." In a low voice, he admitted, "I was thinking about Lisa. She got sick the night Hurricane Hugo hit. Transformers blew like a fireworks show and a hundred-foot tree just missed our house."

"I remember the hurricane. It was awful."

"I thought Lisa was so scared it was making her sick. We stayed in the basement and waited for the storm to pass. It went on for hours.

"When it was over, Lisa was still sick and I realized it wasn't just fear. That's when I started to panic. We don't live far from the hospital. I figured all I had to do was get her there."

He looked blank, and his voice sounded robotic. "It took two hours to go five blocks to the hospital. I thought once a doctor saw her, everything would be okay. But her appendix ruptured and it was too late. Lisa died."

Jill reached across the table and grasped his hand in instinctive sympathy. What a terrible way to lose a loved one.

"I'm guess I'm scared about my situation because I know things can go wrong."

She reached for words of comfort and reason. "E.J., Lisa's death doesn't have anything to do with you. You're not in danger."

He stared down at his hands and didn't reply.

"You're tired and you're letting your imagination run away with you." Jill stood. "I have a class but I'll be back tomorrow. If you need anything in the meantime, Xandralene is over there."

"Yeah."

She knew nothing she'd said had changed his mind. Once he began to get better, he would look back and see he'd been irrational and superstitious. Still, as she left him there alone, she felt helpless for not being able to do more to reassure him.

CHAPTER NINE

XANDRALENE WAS SITTING on the porch steps pulling dog hairs off her oversize black sweatshirt when Jill returned home from her class.

"You look kinda down," Xandralene said. "Did you, like, flunk the test?"

"No, I got a *B.*" Morose, Jill sat down on the steps.

The younger woman plucked a hair from the hem of her pants. "What's wrong with a *B?*"

"It isn't an *A.*"

Xandralene looked dumbfounded.

"I have goals," Jill explained.

Xandralene continued to look confused.

"I want to be at the top of the class. I want to go back to Simmerville feeling good about myself." She had always pushed herself to excel in school. It was part of being a good girl, as if by being perfect she might win her parents' approval. Or at least her grandmother's.

Xandralene shrugged and changed the subject. "Your mother called while you were gone."

Jill felt the tug she always felt toward her mother— love mixed with regret. "Did she want me to call back?"

"No. She was leaving to go to some other country. Canada or Grenada. I forget which. We talked a little."

"What did she say?"

"She said to tell you there are lots of fish in the sea. Was she talking about Darren?"

"I suspect so." Her mother couldn't understand why Jill wanted to reunite with Darren. She herself had always seemed matter-of-fact about shedding one husband and moving on to the next. Maybe she felt grief and sadness at each of her divorces, but she always gave a show of indifference.

"What else did she say?" Jill asked.

"Not much. She called me 'darling' a couple of times and said you can't get good coffee except in the cafés in Paris."

"Yes, that sounds like Mother." Jill smiled and shook her head. "It's hard to believe the same woman who raised me raised my mother. My grandmother still thinks a bride must have a trousseau before getting married and that women should conduct themselves like ladies at all times."

"What did she, like, think of your divorce?"

"That it was a shame." Grandmother hadn't said so, but it had been evident by her look of disappointment.

"But you couldn't keep a marriage together if your husband, like, wanted out," Xandralene said.

"I couldn't stop the divorce," Jill agreed. "But I know Darren pretty well. I've left the door open, and my intuition tells me he's starting to question the divorce. I think he'll call when he's ready."

Xandralene blew her dark bangs out of her eyes. "What if you change your mind in the meantime?"

"I don't think I will." She hadn't known much happiness before Darren. Why wouldn't she want to return to the best life she'd ever known?

"I thought maybe you liked E.J."

"I do like E.J."

For some other woman, E.J. would be the perfect man. Jill was open-minded enough to admit that he had qualities Darren lacked. She couldn't imagine Darren worrying about someone else while he was on his sickbed. E.J. was also more easygoing. He wouldn't get upset if his suits were late coming back from the cleaners.

"Is it because he wears jeans to work and drives a beat-up car?" Xandralene asked.

"No. He just has different priorities from some people." Certainly different from Darren's. He would think E.J.'s casual attire and low-rent car were evidence E.J. wasn't in his league. Jill didn't think that anymore. E.J. really did have different priorities.

Jill tried to imagine E.J. on the golf course schmoozing with the "right" people. E.J. was as likely to tell an important person off. She grinned at the thought. She hadn't thought so at first, but now she saw there was something endearing about his honesty and a sweetness in his lack of pretension. That, of course, didn't mean she wanted him, but E.J. would be a good catch for a woman with different needs and expectations.

Xandralene rose and handed Jill a spray can. "Will you take this into the house when you go?"

Jill read the label. "Herbal Air-Freshener?"

"Yeah. I'm training Fido to attack anyone sprayed with it."

"Why?"

"So he can protect us."

"From bad odors?" Jill inquired.

Xandralene rose. "From bad people."

Jill held her tongue.

"I'm going to start weeding the garden before it gets too dark," Xandralene said.

Jill glanced toward E.J.'s house. He'd been depressed before her class and she had intended to go see him again. But she could visit after she studied. Improving her grade was important. She went into the house, marched to the kitchen table, opened her textbook and began to read.

Fifteen minutes later she heard E.J. shouting. Loudly. She almost overturned the chair in her rush to get to the door. He must have fallen. *Please don't let anything bad happen to his knee,* she prayed.

She wrenched open the back door and rushed outside. Xandralene stood at the bottom of the garden. She wore headphones and was clearly oblivious to the world.

Jill's gaze flew to E.J. He was using his cane to drag himself off the deck toward Xandralene. His face was red and his voice was hoarse.

"What the hell are you doing to my garden?" he shouted.

Xandralene snapped her fingers and bobbed her head in time to the music.

"You're ruining—my garden." E.J. lurched to a halt, leaning heavily against the shed.

Jill ran to him and put an arm around him. "What are you doing, E.J.? Let me help you back to the house."

He didn't take his eyes off Xandralene. "Why is that woman destroying my garden?"

"She's weeding." Jill gently tugged him in the direction of the house.

He didn't move. "Weeding, my eye. I could see her from my back window. She's pulling up cucumber plants."

"It doesn't matter. You need to—"

"It matters," he said implacably.

Jill saw it wasn't going to do any good to argue with E.J.

"I'll go stop her." She ran across the garden toward Xandralene. Prickly leaves snagged her bare legs and she half tripped on a mound of dirt.

Xandralene looked up as Jill approached, and turned off the earphones. "What's wrong?"

"You're pulling up cucumbers."

Xandralene peered at the uprooted plant dangling from her hand. "This is a cucumber?"

"Yes."

"Then what does pokeweed look like?"

Jill pointed to the fat bushes growing up and down the rows. "Those are poke."

"Bummer."

Jill looked up to see E.J. making his way toward them with slow, determined steps.

"Here's the game plan, Jill. You grab her right arm and I'll get her left," E.J. said.

"E.J., Xandralene made a simple mistake."

"She's done more damage than Fido."

Jill looked at his flushed face and her concern grew. "Let's go back into the house and have a cold drink."

Xandralene threw the plant down and brushed dirt from her hands. "Guess I might as well put them on the compost heap," she said brightly.

E.J. glared at Xandralene. Jill touched his arm. It felt too hot. He had overexerted himself coming out here.

"We're going back inside," she said firmly.

He allowed her to lead him back down the row, past where Fido was gnawing a bone, and into the kitchen. By then, E.J. was breathing heavily and his movements were awkward.

Jill pulled out a chair and he sat, shoulders slumping forward.

"Are you okay?" she asked.

"Every stray you take in has it in for my garden," he muttered.

Jill handed him a glass of water and waited while he drank it. Once his color was better, she sat down across from him. "Xandralene is not a stray. She's a sweet girl who doesn't have much gardening experience."

E.J. wasn't so easily placated. "She's an air head. I don't know why you took her in."

Jill pursed her lips. The truth was, she didn't know, either. The Jill of Simmerville would not have saddled herself with a dog or a ditzy roommate. She wouldn't have felt this concern and frustration for a man who was beginning to occupy too many of her thoughts. She hadn't even been able to study, for thinking she should be looking in on him.

She just wasn't ready to take responsibility for someone else's care. She was still too wounded herself.

She heaped the blame back on him. "Being an invalid is making you cranky," she informed him.

He gazed at her. Just when she had braced herself for a retort, he nodded solemnly.

"You're right." He looked at his leg. "I hate being so helpless that I can't even make it to the back of my own garden."

That admission gentled her.

"I know," Jill said. "But things will be back to normal soon. You'll see. You'll feel better once you can walk without the cane. It would dampen anyone's spirits having to hobble around all the time. Once you're better, you can walk Fido around the neighborhood with me."

She would even let E.J. drape his arm over her shoulder. She wanted him to get well because she hated seeing someone so vital and energetic as him frustrated and held back by an injury. And she wanted him to get well because he was beginning to mean a lot to her.

In spite of what she'd said to Xandralene, she did have strong feelings for E.J. They were getting stronger all the time. But they were physical reactions to a very physical man; that was all there was to it.

DARREN ACCEPTED A GLASS of wine and smiled at the bank chairman's wife. The charity fund-raiser was the social event of the year. The ballroom of the hotel was afloat in expensive jewels, tuxedos and low-cut gowns. The chairman's wife wore a black satin thing that barely stayed perched on her generous bosom.

"Alone?" she asked, arching one eyebrow.

"Yes."

"My, my. It's a terrible thing when the town's most eligible bachelor can't find a date."

Darren smiled and sipped at his wine.

"Rumor has it you aren't going out much these days."

He kept his smile. "Is that a question or a statement, Cathy?"

She laughed gaily and the dress slipped lower. It dawned on him that Jill had too much class to wear something that revealing. She had always been too much of a lady to call attention to herself in such an obvious way. That would be the last thing he would

"Well, I do find it curious that you're here alone and that you haven't ever called Becky Phillips again. She was quite taken with you."

"Becky's a nice woman." He looked around for an escape. He'd spent more and more time lately explaining his love life, or lack of it to people who didn't seem to know when to keep their noses out of his business.

He spied Joe.

"It was good talking to you, Cathy."

Darren slipped away and made it across the room to where Joe sat nursing a bourbon and water.

"I saw you over there talking to Cathy. Did she grill you pretty good?"

"Yeah. I think I'm cooked on both sides." Darren sank into a chair beside Joe. "She wants to know why I'm not dating anyone."

"That seems to be the question of the hour." Joe glanced at him sideways.

"Just because I'm single doesn't mean I have to be dating every hour of the day."

"No, but it's a little odd you didn't bring a date to something this big."

"There wasn't anyone I wanted to bring. Becky would have made too big a deal out of it and thought it meant something. She was always analyzing everything I did or said as a test to see if we were going to get serious. I thought about Lucy, but she would have worn something worse than Cathy." Darren put his drink on the floor."

"Hmm."

They were both silent for a few minutes, watching the crowd.

"I talked to Jill the other day." It had been a nice conversation, eased by the fact that they knew each other so well. He could relax with her. With other women, he always felt he had to keep his guard up.

"Ah," Joe said.

"Maybe I should go see her," Darren said.

"Maybe you should."

"YOU'RE GETTING IT, Grace. Now dip a little right here. That's it."

It was a tricky crossover step, and Grace was trying to remember the footwork while she held one arm up prettily. It wasn't easy, but she was getting better. Rick was a patient teacher.

"Do you think I'll be able to demonstrate this tomorrow night?" she asked nervously.

"Of course."

"What if I forget the steps?"

"Just relax and follow me. Have I ever led you wrong?" he asked, giving her hand a light squeeze.

"No."

The music ended. Rick released her, crossed the living room and turned off the CD player he had brought with him. Grace had moved a butler's table to the side of the room, and she and Rick had rolled up the Oriental carpet so they could dance on the hardwood floor. He had been here only an hour and they had already perfected three routines.

"Would you like something to drink?" she suggested when he turned back toward her. "I have some nice iced tea with just a hint of mint. It's my own recipe and people tell me it's very good."

He smiled at her. He had the most dazzling smile.

"That sounds good, Grace."

They sat at the drop-leaf table in the dining room. She served the tea and put gingersnap cookies in a crystal bowl in the center of the table. They talked about dancing and about the people who took lessons at the studio, and he complimented her on her antique furniture.

"This stuff must be worth a lot," he said.

She looked around. The furniture had become so familiar to her, it had lost its charm. She shrugged. "I've never had it appraised. Let me refill your drink."

"No, I'd better not." He glanced at his watch. "I have to go."

"Already?" Grace had hoped he would stay longer. She had even put a pot roast in the oven just in case he could stay for dinner.

"Yes. I'm meeting a man about a job in a few minutes."

A job? Grace swallowed abruptly. "Are you going to quit the studio?"

"Probably. I need to make some money fast."

Grace pushed her glass aside. Suddenly the tea didn't taste so good. "I hate to think of you leaving the Avanti studio."

"I do, too. I like the people I meet there." Rick paused and ran his manicured forefinger around the rim of his glass. Then he looked at her with sadness in his eyes. "This probably sounds dumb, but I feel I make a difference in people's lives."

"You do! When I first started to take dance lessons, I was positive I'd make a fool of myself. You made me feel graceful and you gave me confidence." She blushed at the words but nodded in affirmation.

"Thank you, Grace. I'd stay there if I could, but I've got bills to deal with. I have to be realistic."

"I'll bet they don't pay you nearly what you're worth," she said, and felt a flash of anger at the studio.

"It's not a lot." He looked at his watch again. "Time to go. I don't want to be late."

Grace had always admired punctuality, but she didn't want him to leave. "What sort of job is it?" she asked, to stall him.

"A salesman for a floor-coverings company."

"I'll bet you could make good commissions." With Rick's easy smile and nice manners, he was bound to do well in any line of work. But she wouldn't see him again and that made her stomach feel all hollow.

"I hope I get the job," he said. "Frankly, I don't know what I'll do if I don't. I'm in a terrible bind."

She looked at him helplessly. "I'm so sorry to hear that."

He picked up her hand and squeezed it. "It's nice of you to be concerned. So many people don't care about the problems of others."

"I care," she said passionately.

"I know you do. I'll bet you're the kind of person who helps her friends."

"I do like to help others," she said. "I sort clothing donations one day a week at the charity center downtown."

"You see, that's the kind of thing I'm talking about. I know if one of your friends was down, you'd be there for them."

"Yes, I would." She had taken half a dozen casseroles to E.J. since he came home from the hospital last week.

"I hope you think of me as a friend, Grace."

Her heart fluttered. He was looking at her in that special way again. "Oh, I do."

"Thank you. That means a lot to me."

She was still flushed after he left. He'd forgotten to help put the carpet back, but that wasn't important. She put a Glenn Miller record on and began to dance a box step by herslf in the empty room.

She would be sixty on her next birthday. Rick had barely passed forty. It was ridiculous to think of anything romantic between them. May-December couples always involved rich older men and beautiful young women. Why would someone with Rick's looks care anything about her?

Yet he seemed to.... And he had said he wanted to be her friend.

Grace realized the record was skipping in the last groove. She shut the stereo off and went to look out the window.

The strange girl who was visiting Jill was in E.J.'s backyard doing something with Fido. It looked like she was spraying something. Grace hoped the girl didn't disturb E.J. He had seemed depressed when she went to see him earlier today.

That wasn't like him. Thank goodness, lots of people were looking in on him. His friend Charlie had been by, and so had a number of women. And Jill, of course.

Grace let the curtain drop. She didn't want anyone to think she was a lonely old woman with nothing better to do than spy on her neighbors.

She turned away and went to check on the pot roast she would be eating alone.

IT WAS THURSDAY afternoon when E.J. called Jill.

"I need a favor," he began immediately.

She clutched at the phone. "Is something wrong?"

"Yes. I was just looking at my calendar and I see I haven't been to a movie in over a month. I always go to a movie at least once a month. Let's go."

"Now? I was reading my assigned chapters."

"Jill, if we hurry we can catch the cheapie matinee."

She looked at the clock. The reading had been hard slogging and she was ready for a break. But going to a movie with E.J. sounded an awful lot like a date. Did she want that?

"If we miss the matinee, I won't spring for popcorn," he threatened.

She touched her fingers to her hair. "I can't go just like that. I'm a mess." She looked down at her comfy red shorts and Queens College T-shirt.

"Jill, I don't know what it's like in Simmerville, but here in Charlotte the movie theaters are dark. People won't even see what you have on. I'm heading for the door. I'll meet you at your car."

She went just as she was, right down to the silly thongs on her feet.

E.J. limped out to the car and perused her slowly. "I thought you said you were a mess."

She laughed and was pleased that he thought she looked good. Darren wouldn't have stepped out of the house with her in this outfit.

He got into the car and Jill slid behind the wheel.

"What are we going to see?" she asked, as she backed out of the driveway.

He snapped his seat belt. "Anything with Arnold."

"Ha. That's what you think. We're not going to some silly technothriller. Let's go see that beautiful English movie where he dies at the end."

"I'm not going to watch that sap," he declared.

"Oh, yes, you are. I'm driving."

They ended up in the theater with E.J. sitting in an aisle seat so he could stretch his leg out to the side. The lights went down and Jill pulled out a tissue in readiness.

"Jill?"

"What?"

The music swelled with the opening credits.

"I lied."

"What are you talking about?" she whispered, even though they were practically the only people in the theater.

"I don't go to movies every month. I was looking for an excuse to be with you."

She felt that same spurt of joy she'd had in third grade when she was picked first for the kickball team. It felt good to be important to someone; but she warned herself she couldn't invest his words with too much meaning.

"I know you were getting bored at home and you wanted to get out," she said.

On-screen, the heroine met the English gentleman for the first time. Their gazes met and lingered.

"I didn't want to get out with just anyone, Jill. I wanted to go with *you.*"

The characters in the movie were dancing together. They couldn't take their eyes off each other.

Jill looked at E.J. Any woman would be flattered to have a man this handsome express interest in her. Jill was flattered, too. Did her excitement amount to more than that?

She looked back at the screen. The couple was still dancing, still exchanging hungry looks. She felt their need.

He had been truthful with her; she had to be honest, too. "I like you, E.J., and I have thought about us in, well, in ways other than friendship." In ways that were very man-woman and sexual—but she didn't say that.

"Then why are we holding back?" he asked.

Jill kept her gaze on the screen. As the couple parted, they looked back toward each other.

She sighed. "Because I'm not sure we're compatible even if I were ready. Anyway, it doesn't seem right to date someone else when my ex-husband is calling me."

"Tell him to quit calling."

"Honestly, you have an answer for every problem. But life isn't that simple."

Jill suspected that dating E.J. could get compli-cated. Her physical needs had gone unmet for many months, and she had already experienced the fleeting temptation to find relief and pleasure with E.J. But that wasn't the basis for a real relationship. And she meant it when she said she wasn't ready for one, anyway.

He took her hand and held it. "It *is* simple. You just have to let it be." He locked his fingers with hers.

The fit felt good and she didn't pull her hand away.

On-screen, the man and woman met again. He told her he couldn't see her again. He was dying and he couldn't make his pain her pain.

Jill dabbed at her eyes. "I can't handle anything too serious between us, E.J. We have to keep it light."

"Sure. We'll start there."

She turned back to the screen. Now wasn't the time to argue about how serious. But she trusted E.J. enough to know he wouldn't press too hard if she didn't want him to.

E.J. leaned toward her. "Since we already know he's going to die, can we leave now and go see a real movie?"

She swatted at him, but she was secretly relieved. E.J. would keep it light and fun, so why not have a few casual dates? Jill would welcome the chance to escape from her apartment, and E.J. needed to get out, too. Why deny them both something pleasant and innocent? Being together couldn't slip into something heavier unless they allowed it, and that wasn't going to happen.

CHAPTER TEN

DR. FINDLEY PUSHED HIS chair away and picked up a clipboard.

"So, how's it look?" E.J. asked.

The white-haired doctor continued scribbling. "Knee surgery is always difficult," he said. "The knee is a highly modified hinge joint. It has two degrees of freedom—flexion-extension movement and rotary movement. It's vulnerable because of the capsular and ligamentous components."

"Give it to me in layman's terms. I'm doing the exercises but I don't seem to be getting back mobility. Is that normal?"

The doctor frowned. "I'm going to send you for more X rays."

A red flag fluttered in the pit of his stomach, and E.J. could almost see an enormous bull getting ready to charge at it.

"Is something wrong?" he asked.

Dr. Findley put the clipboard under his arm and rose. "I don't know. I need more information."

E.J. sat, stunned, as the doctor left.

Finally he dressed and went out into the waiting room. Jill stood and smiled at him. His spirts lifted infinitesimally. He was glad she had driven him. He needed her next to him, talking in those soft accents and offering her arm.

"Ready to go?" she asked.

"Yeah."

"Good." She smiled.

Seeing that smile helped E.J. push the worry monster into a closet in his mind. He slammed the door and pretended there were no monsters.

They started toward the parking lot. His cane *thumped* in time to their steps and she kept her arm tightly around his left arm. Her touch comforted him.

He didn't want to go home and have to face his fears alone. He wanted to put off that moment for as long as he could. When they reached the car, he suggested, "Why don't we have some lunch while we're out?"

She shook her head. "I can't. I have a class in an hour."

He thought about playing on her sympathy and telling her the news at the doctor's office hadn't been good. But he wasn't ready to admit aloud that there might be problems.

Jill bit her lower lip as she braked at a stoplight. "I guess I could skip my class. I wouldn't be so reluctant, but I'm only getting a *B* in the course."

"Missing one class won't hurt." E.J. didn't care if he was being selfish. He wanted to be with her.

Jill put her foot on the gas as the light turned green. "I guess I can be bad once in a while."

"That's the spirit."

She guided the car to a deli with a striped awning out front and little bistro chairs inside. They ordered at the counter and took their sandwiches to the only empty table. E.J. leaned his cane against the edge of the table.

"How much longer will you have to use the cane?" Jill asked as she removed the lettuce from her sandwich.

"Hard to say." *Forget the doctor and the worry rattling around in your gut,* he told himself. *Think about something else. Jill, for instance.* She looked especially pretty in the light filtering through the window. Her skin was fine grained and flawless, her mouth a moist pink.

"Have you talked with Mrs. Casey lately?" she asked, as she fitted both hands around her sandwich.

"I talk with her all the time," he replied.

"I mean about this man who's teaching her to dance. Rick."

"Yeah," he said. "She mentions him. She seems to really like him."

"I'm afraid she does." Jill nibbled at a potato chip.

"What's wrong with that?" he asked.

"Maybe nothing."

He snitched one of her chips. "Look, Jill, if you're going to cut classes and sin, you might as well sin all the way and gossip."

She looked as if she were about to make a self-righteous retort. Then her face relaxed into a grin. "I'm not sure I like Rick."

"Ever met him?"

"No."

"Then why wouldn't you like him?"

"I have a feeling he wants something."

"What?"

"I don't know."

E.J. dug into his sandwich. Women's logic always eluded him.

Jill sighed. "I've seen him leaving her house. He's much younger, but she talks about him as if it's a romance."

He shrugged. "Younger men date older women all the time. Do you want your pickle?"

She handed it to him. "Maybe I'm too suspicious."

"Probably."

The worry monster stuck its foot out of the closet and E.J.'s thoughts veered away from Mrs. Casey. He quickly banished the monster again.

"Have you given up trying to get rid of Fido?" he asked, to distract himself.

"No. Certainly not." Jill looked away from him. "It's just that, well, placing a dog is like placing a child. I can't just put him in any home."

"Why not?"

She shook her head in exasperation. "Because it might not be the right fit."

"Are you getting any calls?"

"No. I'm going to run another ad, though. I need to be more specific and target my audience more. I know Fido has been in your backyard a long time, but I'll place him soon."

"Those ads must be costing a bundle."

"I don't mind."

They finished their lunch and left. The monster was pounding on the door of E.J.'s mind as they stopped at his house. He knew he faced a hard night.

"OH, RICK, THAT'S AWFUL!"

The blond man shook his head. "I couldn't believe it myself. I had just paid off all my debts." He looked quickly at her. "I really appreciate the money you loaned me. I'm going to pay it back, you know."

"Of course, I know that."

"This new thing has come at me out of the blue."

"How can your ex-wife get a judgment for all that money when you've been paying support all along?" Grace asked as she stood, distraught, in the middle of her living room.

He waved his arm helplessly. "She got some slick lawyer and they found a loophole. You know how these things are. She's so vindictive. I've tried to be friends for the sake of the kids, but if you want to know the truth, I think she's still in love with me and this is her way of hurting me because I just don't love her back."

"That's terrible."

"What's terrible is that they're going to put me in jail if I don't pay the money."

A chill ran through her.

Rick looked at her mournfully. "I hate to ask you for more money, but this is an emergency."

He looked so pale and drawn. Poor man. Grace could just shake his ex-wife.

"But you said you own a house with her?" she asked.

"Yes. The house is on the market and as soon as it sells, I'll have the money to pay you back."

Not that she was suspicious of Rick, but it was reassuring to know his money would be available soon.

"I'm willing to sign a note if you want that, Grace."

"It's not that." She knew her husband would have insisted on a note, but that would imply she didn't trust Rick. Still, before she lent him the kind of money he needed, she had to ask more questions.

"I still don't understand about your wife getting a judgment. It seems—"

"Grace, I'm sorry to cut you off, but it torques me off to think about it, and I don't want to discuss it."

He seemed so perturbed that she didn't press further. "Of course." Still, he was asking for an awful lot of money.

"I don't know, Rick," she said unhappily. "I'll have to think this over."

"Of course." He bent to roll the carpet back into place. "Everything would have worked out if I'd landed that other job, but I didn't, and I'm still at the dance studio."

She was secretly glad he hadn't got the other job, even if it would have paid more money. But wasn't it selfish to want him to stay at the dance studio when she wasn't willing to help him financially?

"I don't want to take up your whole day," Rick said. "I'd better go."

At the door, he turned to her with a bittersweet smile. "You're going to think I'm nuts, but Rainbow Cruises has a ship headed for the Caribbean next month. I want to go—you know, to help me forget this whole mess with Helen—and I'd like you to go with me."

He was asking her to go on a cruise with him! Grace's heart did a fast, excited samba.

"Have you ever been on a cruise?" he asked.

"No, never." Her husband would never have spent money on such foolishness. Grace could almost feel the ocean swaying beneath her. She thought about dancing in Rick's arms beneath the stars on the deck of a ship. The idea was rash and romantic and she loved it. It flashed through her mind that Rick didn't have the money to go on a cruise, but surely his house would be sold by then. Besides, money wasn't the issue. The important thing was that he was asking her to go with him. He was as much as telling her he saw her as more than a friend. Grace was positively breathless with the thought.

"What do you say?" Rick asked with that tender-teasing note she loved.

"Oh, Rick, I'm just overwhelmed."

He put his index finger to her lips. "Don't say anything, then. I'll call you later."

THE DAY AFTER JILL took E.J. to the doctor's office, she was finishing her lunch when Mrs. Casey arrived. Jill had considered walking to the grocery store but decided not to. The sky was a leaden gray. Every once in a while the heavens growled to let her know they were serious about raining.

"I'm not interrupting you, am I, dear?" Mrs. Casey asked.

"No. Is something wrong?" The older woman's cheeks were fuchsia pink and her eyes looked a little wild.

"Nothing's wrong." Grace stepped through the door Jill held open for her. She glanced around. "I like the way you've decorated. Those pinks and reds look so pretty together, and I love the cabbage roses on the throw pillows."

"Thank you."

Mrs. Casey lowered her voice. "Are you alone?"

"Yes, Xandralene has gone to the art gallery. Sit down. Please."

Mrs. Casey sat in the wing chair. "Rick just left. He's my dance instructor."

"Yes, I know." Jill eased herself into a chair and waited.

"He's a very sweet man." She rubbed her hands together. "He's having a few problems right now."

"Oh?"

It all came spilling out then. Wretched ex-wife. Lawsuit. Jail. Injustice. The fact that Mrs. Casey frequently backed up to clarify a point made it hard to follow everything, but Jill got the overall picture. Rick wanted money.

"He's willing to sign a note, but that seems so unnecessary. I believe a man's word as a gentleman is enough."

Was Rick a gentleman? Jill wondered. But she knew it would get her nowhere to ask that question.

"Lending money is tricky," Jill began in her most diplomatic voice.

"Oh, I almost forgot! He wants to take me on a cruise to the Caribbean."

Jill's warning system went on full alert. This guy was not to be trusted. But how to tell Mrs. Casey something she clearly didn't want to hear?

"A cruise costs money," Jill began carefully. "It doesn't sound as if Rick would be able to afford it. At least, not right now."

"Does it matter who pays?" Mrs. Casey demanded passionately. "Besides, he'll have money once his house sells. If his awful ex-wife doesn't do something to steal it from him." She rubbed her hands more rapidly. "You don't need to worry that I would do anything, well, scandalous. I wouldn't go away alone with him. I'll find someone to accompany us as a chaperon."

The propriety of the cruise was the last thing on Jill's mind. She was more worried about a shyster getting into Mrs. Casey's pocketbook. Yet Jill knew she must pick her way carefully through this briar patch of longing and bad judgment.

"I think you need to consider this very carefully," Jill said. "Caution is a good thing."

A look of rebellion swept over Mrs. Casey. "I've been cautious all my life. My husband and I pinched pennies and invested wisely. Why shouldn't I do what I want with that money now?" She stared at Jill, daring her to disagree.

"It's your money, of course, but you want to be sensible with it."

Mrs. Casey looked away. Jill knew she had lost her. She didn't think anything she could say would bring her back. It was hard to compete with visions of a starlit cruise. Jill just didn't want to see a good woman taken advantage of.

Grace rose and started for the door. "Thank you for talking to me, dear. I won't take up any more of your day. Goodness, look how dark it is outside. It's going to pour any minute."

As Jill watched her leave, she suspected her landlady was going home to look through her wardrobe for cocktail dresses and cruise wear.

Well, what could Jill do? It wasn't her problem. But her conscience said otherwise. She'd feel miserable if this guy took advantage of Mrs. Casey. Sighing, she pushed herself out of her chair and headed for E.J.'s house. He had known Mrs. Casey longer. Maybe he'd have some ideas.

She wanted to see E.J., anyway, she realized as she stepped outside. She hadn't seen him since their lunch yesterday. She had thought after their afternoon at the movie that he might start to pressure her for more of a romance. He hadn't. He had held back as if waiting for a signal from her.

As she opened the gate to E.J.'s backyard, the wind blew the undersides of the leaves up. Large splatters of rain began to fall.

Jill hurried to E.J.'s house and dashed in the back door without bothering to knock. As she slammed the door, the skies opened and the rain pelted down in noisy earnest.

"Hi," she called, and headed into the living room.

E.J. was sitting in a chair doing the exercises the physical therapist had prescribed. He was wearing a pair of red shorts and a gray T-shirt with the collar torn out. His legs were muscular and hairy. His arms glistened with sweat. She felt something stir within her.

Jill almost forgot why she had come over.

He looked up at her. "Be finished in a sec."

"No problem." She sensed a recklessness in him today. It was in his face and in the way he moved his body, as if he were pushing himself with determination. She wondered why, then lost the thought as she watched him bend and flex.

The constriction in her midsection tightened further. Thunder boomed and she jumped.

"That was close," he said.

"Yes."

Fido howled in the background.

Jill looked guiltily over her shoulder. She hadn't even thought about the dog being out in the rain.

"Don't worry," E.J. said. "I had Xandralene put him in the shed earlier. He won't get wet."

"Thank you."

E.J. finished the exercises and made his way to the sofa, holding on to furniture as he went. He patted a place beside him. "You must have something burning a hole in your mind to come out on a day like today."

"Actually, I do." Jill wondered if it was wise to sit so close to him, then realized she was being ridiculous. She was letting the fact that she noticed him as a man cloud her judgment. It was normal for women to notice men. Why make a big deal out of it? She sat down beside him.

"I'm worried about Mrs. Casey," she said. "This guy Rick is trying to con money out of her."

"She told you that?" He leaned back into the cushions and watched her.

"Naturally, she didn't use those words."

"What did she say?"

"He wants to 'borrow' the money and he intends to pay her back."

"Maybe he does."

Jill shook her head. "You haven't heard the whole story. He wants to take her on a cruise. I think he's playing on her hope that this is a romance and that he cares for her."

"He might, Jill."

Were all men so gullible? she wondered, then jumped when thunder crashed even closer.

"Does thunder scare you?" he asked.

She sensed that recklessness in him again, and maybe something more, almost as if there was a suppressed tension in the air. Now that she thought about it, he had seemed different when he left the doctor's office.

"It scares me when it's that close," she said.

He put an arm around her. "Feel better?"

Yes. In fact, his touch made her feel *too* good. It was time to go. "I'd better get back to the house." She started to rise.

He pulled her back beside him. "In this rain?"

"I think it's letting up."

Lightning seared the sky outside the window.

"Yeah, right," he agreed sarcastically.

She subsided back into the couch. It *was* storming outside. There were, however, storms of a different nature brewing inside the house, and she wasn't sure she wanted to deal with that, either. She tried to put their conversation on a less personal footing. "I still don't like this whole thing with Mrs. Casey."

"Don't worry about it. Concentrate on your own life."

A low moan of thunder grew to a crescendo. The lights flickered, made a valiant effort to burn, then died. Jill found herself in pure darkness.

"I *am* concentrating on my life," she said defensively into the void. "I'm taking classes and going to art museums and reading literature."

"That's just passing the time." E.J.'s voice sounded thick and substantial in the blackness. "Living is experiencing things."

"Such as?" she challenged.

"This." He ran his hand slowly up her back. His touch was warm and sure.

Pull away, Jill, a voice warned. But it felt so good. His palms exerted just the right amount of pressure and his touch lingered in each place just the right amount of time.

"Or this."

His hand reached the top of her spine, and he began to massage the base of her neck. Heat radiated out from his touch. As he continued massaging, he tried to draw her closer against his body.

She tensed and stayed where she was.

"Relax, Jill."

"I can't. I don't want to be here." Her words were a mere thread of coherence.

"Why not?"

"Because..." Because she was committed to some- one else? But Darren had left her. And if she still felt committed to him, why had she been so aware of E.J. as a man when she came in? Why did his closeness make her body tingly and her thoughts gummy?

"I want to hold you," he said.

This time she let him pull her against him. She knew he wanted a lot more. She could sense his need in the way he touched her, and hear it in the rough tenderness of his voice. This was not a moment of friendship; this was a prelude to something infinitely more compli- cated. This was the beginning of passion.

"Are you trying to seduce me?" Jill didn't mean for her voice to sound husky, but his touch was changing her body in many ways.

"Honey, if you have to ask the question, I mustn't be doing a good job." His kiss sent hot currents across her ear. "What do you want me to do that I'm not do- ing?"

She wanted him to stop. Didn't she? Only her mouth couldn't form any words. She had never known the skin below her ear was so sensitive that a kiss there left her light-headed. And hungry for more.

Jill fought to clear her mind. She couldn't be inti- mate with a man solely to experience physical passion. There had to be more. As E.J. feathered a line of kisses across her cheek, Jill admitted there was more between them than simple friendship. She cared for him.

There was a loud crack of thunder, but the noise barely intruded on her consciousness. She was losing track of the world around her. She was drawing into herself and bringing E.J. with her. Was that the right thing to do? It seemed so. In fact, it seemed important.

In the midst of his kisses and touches, Jill couldn't analyze rationally. But she knew this was a not a casual thing. It had begun when they first went to the mall. It had grown during the night they spent at the gallery crawl. It had continued to grow during all the little events and exchanges that had marked their lives since then.

E.J.'s mouth played a pattern of kisses on her neck and up the lobe of her ear. Little streams of pleasure flowed up and down her body. He drew her closer against him.

It was do or die. Now was the moment to tell him she wasn't going to allow him to seduce her. Now was the moment to take a stand. Now, while his hand was moving along her ribs and beginning to explore the underside of her breast. If she didn't call a halt, E.J. would surely move those caressing hands farther upward. He might even push her clothes aside and take her nipple into his mouth, teasing it the way he'd teased at her ear....

"E.J., I—"

"Yes, tell me what you want." His voice was a low, throbbing murmur.

"This isn't right."

"Tell me, then. I want to do it right."

His mouth hovered above hers so that when he talked his breath invaded her body. It was an incredibly intimate feeling. His hand cupped her breast more firmly, moving upward as she had known he would. Instead of wrenching away, she tensed with anticipation at the pleasure to come.

But he didn't do anything. He remained motionless, as if waiting for her to continue.

"I won't force you," he said. "You've got to want this as much as I do."

She did want it. The possibility that he might stop alarmed her. Jill knew, then, that she was already committed. She couldn't get up off the sofa and walk away. Something was happening between them that was more than desire, more than impetuosity.

Her decision made, she moved her mouth that millimeter closer and their lips met.

They kissed.

It was a simple act, really. Men and women did it all the time. She had kissed and been kissed before, but never with such results. This was fire and fever, demand and desire. As his tongue moved inside her mouth, the little streams of pleasure grew into rivers of passion.

Thunder sounded a deep, escalating drumroll outside. Their kiss matched it, growing fiercer and more demanding. Lightning struck. The ground opened up below Jill, exposing a well of need. She had a sudden, blinding fear that the well was too deep to fill. She wrapped her arms tightly around E.J.'s neck, wanting to hold on to him and to this moment. He put both arms around her and held her close. Their kiss expanded.

Jill let herself spin at the mouth of the volcano for several minutes before she pulled back. E.J., for all his evident need, was still recovering from surgery, and she didn't know what he could and could not do.

She took a deep breath. "I don't want to sound too technical, but what do you need me to do?"

"It's probably easier on the floor and easier if I lie down. There's some protection in that drawer over there." She didn't hear any embarrassment in his voice, just a hoarse need.

They moved to the floor and lay side by side.

There he pushed aside her blouse and kissed the bare flesh of her midriff. Lightning shimmered outside the window. She gave herself over to his moist kisses on her stomach. Then he searched higher, skirting her breast before coming to rest on her nipple. She closed her eyes and slowly exhaled.

Jill combed her fingers through E.J.'s hair and felt the thick texture.

With E.J., everything was new. All she knew about lovemaking was centered around one man. Yet it felt good to be here with E.J. and to learn about him and about herself.

Learning about herself was the scary part, and for a moment Jill faltered. What if she was doing this for the wrong reasons? As much as she liked E.J., was she ready to cross with him into uncharted territory? Was she ready to be vulnerable with him?

Yet he'd said nothing would happen unless she wanted it to. By giving her control, he'd already made himself vulnerable. Could she do less? No. And she didn't want to.

Sanity became a tangled skein as E.J. continued to caress her breast.

Then he pushed her skirt up and his hands began to explore. Anticipation rippled through her. Warm, liquid sensations curled out from the intimate part of her where his fingers played. She felt suddenly, starkly hungry with the need for him. Hungry for fulfillment.

Whatever reservations she'd felt were cast aside. She wanted him. Now.

As if he sensed her rising urgency, he stood and shed his clothes. Thunder rumbled now and again, and lightning flashed, illuminating him standing naked and throbbingly male. Then all was blackness again, but the vision remained imprinted on her mind's eye as she removed her own clothing. No barriers remained between them as E.J. lay back down and pulled her to him.

He covered her mouth with his and she was lost in his kisses, in the rising tide of wanting and in the feel of him waiting to enter.

He waited for the longest time, tempting and tantalizing her as their kisses became a hot frenzy. Still he waited, as if for the moment when neither could stand it any longer.

Dear Lord, Jill felt that moment fast approaching.

She moaned and pressed closer.

A roll of thunder played in the background as lightning flashed around the room. Then, E.J. slid inside her and she sighed blissfully, knowing that something even better awaited her. She felt flushed and frantic and desperate for her need to be filled.

But E.J. clearly knew what she wanted. He knew what she needed. He proved that as he began to move with quickening thrusts. He kissed her with darting movements of his tongue, probing the satin lining of her mouth even as he explored the other recesses of her body. His hands bound her against him with an intensity that would have kept her from escaping even if she'd wanted to.

That was the last thing on her mind.

She gave back kiss for kiss as his every thrust took her into swifter currents. She was losing control. That had never happened before. Before, even in the midst of passion, she had always preserved a part of herself.

Panic erupted, followed almost immediately by exhilaration. She didn't want to be safe. She wanted to swim the dangerous currents with E.J. She wanted to be swept away with him into the dark water.

Her desire was followed almost immediately by the reality. The lightning was inside her now and not part of the storm that raged outside. He dug his hands into her back and clasped her closer into an embrace of passion. She held on to him and she saw him in her mind's eye as the lightning had revealed him earlier: naked and taut with erection.

The memory was enough to lift her up into a climax of whirling velocity and aching intensity. Her whole body throbbed and retreated, throbbed and retreated, and her only lifeline was E.J.

CHAPTER ELEVEN

WHAT HAD SHE DONE?

It was three o'clock in the morning and Jill was wide-awake. E.J. slept beside her on the carpet beneath the afghan they had pulled from the couch after their love-making.

She shifted restlessly and was racked by doubts. She had wanted this to happen, but implications that had been blurry in the midst of passion stared unblinkingly at her now. While the rain pattered steadily outside the window, she tossed and worried. Had she had sex with E.J. because she wanted to experience lovemaking with someone other than Darren? What were her *real* feelings for E.J.?

Sex had clouded the issue. She couldn't avoid comparisons between the only two men she had ever known intimately; lovemaking with E.J. had been more powerful than it had ever been with Darren.

Usually, something that good was wrong.

E.J. was a good lover. He had the experience and sensitivity to bring her to new heights of passion. But that didn't mean he loved her. And she certainly didn't know that she loved him.

Sitting up, she pushed a hand through her hair. In a few hours he'd be awake. How was she going to act toward him? She didn't even know what to say to herself, let alone what to say to him.

She had grown up trying to do the right thing and behave like a good girl. Yet she'd made a conscious decision to be with E.J. without ever deciding to give Darren up. How had she allowed herself to do that?

Besieged by doubts, she knew she wasn't ready to face E.J. Quietly she lifted the afghan and rose. She slipped into her clothes and left by the back door. Later, after she'd had time to sort this out in her mind, she'd be able to talk with E.J. But not yet.

Jill let herself into her apartment and crept past the sofa where Xandralene slept.

"What time is it?" Xandralene asked sleepily.

Jill stopped guiltily. "A little before four."

Xandralene turned on the light. "The electricity is back on," she said. "It was out all over the neighborhood for a real long time."

"Yes, I know."

"Jeez, what did you do over there at E.J.'s in the dark until this hour and..." Xandralene looked at her and understanding dawned. "Uh-oh. Forget I asked."

"Go back to sleep."

"You seem kind of bummed. I guess things turned out bad," Xandralene mumbled sleepily, and switched off the light.

Jill hesitated in the doorway of her room. That was the crux of the problem. Everything had been *too* good. Even now, by the light of reason, goose bumps rose on her arms at the memory of how enjoyable and erotic it had been.

"I didn't have any business being there with E.J.," Jill said, not sure why she felt compelled to explain to Xandralene. Maybe she just needed to talk.

"'Cause of, like, Darren, you mean?"

"Yes." Even as Jill groped for an image of Darren, he seemed gray and insubstantial. It was E.J.'s face she saw. E.J.'s laughter she heard. E.J.'s body she remembered.

"But you're divorced. There's nothing to stop you from seeing other dudes."

Jill sagged against the doorframe. "I may be divorced, but I hadn't given up trying to renew my relationship." She wanted the words to sound strong, but it was as if they were weakening from use. Maybe they were. Otherwise, how could she have slept with E.J.?

"I knew this guy once," Xandralene said, "and I was real crazy about him, but then we quit seeing each other and pretty soon I forgot all about him."

Jill's friends had also advised her to forget Darren. Her mother insisted on it. But Jill hadn't been able to face the thought of being alone. She wondered if she could now. She wondered if it wasn't love for Darren but a love for the past and a fear of the future that had made her cling to him.

Or maybe she was just so confused right now, she was looking for explanations for how she could have let this thing with E.J. happen.

Jill took a step in the darkness, then turned back. "Would you mind feeding Fido for a while?"

"You avoiding E.J.?"

"I guess I am," she admitted. "I think it would be less awkward for both of us if I didn't see him for a day or so."

"Sure. Whatever."

Jill knew this wasn't the best course, but it was the only one she could face right now.

E.J. SAT IN THE FRONT seat of Charlie's truck with his leg stretched stiffly out in front of him.

"How come you're so cranky?" Charlie demanded as he turned right on a yellow light. He flipped a hand sign to a driver who honked.

"I'm not cranky," E.J. said. "Watch your driving."

"My driving is fine. Boy, are you in a foul mood."

Okay, he was in a foul mood. He had been since the day before yesterday, when he'd awakened to find Jill gone. His first thoughts on rousing had been the sheer physical pleasure he'd shared with her.

He'd figured there had been a good reason for her leaving. She would be back. She would call. She would send a note by carrier pigeon.

He hadn't seen or heard from her since.

Charlie wheeled the full-size truck into a spot marked Compact Cars Only.

"Here we are," he announced like a cheery tour guide.

E.J. climbed out, his thoughts still on Jill's abandonment. The least she could have done was wake him up to say goodbye. He wouldn't have been crazy about that, but he sure didn't like waking up after a night like the one they'd spent and finding her gone. He didn't know if she was scared or if she regretted what had happened, but he was tired of playing Mr. Nice Guy to her skittishness. She owed him more than two days of silence.

Besides, he had needed her support during those long, worrying days when he waited for the final results of the X rays.

"Need help?" Charlie asked from beside him.

"No, thanks." He was tired of pity and sympathy. Tired of the constant ache. He just wanted to get well.

They went inside the doctor's building. After a short wait, E.J. was taken to an examination room. A few minutes later, Dr. Findley came in.

E.J. took one look at his face and tensed. "Something's wrong, isn't it?"

"Why don't you sit down, Mr. Robbins."

E.J. sat woodenly, his cane perched on the edge of the chair.

"I'm afraid there is a problem."

While E.J. sat motionless, the doctor turned out the light and pointed at things on the X ray. He explained about the trochlea and the femoral condyles. He talked about the patella and about the delicacy of knee surgery and the fact things could go wrong. Some injuries were permanent.

E.J. felt denial build inside him. He wanted to shout that the doctor was wrong.

But how could he deny what he had known all along? His premonition had been dead right. He wasn't going to get well. A sick feeling was closing in on him.

"So you see, Mr. Robbins, I believe—"

"The bottom line is that I'm not going to be cured," E.J. snarled.

Dr. Findley folded his hands in front of him. "I'm afraid so."

"What about another operation?"

The surgeon shook his head sadly. "We can't take the chance of making things worse."

E.J. laughed bitterly. "How much worse can things get?"

"You can walk now, even if you do have a pronounced limp."

That sobered E.J. "You're saying I'm going to have this limp for the rest of my life?"

"Yes."

He had to get away. E.J. tried to push himself out of the chair but couldn't rise without the cane. He snatched it up, angry at the doctor and at his X rays and at whatever mean and unfair fates had brought this on him.

"Mr. Robbins, I'm very sorry. I wish I could have had better news."

E.J. couldn't reply. He went back out to the waiting room.

Charlie looked up from the magazine he was reading. "Listen to this. It says here—"

"Let's go, Charlie."

He headed out of the building without looking back to see if Charlie was following.

They drove home in silence. Charlie offered to come in, but E.J. shook his head.

Alone inside his house, he considered calling Jill. *Real smart, E.J.* He still had some self-respect.

He also had anger. It wasn't fair that this had happened to him. Thousands of people had operations every day and everything was fine.

A short time later, someone knocked on the back door. He looked up to see Xandralene waving at him. She entered without waiting to be invited.

"Your friend, that Charlie guy, called and asked me to check on you."

"Tell him I'm fine," he said shortly.

"Oh, he's not on the phone or anything. He just said you were in a bad mood and might need some company."

"Where's Jill?" he demanded.

"She's, uh, busy."

Good eye contact, Xandralene. He hoped she didn't go into a business that required her to lie. Okay, so Jill didn't want to see him. He'd already figured that out. But he was mad at the world and at her in particular for deserting him when he needed her.

Xandralene flaked red polish off her nail. "She's got classes and stuff."

"She's even too busy to feed Fido, isn't she?" he countered sarcastically.

"Yeah."

He ought to tell Jill to get the dog out of his backyard. He ought to demand that she sit down with him and talk about what happened between them. But did it matter?

Her silence and absence told him everything.

It wasn't as if he was in love with her. He liked her, or he had, and the sex had been good. But she wasn't the only woman in the world.

The mail dropped through the slot in the front door and provided a needed distraction. Xandralene picked it up and carried it over to him. "Looks like a bunch of bills and this one big envelope."

He opened the manila envelope first. An editor was returning a short story he'd submitted a few weeks earlier.

Xandralene read over his shoulder, "'We regret that this does not suit our needs. While the characters have potential, the story bogged down in clinches. We wish you luck in placing it elsewhere.'" She made *tsking* noises. "Too bad they didn't buy it. What do they mean by too many clinches?"

"Clichés."

"You don't have to shout."

"They're necessary to the story," he told her belligerently. "That's how people talk. Don't those bean-brain editors know anything?"

"Gee, I don't know."

He grabbed the phone and called the number on the masthead. "Mr. Mitchell, please. This is Mr. Mitchell? Good. This is E.J. Robbins."

Xandralene flaked off more nail polish. It fell in red pieces to the carpet.

"I'm calling about my rejection of 'A Day at the Beach.' You say you don't want it because it's full of clichés." As he talked, the full impact of the doctor's words began to hit him. This was forever.

"That's right," Mr. Mitchell agreed pleasantly.

He wasn't going to climb up into attics again. "In the real world people talk in clichés," E.J. snapped.

"Well, they don't in our magazine and they never will. We look for freshness."

"Fresh as a daisy?" E.J. suggested.

"Yes."

"That's a cliché."

"I don't have time for this."

"Your time is too valuable?"

"Yes, it is," the editor said testily.

"That's another cliché, Mitch. You're going to have to watch that if you want to stay fresh."

"I don't believe I can help you. Oh, and Mr. Robbins, don't send us any more of your short stories. I don't believe we will be buying them."

E.J. hung up. Jackass. It was a wonder the publishing world muddled along as well as it did when they had idiots like that running the show.

"Did you talk him into buying it?" Xandralene asked innocently.

He glared at her.

"Well, I'd better get back. Jill will be wondering what's keeping me so long. She always asks a lot of questions about how you're doing and everything." Then, as if she'd said something she wasn't supposed to, she finished lamely, "She'd come and see you herself if she weren't so busy."

"Right," he said through gritted teeth.

Who needed her, anyway?

Jill Howard had shown her true colors when she left him in the middle of the night. He wouldn't be thinking about her at all if he weren't feeling so lousy. He wouldn't be thinking about her at all if he didn't keep remembering how great it had been between them.

THREE DAYS AFTER THE storm, Jill stood at her kitchen window and looked across to E.J.'s house. Isaac's battered truck was parked in the driveway.

She took a deep breath and started toward her door. She couldn't avoid E.J. forever, and it would be easier to visit while he had other company.

Jill found the two men sitting on the front porch. The swing creaked as E.J. rocked back and forth. Isaac sat on a kitchen chair and played a dulcimer. He returned her smile with a nod and continued playing the delicate little hammers across the dulcimer strings. Jill turned toward E.J.

"Hi." She tried to up the voltage, but her smile felt strained and unnatural.

He didn't say anything. He just gave her a long, considering look.

Trying to ignore the tension, she sat on the top step and listened until the tune ended.

"That was beautiful," she said to Isaac. "I used to play the violin, and I've always loved the dulcimer."

"The violin?" Isaac's eyes twinkled. "Ain't that just a fiddle that went to college? I've got a fiddle in my truck. Let's see how good you play."

"Oh, I haven't played for a long time and—"

"Go ahead, Jill. You don't have to be shy around us," E.J. said. The tone of his voice suggested other meanings.

She looked at E.J. as Isaac left to get the violin. He returned her gaze coolly.

"I'm sorry I haven't been over to see you. I felt that, well..."

"That you'd got what you wanted from me?" he suggested.

She stiffened. "You know that isn't it."

"I don't know anything except that we had a good thing and then you disappeared."

She heard Isaac shuffling back. "I needed some time. I figured you did, too."

Isaac reached the porch. Jill couldn't explain now, but she felt she couldn't leave the matter without a final word. "Can we talk later?" she asked.

"If you can work me into your schedule." The blue eyes were like chips of ice. "I know how busy you've been lately."

"Here's ye fiddle," Isaac said.

Jill took the instrument and ran her fingers across the handmade top. Her thoughts remained on E.J. She'd known he would be unhappy with her, but she hadn't anticipated the hostility she saw in his eyes. Nor had she expected the misery that had marked her separation from him. She had missed him.

"What tunes do you know?" Isaac asked.

"Classical things."

"You must a been schooled by some fancy teacher. Let's see if you can follow a little down-home style." Isaac began to play the dulcimer.

Jill tucked the fiddle beneath her chin and ran the bow across the strings. She picked up his lead easily. The years of lessons paid off. She would have played even better if she hadn't been so distracted by E.J. and by the melancholy of the old-time Appalachian music.

When the tune ended, Isaac grinned at her. "You're not half bad, gal." He took the violin. "I must be gettin' along. I'll leave you to the care of your pretty friend." He clapped E.J. on the shoulder and was gone.

Jill sat silently. "I know I didn't do the right thing," she finally said. "But I hadn't planned for anything to happen between us and I didn't know how to act around you after it did."

"You could have been yourself." He was still watching her with a coldness that was new to her.

She shook her head. "It isn't that simple."

"Yes, it is. We were attracted to each other and it went from there. End of story."

His words cut. Jill thought he wanted them to. "Maybe it was the end for you, but that night meant something to me," she said.

"Is that why you left in the middle of the night?" he demanded.

"I said I was wrong. What do you want from me?"

"Nothing. I never expect anything from one-night stands."

Jill felt the color drain from her face. She started to rise, then deliberately sat back down. "I don't know what kind of person you think I am, but I believe in commitment and respect, and I don't have one-night stands."

"Oh?"

Ignoring his sarcasm, she continued, "I was confused. I felt disloyal to Darren."

"Yes, let's talk about him. I'm always glad to hear what a wonderful person he is."

"I felt disloyal," she repeated. "But I also felt defiant, like I was striking out on my own." Where did that path lead? She had asked herself that a lot over the past couple of days. It might lead away from Darren, but that didn't mean it led to E.J.

"Look, I'd love to stay and explore your guilt, but I've got things to do." He got to his feet.

Jill shot up and blocked his path. "All of this anger can't be about me."

He was silent. They stood toe-to-toe in tense silence. Finally he said, "You're right. I'm mad at the world."

"Why?"

He looked away, as if it took an effort to find words. "I saw the doctor yesterday. The operation was a failure."

"Oh, E.J." Her anger wilted like a weed in the summer heat. "Now I feel even worse that I avoided you."

He chuckled ruefully. "Good."

"I mean it. I wouldn't have left you if I'd known. You should have called me when you found out."

He looked at her then, and she saw the male pride in his clear blue eyes and the hurt he'd carried.

"Never mind," she said. "I know you couldn't call. I guess I wasn't a very good friend." She wanted to hold and comfort him for the disappointment he was going through. But comfort could lead to too many other things, especially with the electricity already arcing between them as if they were two poles of a magnet.

Instead, she took a step back. "I want to be your friend, but I'm not ready for anything else, E.J. I'm simply not sure what I want."

That was a vast understatement. Her mind was a pinwheel of needs and desires and faint hopes and memories.

"I figured that," he said.

He was upset that she'd left, but if she'd stayed, would they have mapped out a future relationship? On top of her uncertainty about her own feelings, she had no idea what E.J.'s feelings were.

"I know it sounds corny," Jill said, "but I want to be friends."

He didn't say anything.

"E.J.?"

He combed his fingers through his hair. "I don't know if we can go back to being friends."

"Yes, we can." She said the words emphatically, wanting them to be true.

"What about that night? That was good, Jill. You can't ignore something that good."

She took a deep breath. "If people made decisions based strictly on sex, we'd still be living in caves."

A grin pulled at his mouth. "Sounds good to me."

"No, it doesn't, E.J. Robbins, and you know it."

At least the anger between them was gone. She knew much of E.J.'s turmoil didn't have to do with her. It was rooted in his disappointment over his surgery. She hadn't meant to drop that subject so quickly and she would talk about it with him later. Right now, though, it was important to conclude this discussion.

"Friends?" she prompted.

He lifted his head and gazed down at her from beneath the fringe of his dark lashes. "Yeah."

RICK LOOKED INCREDIBLY handsome in a white tux with a black bow tie and a black satin cummerbund. Grace watched him move around the corners of the room as he prepared for the exhibition dance.

Couples were just starting to come into the Avanti studio.

Rick's hair looked a little stiff, but Grace knew he had to use hair spray or it would flop all over the place when he danced. He was wearing the cologne she had bought him. It was expensive, but once she found out it was his favorite, she couldn't resist buying it.

He was so sweet when she surprised him with presents like that. He'd look at her with that you-shouldn't-have expression and she'd just melt.

"Grace, don't forget you're my first partner tonight," he said as he breezed by. "Where did I put the samba record?" he wondered aloud, as Edith and Bill stepped through the door. "Edith, you look beautiful."

Grace looked at Edith's pale blue dress. Grace's own dress was white and silver and she suddenly wondered if it was too fancy for the evening.

Rick returned to her side. "Doesn't Edith look pretty, Grace?" He bent to whisper. "Not as nice as you. Promise me you'll take that dress on the cruise. I love it."

"Yes, of course." She'd been making a list of the clothes she could take on the trip and had gone out yesterday and bought two new pairs of shoes.

"Hey, Dottie." Rick waved gaily to a newcomer.

Grace watched from her chair and tried not to feel resentful when Rick gave his attention to others. It was his job as a dance instructor to make people welcome. And tonight, with the exhibition dance, he had to be doubly charming. The studio depended so much on Rick. It was a downright sin they didn't pay him more.

As she waited for the music to begin, she wondered again if she might have loaned Rick too much money. He was going to pay it back, of course, once his house was sold.

Edith sat down beside her. "Ready for your big number?" she asked.

"Yes, we've been practicing it."

"I wonder if Rick gets bored teaching these steps over and over to old people like us?" Edith said.

Grace stiffened. "I don't consider myself old."

"Oh, I don't mean old-old. But Rick's a lot younger than us. He's probably got some pretty young thing somewhere."

Grace felt a flutter of unease, a prickling warning that she didn't want to listen to. She sat up straight and crossed her arms. "I think Rick appreciates mature women."

Edith gave her a curious look and went to sit somewhere else.

Let her go, Grace thought. She was a silly woman who didn't understand the first thing about Rick. He didn't want some flighty young thing. He appreciated maturity, and she and Rick were going to have a wonderful time on the cruise together. She wasn't going to let Edith's foolish remarks ruin her evening.

Grace deliberately turned her thoughts to the cruise. The question of a chaperon still loomed in her mind. She had to take someone. It wouldn't be decent to go alone with a single man, but she didn't know whom to ask. She'd considered a couple of people from her church, but she didn't know them well enough to invite them.

Rick returned to her side. "Almost ready. We'll do our little warm-up number first." He started to leave, then turned back. "Grace, you have got to wear that dress on the cruise. I have never seen you looking better."

She smiled and almost forgot Edith's words.

"Oh, and by the way, here's some of the money I owe you." He reached into his pocket.

"Not now, Rick." She looked around uncomfortably.

"You're right. I don't know what I'm thinking." He glanced up at the clock on the wall. "Time to start."

Edith and Bill were shaky on their number and Dottie was badly off the beat, but Grace's dance with Rick was flawless. One time she forgot the steps, but he led her through it smoothly.

She was heady with the excitement of the evening when Rick drove her home. He walked her to the door like a gentleman, gave her a fleeting but sweet peck on the cheek, and left her feeling euphoric.

She didn't even realize he hadn't given her the money until the next morning. Oh, well, there was plenty of time to collect. Meanwhile, she turned her thoughts to the cruise.

CHAPTER TWELVE

JILL WAS ALONE IN THE house the day after her discussion with E.J. when the phone rang.

It was Darren. Her hesitation at hearing his voice was because she was surprised, wasn't it? She was also optimistic. Maybe this call would lead somewhere.

"Did I catch you at a bad time?" He sounded tentative. Jill wasn't used to hearing uncertainty in his voice.

"No. I can talk," she said. "Is there a problem with the house?"

"No." Darren took an audible breath. "I called to talk about us."

Jill twisted the phone cord around her fingertip and waited. She had intended to call Darren herself. If she was going to take control of her life and her emotions, she couldn't keep waiting for him to decide what *he* wanted to do. But he had called her before she'd ordered her thoughts and emotions.

"I've been doing a lot of thinking and I believe we have some things to discuss."

Jill knew this call was hard for him to make. She wanted to make it easier by reassuring him, but she was no longer sure of herself. If he had called a few weeks ago and said those words, she knew exactly what she would have said. But things had changed. She had been with another man since then.

"Jill?" he prompted.

"Yes, I heard you."

"What do you think?"

"I think we have some things to discuss," she said slowly.

"Good." She heard his relief.

"I want to come and see you," Darren said.

Yes, she wanted that, too. Maybe the sight of him, the touch of him, would answer her questions and resolve things once and for all.

"When?" she asked.

"I'd like to come this weekend...."

The hope grew firmer. Darren's impatience to see her was a good sign. Maybe her small reluctance about seeing him was guilt about E.J. instead of real doubts about Darren and herself.

"I'll be here this weekend," Jill said.

Darren sighed. "I was going to say I wish I could come then, but I can't. I've already made other plans."

She stared into the pale blue flowers on the wallpaper. A date? The familiar flutter of jealousy was followed by a new emotion. Resentment. She felt cheated that he had called her to say he wanted to get together and then he wasn't available.

"I can make it next weekend," he said. "Is that okay?"

She ought to tell him no, she thought spitefully. But a more rational side of herself took over. She couldn't let pride stand in the way. If they were going to talk honestly, they were both going to have to put aside bitterness and act like adults.

"That will be fine," Jill said.

"Great."

Next weekend was better anyway, Jill told herself. It would give her time to sort out her conflicting emotions.

"E.J., YOU NEED TO GET away for a while. You listening to me?" Charlie demanded.

E.J. forked at the lettuce in his salad bowl and nodded. "Yeah, I'm listening."

It was half a lie, because he was also thinking about his conversation with Jill yesterday. They had decided to be friends. That was probably for the best. Being permanently disabled gave him enough changes and problems to deal with. He still thought about those green eyes, that sweep of dark hair, that body lying next to him. But she had begun shying away almost immediately after they'd made love. One couldn't push a string and he wasn't going to try.

"I'm talking about going to the mountains," Charlie said. "You and me. Pay attention."

E.J. put down his fork. "I'm not in the mood for a vacation."

"That's exactly why you need to get away. You're upset. Hell, I don't blame you. You thought you were getting fixed up good as new and then you find out it ain't so. It's a drag. But you gotta get away and relax."

"What am I supposed to do in the mountains, Charlie? I can't hike."

"Sit on the front porch with a bottle of beer and mellow out."

It sounded boring. And he'd have way too much time to think. "I don't think so."

The waitress stopped. "Need anything?"

"Do you have good sense on the menu?" Charlie inquired. "My friend here is a little shy on it."

The waitress smiled and glanced at E.J. He saw the look of mild interest he sometimes got from women. Then he saw her gaze drop to his cane and he read sympathy and regret.

"Sorry. The best I can offer is pie and coffee."

He shook his head and she went away.

"I've already rented the rooms, E.J. Five whole days. Paid for it myself. I thought you'd be happy." Charlie looked hurt.

E.J. didn't have a lot of other great plans for the future. He'd been cranking out some short stories, but given his track record, he was losing hope they'd sell.

"Oh, all right," he said.

"Atta boy. I'll pick you up on Friday." Charlie leaned into his coffee. "How's that pretty little neighbor of yours? Does she stop by to see you?"

"I see Jill now and again," E.J. said vaguely. He didn't want to talk about her or wonder why she attracted him in ways other women didn't.

"'Now and again.'" Charlie curled his lip. "What's the matter with you, bubba? You're home from work. You've got all the time in the world to spend with her. Ask her to come over and give you a back massage."

"My back is fine. I'm not going to resort to cheap tricks just to see some woman."

Charlie fiddled with the salt-and-pepper shakers. "I thought you were interested in her."

"I was, but there's nothing between us now."

And they had agreed there wasn't going to be. She'd said yesterday she felt their night together had been a betrayal of Darren. E.J. had too many of his own problems to help her deal with hers. And he didn't want to set himself up to be odd man out in some threesome.

"You going to eat that last roll?" Charlie asked.

E.J. handed it to him.

"Thanks. Anyway, I figure we can leave as soon as I get off work on Friday. Have your stuff packed and I'll pick you up a little after five."

E.J. nodded. Maybe a change would do him good. "Friday," Charlie reminded him before he left to get into his pickup.

E.J. took the bus home. He wasn't ready to have his car installed with the adaptive equipment that went with having a knee that couldn't operate the clutch. That was one of the things he'd eventually have to deal with. Maybe when he got back from the mountains he'd be ready to make concessions to the fact his life had changed. Not yet, though. Not yet.

Friday afternoon, E.J. was packed and waiting. It was almost five when the phone rang. It was Charlie.

"E.J., you ain't going to believe this."

"What?"

"I've got the flu and I can't go."

Disappointment pinched him, but E.J. said nonchalantly, "No big deal. We'll go some other time."

"*You're* still going," Charlie said. "I'll be okay in a couple of days and I'll come up then."

"Charlie, I can't drive." What did this guy use for brains?

"Jill will drive you. I just got off the phone with her and it's all arranged."

"I don't intend to go with Jill," E.J. stated flatly. Sure, they'd agreed to be friends, but why take a chance on getting burned by playing too close to the fire?

Charlie sighed raggedly into the phone. "I don't feel like arguing, E.J. I've been puking all afternoon and I want to go back to bed. I've already paid for the place and can't get my money back. Besides, there's not one good reason you can't go."

"I'll give you one. I don't want to go with Jill." That wasn't entirely true. He *did* want to go with Jill, but he was too smart to do it.

Charlie stopped to wheeze pitifully. "You said there's nothing between you two. I figured it would be safe to get her to drive you."

"You figured wrong."

"What's with you, E.J.? Are you just going to sit around feeling sorry for yourself the rest of your life?"

That stung, especially since E.J. had spent the past few days brooding. He didn't want to become someone who was absorbed in self-pity.

"She's only going to drive you up there," Charlie continued. "You're not sharing a room or a cozy cottage. The place is a run-down shack, but I've gone to a lot of trouble to arrange this."

E.J. didn't often hear Charlie sound so aggrieved. The truth was, he'd looked forward to getting away for the weekend. He knew going with Jill would be tricky, but it wasn't as if they'd be in some romantic bed-and-breakfast together. Charlie made the place sound like a flea trap.

E.J. raked his fingers through his hair. *Go for it.* "You win."

"Thank heavens you're showing some sense. She'll be over shortly." Charlie hung up.

E.J. put down the receiver and looked at his luggage. He'd packed flannel shirts and jeans and left out his razor, with Charlie in mind. A weekend with a woman demanded different stuff.

"No, it doesn't," he told himself irritably.

Sure, Jill's jeans tucked and fitted in places Charlie's jeans would never have managed, but the weekend wasn't about the differences between men and women. It was about companionship. He was going to sleep in a separate bedroom and let his face get scratchy, just like he would have done with Charlie.

His life was messed up enough already without complicating it with woman problems. He was a nineties man who had plenty of women friends. Jill would be just one more. He was intelligent enough to ignore his lust and follow his logic.

Forget eyes that could darken to forest green and a body that had arched against his in passion. Forget skin like soft cotton.

"Oh, hell." He leaned against the wall. This wasn't a good idea. On top of everything else, he wondered why Jill had agreed to go. Had Charlie made her feel pity for him? He didn't want that.

He was going to stay home like a sensible man even if he was bored and ready for any diversion.

"I'M CRAZY," JILL TOLD Xandralene as she stuck her toothbrush in her flowered cosmetic bag.

Xandralene stood in the bathroom doorway and looked vacantly at the ceiling. "I need to buy some new herbal air-freshener so I can, like, work more on training Fido."

"Why else did I let Charlie talk me into this?" Jill continued aloud as she rummaged in the cabinet for her nail file and tweezers. And why was she so excited about going?

Xandralene looked at her vaguely. "Oh, you're talking about the trip to the mountains."

"Charlie did sound awful." Jill stuck the gadgets into the bag. Otherwise, she would never have agreed to go. Never.

"Then why didn't he cancel the trip?" Xandralene asked.

"Because Charlie says E.J. has his heart set on it."

He probably did need to get away, Jill thought with a pang of sympathy. She leaned against the bathroom sink and felt ashamed that she'd objected to driving E.J. The man had recently received devastating news about his future. Was her need to keep her distance so strong that she didn't have any compassion for his suffering? Besides, if E.J. was comfortable being with her, surely she could show the same sophistication.

And she *was* just going because Charlie was in a fix.

Oh, who was she kidding? She would enjoy being with E.J. But that didn't mean she was going to let down her guard again. She would see Darren next weekend, and she intended to do that with a clear head and a clear conscience. She didn't want to drag in guilt about some weekend fling.

"You're going today?" Xandralene asked.

"As soon as I get packed. E.J. is already waiting."

"Cool. Have fun." She wandered away.

Jill finished packing and carried her bag out to her car, then went to E.J.'s back door and knocked.

She heard his cane hitting the floor and his bad leg dragging after it as she waited.

He opened the door. He was wearing a pair of pleated pants she hadn't seen before and a blue knit shirt. The color matched his eyes perfectly.

She smiled at him and expected an answering smile. She didn't get one. E.J. regarded her as if she were a pesky salesman.

Her smile faded. Maybe he didn't understand why she was here. "Charlie called me."

"Yeah, so he told me."

He didn't move or say anything else. Jill frowned. Had there been a misunderstanding?

"I'm going to drive you to the mountains, E.J."

"How come you can go on such short notice?"

His tone of accusation caught her off guard.

"Well, I don't have any tests next week, and I've already finished my paper."

This wasn't the warm and fuzzy welcome she'd expected, and she was beginning to fume under his sharp questions.

"Did Charlie force you into taking me?" he demanded.

"He asked me if I would." It occurred to her that E.J. was acting this way because he feared he was taking advantage of her. Part of her wanted to touch his hand and reassure him. Another part wanted to shake him for being such a jerk.

"Look, we don't have to go," he said. "To heck with Charlie."

She bit at her lower lip. Obviously E.J. wasn't nearly as eager to go as Charlie had said. But if Charlie had been so intent on making these arrangements, he must think E.J. needed to get away.

"Charlie's already paid for the rooms," she said.

"So what? I'll pay him back."

Jill persisted without being sure why. "Charlie said you wanted to go."

E.J. laughed without humor. "Looks like he conned us both."

So that was it. Jill suddenly felt foolish. She had rushed over thinking she was saving E.J., but he didn't even want her here. She felt even more foolish, knowing she had relished the notion of being with him. He clearly felt no such desire to be with her.

"You don't really want to go, do you?" His voice was half challenge. "I mean, you're going because Charlie convinced you I wanted to."

"That's true." But she hadn't agreed to go solely out of kindness. She needed to know if what had happened between her and E.J. had been infatuation or something stronger and deeper, and she needed to know before she saw Darren.

She needed an end to her confusion, she suddenly realized.

"I know you rushed around and packed and got your adrenaline going." He laid the cane on the counter and leaned his hands against it, as if for greater support. "It would feel like a letdown to you to go back and sit in your apartment. Why don't you go ahead by yourself?"

Jill shook her head. "I wouldn't feel right doing that. Charlie arranged this weekend for you." And she didn't want to go alone.

"Then let's decide this like mature adults. We'll flip a coin. Heads we go, tails we don't."

Only a fool would make a responsible decision based on a game of chance.

"I have a quarter in my purse," she said.

It turned up heads.

They drove out of Charlotte on the expressway. E.J. had brought a portable CD with country-music discs. Garth Brooks. George Strait. Reba McEntyre.

"Don't you have any Michael Bolton?" she asked.

He stared at her. "You're kidding?"

"No. I like him." She flicked a look at E.J. and saw his hair tumbling over his forehead as he searched through his stack of discs. She remembered how soft his hair had felt to her touch. Quickly she turned her attention back on the road where it belonged.

"Sit back and relax," he said. "I'll teach you to like the good stuff."

Music chauvinist, she silently accused.

As they drove, she suffered through the country wailing. She even liked some of the lyrics, although she didn't tell E.J. that. Every now and then she stole a look at him and saw the strong masculine lines of his profile. He was a good-looking man, no question about it.

Her mother would applaud her decision to be here.

Her grandmother would purse her lips in disapproval.

Jill herself wondered if she would look back with regret or satisfaction. But she'd made a decision. She was going to spend the next three days relaxing and enjoying E.J.'s companionship and offering whatever support she could to offset the prognosis on his knee. And she was going to sort out her own feelings about this perplexing man.

"Let's take the back roads," he suggested. "They're more scenic and we're in no hurry."

"Sure."

She drove the car off the expressway at Shelby and threaded along the curving roads and denser growth of trees that carried them to Lake Lure. They skirted the shore of the blue lake, driving by a bevy of restaurants, antique stores and roadside stands, then left the lake behind and headed deeper into the mountains.

"I still miss Michael Bolton," she said as he fished for another disc to put into the player.

He looked soulfully at her. "I'll sing to you."

He sang "You Are So Beautiful" in an over-wrought, note-grinding voice, filling in the words he didn't know with nonsense words.

"You are so beautiful." He just happened to pick that song, those words, Jill told herself. It didn't mean anything. Neither did the intense, searching way he looked at her. That was just more playacting.

Wasn't it?

Sometimes, yes, he did look at her in ways that suggested he thought she was beautiful. But she couldn't keep thinking that everything he did was steeped in significance. And she couldn't keep thinking about their night together when the truth was, things had changed substantially since then. Darren had reentered her life, and E.J. had received news that was going to deeply affect his own.

When E.J. finished singing, she tried for a light tone. "Let's have some more country music. I'm beginning to like it a whole lot more."

"More than my singing?"

"Yes."

She was thankful when he put a disc in and they didn't have to talk anymore.

Outside Asheville they took a road that wound upward into the mountains. Vegetation grew lushly along the road, sometimes brushing the car.

Jill told him about Xandralene's plans to move to the country to live with eight other people.

"Where are they moving to?" he asked as he rubbed his knee.

"Somewhere near Derita. They won't have a phone out there," she said.

"Savages."

"The place may be primitive, but Xandralene is young and adaptable. She plans to take Fido, too."

"This is where you turn," E.J. said. "Make a right. The inn is at the top of the hill."

She followed his directions. After a steep climb they emerged onto flat ground, where a large old Victorian-style house looked out over the mountains.

"It's beautiful," Jill said. In fact, it was breathtaking. Wisteria wrapped around the sprawling porch of the white clapboard inn, and in the distance the mountains rose and fell like purple waves.

E.J. scowled.

"Don't you like it?" she asked. "I think it's lovely."

"That's exactly what it is. And it seems to me it isn't the kind of place Charlie would have picked out for a couple of men to spend a few days."

She could clearly see that Charlie had manipulated them, but they were here now. Was it so bad to be here with her?

Jill looked at E.J., wanting him to smile and joke about the situation.

He just sat, stone faced, while she parked in front of the inn. She waited until E.J. got out of the car, then followed and saw him struggle to make it up the steps while leaning heavily on the railing. She didn't offer assistance because she sensed he didn't want it.

A kindly gray-haired woman greeted them and helped them register.

"You're both on the second floor. I'm afraid we don't have anyone to carry in your bags," she said with an apologetic glance at E.J.

"We can manage," Jill replied.

"There's a lovely balcony at the end of the hall," the woman added. "We have two other guest rooms on the second floor that all share the bath."

"Thank you." Jill smiled at her and turned to go.

E.J. limped back out to the car. "I'm sorry," he said.

She lifted her suitcase out. "Why?"

"I feel useless not even being able to carry my bag upstairs."

"E.J., this is one of the reasons I came. It's no big deal."

But his expression said it was a big deal to him. She realized this was one of the tangible ways in which his life had changed. She also knew he'd never be able to ride his bike again or play in a game of basketball, and that knowledge tugged at her heart.

She couldn't dismiss or minimize his new limitations. She wondered how she would feel if she were facing what he faced.

Jill picked up her bag and looked at him. "I know this is hard for you. I wish there was something I could do to help."

"You can beat up Charlie for me when we get back," he said.

"It's a deal."

A smile dawned and something caught in her throat at the sight of it. They stepped inside the inn together.

"It *is* a neat place," E.J. said as he touched the smooth wood of the banister railing at the foot of the stairs.

"Yes." She ventured a smile. "Let's enjoy ourselves here just to spite Charlie."

"Yeah. Let's do that."

E.J. WENT FOR A SOLITARY walk shortly before dinner. He wasn't able to go far, but it was enough to satisfy his need to get away from Jill.

Not that he *wanted* to be away from her. That was the problem. He wanted to be closer to her. He wanted to hold hands with her and exchange kisses and sleep in her bed in the room at the other end of the hall from his.

Later, lying in bed that night, he thought about Jill in that room down the hall. He'd seen her leave the bathroom wearing a pink satin robe that fluttered open to reveal her legs.

How could a guy sleep for thinking about those legs? Or the cotton-candy puffs of her freshly scrubbed cheeks?

They were here in a cozy hideaway and nothing would stop him from pressing that advantage. Nothing, that is, but the ghost of an ex-husband and the grinning ghoul of a limited future.

Knowing he couldn't have her didn't kill his urge to trace the curve of her mouth or tangle his fingers in her hair. It didn't keep him from wanting to feel her skin gliding against his.

He shifted restlessly on the bed and tried to think of other things. His first random thought was of Isaac. E.J. would no longer be able to help people so directly. The government wouldn't fire him, but they would reassign him to a desk. No more dirt under his fingernails. No more gritty involvement in making a tangible difference in someone's life.

E.J. was going to be forced to become the office type he had never wanted to be.

He got out of bed and pulled on his terry robe. The landlady had mentioned a balcony. Maybe some cool night air would get his thoughts on something else. He picked up his cane and made his way to the balcony at the end of the hall. He opened the door and stepped out into the coolness.

It was a cloudless night and countless stars shone white against the black sky. He'd gone camping under those same stars, backpacking into remote areas and setting up a little tent. He wouldn't be doing that again.

"Are you okay?"

He turned to see Jill leaning against the doorway. The light from behind her made the thin satin of her robe transparent. He saw every contour of her body. He remembered touching those curves, kissing those breasts.

"No, I'm mad at the world."

"It's normal to be angry," she said quietly. "That's one of the stages of grief."

He hadn't thought of himself as grieving until now. The concept left him silent.

"Do you want me to leave?" she asked.

"No."

He let himself look at her again. He saw more than the woman's body unconsciously revealed in the light. He also saw a lovely, caring woman. He'd be stupid to turn away her support.

"It was nice of you to come and see about me. I appreciate it, Jill," he said simply.

She nodded.

"What comes after grief?" he asked after a few moments.

"Acceptance."

"How come you're so smart?"

She took in a deep breath. "Because I've been there."

"Ah." But she had never reached acceptance, E.J. thought. Otherwise, it wouldn't still mean so much to her to be back with Darren.

Well, he was going to reach acceptance because the doctor had made it clear there was no changing this. E.J. didn't intend to spend the rest of his life pining for the past. It was gone, and he must find a way to be comfortable with the future.

JILL WAS UP EARLY the next morning. E.J. was already outside.

From behind the lace curtains in her room, she watched him make his way slowly through the sloping garden. He paused occasionally to lean against a tree and rest.

She wanted to go out into the garden and join him but she sensed he didn't want that, just as she sensed he hadn't wanted her to join him yesterday when he went for a walk.

She missed those days when they'd exchanged casual remarks while she fed Fido. She missed E.J. smiling at her with the camaraderie of a good neighbor. There were barriers now that hadn't existed before.

Some of them had been of her own making. But E.J. was putting up walls, too. He hadn't asked her to join him on the walks, and she wasn't sure he had wanted her on the balcony last night. But when she had heard him moving down the hall, she couldn't stop herself from making sure he was all right. She *had* stopped herself, though, from putting her arms around him and drawing him to her to whisper words of comfort.

Her role here was to help E.J. enjoy himself and to have a good time herself. Nothing more.

With that in mind, she dressed in a green sweatshirt and beige slacks and went downstairs to breakfast. Plates and gleaming silverware waited on an antique sideboard, along with a basket of fresh muffins and an urn of hot coffee. A plate of fresh fruit and choices of cereal sat beside the urn.

Jill poured herself a cup of coffee and sat down at the dining room table. A few minutes later some other guests came in, chatted a few minutes while they ate muffins, then left to go for a hike up the nearby mountain. Jill was alone when E.J. returned from his walk.

He sat down at the table.

She scanned his face quickly. He looked stressed. But he smiled.

He reached for a blueberry muffin and she refilled her coffee cup.

The silence between them didn't feel strained. Jill was content to listen to the soft classical music coming from the kitchen as she looked out the window at the purple blue accordion folds of the mountains off in the distance. This was the kind of peaceful morning she and Darren had shared early in their marriage.

"You're awfully quiet," E.J. said.

"I was thinking about—" She stopped uncertainly.

"Go on."

There was really no reason not to share her thoughts. "I was thinking about marriages and how things change. Sometimes the changes are so subtle, so small, you don't see when they happen until you look back."

She transferred her gaze from the mountains to the blue of his eyes. He was watching her with total attention.

She hadn't intended to reveal so much of her private thoughts. Embarrassed, she ducked her head. "I'm rambling."

"No, you're not. You're talking about something important."

She was grateful for that acknowledgment. It encouraged her to continue. "Darren and I had calm mornings like this when we were first married. But then the pressures of his job and the more hectic pace of our lives changed things."

"Lisa and I never had calm mornings. She was full of energy and ambition, and didn't have time to do more than grab a cup of coffee on her way out the door."

"That doesn't sound like the kind of woman you would have married. Although I'm sure she was a wonderful person," she added quickly. She hoped he wouldn't think badly of her for making comments about his wife. In fact, Jill was curious to hear more about this woman who had shared E.J.'s life.

"She was wonderful. But you're right. She needed to conquer the world and I didn't. It bothered her that I just wanted a simple, honest job where I was helping people. I didn't care about mergers and acquisitions and going to night school to get an M.B.A."

"And she wanted that?"

"She thought it would be nice, yeah, but I think she finally understood it wasn't me."

Jill knew E.J. wouldn't trudge around a golf course every Saturday like Darren just to make the right contacts. She had always been proud of Darren's ambition, but now she wondered what truly drove him. How many men had E.J.'s courage to make up their own mind what they wanted and not let the opinions of others sway them?

"Did she ever want a family?" Jill asked. Maybe she shouldn't have asked, but she was so curious.

"Someday. Lisa was never very specific about when."

"Did *you* want one?" Jill held her coffee cup near her lips but she was too intent on watching him to drink.

"Yeah. I did."

He spoke in the past tense. Did that mean he no longer did? It hadn't occurred to her that men might change their minds about such things. Darren had wanted children, too. But after her devastation over the miscarriage, did he still want them? That was a fear she didn't want to consider. She still wanted children very much. Before she could commit to any relationship, the man must want them, too.

In the empty quiet of the breakfast room, Jill asked E.J., "Do you miss her still?"

"Yes."

She ached at the simplicity of that answer. His love had survived differences and finally death and was still intact. Well, hadn't her own love survived a divorce and the months that had separated them?

What if it hadn't, though? What if she was clinging to the life raft of her old life because she was afraid she would go under without it? Maybe she was simply afraid to go on with a new life because there were too many uncertainties.

Could a new life include E.J.? As hard as she tried to maintain defenses against him, she was still attracted to him. His smile warmed her and the memory of his intimate touches ran like wildfire through her nervous system.

"I have to tell myself sometimes that Lisa would be different now than she was when she died. I'm different," E.J. said. "But I still think we'd get along okay. We were good at working out problems together."

"Darren and I were, too," she interjected quickly.

She was sure that was true. Yet, when she looked back on the major issues in their marriage, the compromises had been on her part. She was the one who had quit school before graduation so Darren could take the job he wanted. She was the one who had done volunteer work and devoted herself to helping him succeed in his career.

"Compromise is what it takes to make things work," E.J. noted.

Had things stopped working when Jill was no longer able to compromise and do things the way Darren wanted them? Had things stopped working when her own needs became so great that Darren was unwilling or unable to meet them?

They fell back into silence as Jill examined her thoughts. After a time, E.J. rose.

"I think I'll go up and read."

Jill was left alone in the room. She felt the isolation even more after their exchange of private thoughts. She hoped E.J. wasn't going to retreat from her again and spend his weekend in solitary walks. But she feared he would.

CHAPTER THIRTEEN

LATER ON SATURDAY, Jill and E.J. went into Asheville, where they browsed through the shops. Jill bought a print to hang in her bedroom. E.J. found an old hardware store and lost himself in its musty interior. The thousands of mysterious metal objects that appeared useless to Jill, fascinated E.J.

Afterward, they went into a bookstore with a coffee shop in the basement. He found a book on composting. Jill furtively bought one on dog obedience. Not that she was planning to keep Fido, but just in case.

They left and headed back down the narrow street. Sometimes they talked about interesting things or unusual people they passed. Sometimes they were quiet.

It was an easy day; neither made any demands on the other. Jill was thankful for the simple, unquestioned companionship.

Yet, when they returned to the inn, E.J took another of his solitary walks. Jill knew it was ridiculous to think they should spend all their time together, but she felt left out.

Charlie arrived at the inn on Monday, looking surprisingly fit for a man who had just recovered from the flu. Jill didn't question him. She just exchanged a few pleasantries with him and put her suitcases into the car.

As Charlie headed into the inn, E.J. remained beside her car. His face showed the effects of three days of not shaving. The dark little bristles were roguishly appealing. She wondered how they would feel against her skin. It wasn't the first time that weekend she had thought about his touch, but she'd been careful not to act on those thoughts. In any event, he'd given her no encouragement.

"Thank you for driving me up," he said.

"You're welcome." The atmosphere felt stilted.

"I'm glad we had this time," he told her. "It makes me realize what a good friend you are."

He didn't move forward to kiss her or offer a friendly hug. Maybe the cane made that too awkward, Jill told herself, but she thought there was more. He was putting up barriers as surely as road crews set out orange barrels.

She headed back to Charlotte alone.

It felt odd to be by herself after spending the past three days with E.J. It was only loneliness, of course. Sometimes, though, she feared it was a deeper ache, a sense of loss so profound that she wasn't yet ready to look it fully in the face.

However formal E.J. may have been with her this morning, she couldn't forget the times she'd seen him looking at her the way he used to. Even with his impaired mobility, there was something come-hither and compelling about him. Something elementally male.

But he'd behaved like a perfect gentleman all weekend. If he had really wanted to be with her, wouldn't he have swept aside any objections and seduced her? But he hadn't. He'd always kept that careful, safe space between them. And sometimes, just when she thought they'd shared an especially nice moment, he'd disappear down the road again on his slow, private walk and she was left behind, uninvited.

A car honked and Jill turned her attention to the traffic.

This weekend was over, she reprimanded herself. She was back in Charlotte and it was time to think about the upcoming weekend. She hadn't told E.J. about Darren's visit. There had never seemed a time or a way to work it into the conversation.

After this morning's parting, she realized it wouldn't have mattered. Lovers were obligated to share such facts. Friends were not.

On Tuesday evening, Darren called to say he planned to arrive at seven on Friday. He sounded so enthusiastic that Jill's anticipation increased.

She kept busy.

She cleaned the apartment and helped Xandralene move Fido to the country. She had lunch with Mrs. Casey and heard more about how wonderful Rick was. She threw herself into studying for the big test.

Jill wondered how she would feel when she finally did see Darren again.

On Thursday her mother called.

"I phoned last weekend and your roommate told me you'd gone away with a man," her mother began. "Good for you."

"It wasn't like that."

"Is he handsome?"

"E.J.?" He wasn't male-model perfect but his face had character and charisma. Jill remembered the stubble on his face when they'd parted and how she had longed to feel the roughness of it against her cheek. To her mother, she said blandly, "He's not a love interest."

"Well, make him one, darling. You are my daughter, after all. Surely you know how to do that."

No, Jill didn't know how. Anyway, E.J. wasn't any more available for romance right now than she was. She had things to work out with Darren, and E.J. was occupied in dealing with his own problems. They'd both known that when she left the mountains on Monday.

So there was no reason for this dull ache she felt every time she thought about that parting.

"Darren is coming this weekend, Mother," she said brightly. "He and I are still keeping channels of communication open."

"Oh, pooh."

"I know you don't think we can work things out, but I want to talk with him."

"He won't change," her mother announced. "Men never do."

"I'm not asking him to change."

Was she? But Jill herself had changed. She had come to Charlotte intent on improving herself so she could return home a better, more interesting person. In the short time she'd lived in Charlotte, she had created a niche for herself. She'd met people in her classes. Xandralene and Mrs. Casey had become her friends. She had even decorated her apartment so that the wallpaper and sofa cushions and throw rugs complemented one another—and all to her taste, not Darren's.

"Dear, I've always found that sleeping with an ex is never a good idea."

"I'm not going to sleep with him," Jill said tersely. She had already put sheets on the Hide-A-Bed sofa in the living room. Darren would understand. Surely he didn't expect anything more so soon.

"Then what's the point of getting together?" her mother demanded.

"There's a lot more to a relationship than the physical side." Jill suspected most daughters wouldn't have to explain that to their mothers.

"Don't kid yourself, darling. If that's not there, nothing else works."

Jill saw no point in prolonging the conversation. Her mother was only going to argue with her and Jill would have to defend a decision she knew was right.

"I'll talk to you after the weekend, Mother."

"At least don't make any foolish promises to him. I let my third husband pressure me into just that sort of thing after we separated. You've got to keep other options open, dear."

Jill wasn't going to be like her mother and be led by every whim of her heart from one man to another.

As FRIDAY APPROACHED, Jill's anticipation edged toward panic. It was as if her whole future was riding on this visit. If she discovered it was over between her and Darren, where did that leave her?

Jill remembered all those times as a child when she'd prayed that one of her parents would take her to live with them. Those dreams never did come true and she grew up in limbo, with no reassuring plans for the future and no promises of security. She felt that same hollow fear now.

Those thoughts sent her spiraling back into anxiety.

Friday night at seven, Jill heard Darren's car pull into the driveway.

She took a deep breath and went to the door. She stopped with her hand on the knob and looked at herself in the oval mirror. Her hair was longer than when Darren had seen her last, and the style more carefree. Her blue flared pants were fashionable, and the matching blue-and-green top was vibrant with color. She'd been excited about the outfit in the store. Now she wondered if it was too bold.

A knock sounded. Jill touched her hair, then opened the door.

Darren was more crisply handsome than she had ever seen him. His blond hair was perfectly in place, and he was dressed in a white polo shirt and razor-creased gray trousers.

She waited for the rush of pleasure at seeing him. She only felt nervous.

"Hello, Jill."

"I— Come in." She realized she was blocking the way and moved back so he could enter.

"Sit down," she said.

He sat on the apricot sofa. Jill was at a loss for words even though she'd spent days choreographing this scene. *Sit,* she told herself, and made her way to a chair across from him. That was better. She felt pleasure, or at least relief, that he was here.

"Did you have a good drive?" she asked.

"Yeah. I made great time." He chuckled in that easy way of his. "I sped a little. I guess I was impatient to get here."

That warmed her and helped relax her further.

"I thought we'd go out for dinner," she said. "Is that okay?"

"Of course. Whatever you like."

Darren had always been accommodating. On nights when she hadn't wanted to cook, he'd been willing to pick up at a moment's notice and go out.

"I'd like to relax a few minutes before we go," he said. "I'm a little tired."

"Of course." She sat back in the chair and saw him watching her.

"You've changed, Jill." There was no mistaking his look of appreciation. "New hairstyle. Snappy clothes. You look good." She touched her hair. Those were superficial things, but she reasoned it was too early for him to see the more subtle things. He didn't know that she wasn't as concerned with being a top student as she had once been. He didn't know it wasn't as important to her whether or not people liked her. He didn't know she had decided she didn't have to be perfect.

Darren's attention had shifted to the apartment. She saw him glancing around. "One bedroom?" he asked.

"Yes."

She knew how small the place must look to him. After their divorce, Darren had moved into a big new house in the best part of town. She couldn't picture him in a cramped apartment.

"Well, it's not permanent," he said.

Jill looked around. The rooms were cozy and she had decorated them to her liking. She hadn't realized it until now, but the place was good enough for her. In fact, it was home now.

Silence fell between them. Jill felt as if they were strangers on a first date. She had hoped for some blinding realization that he was the only man for her. That didn't come, and she was left in awkward silence. *Then do something about it,* she told herself. Darren had driven all the way up here to be with her. It was her turn to initiate something.

But he spoke before she could find something to say.

"Are you dating?" he asked.

She hesitated. She wasn't dating E.J. But she had spent time in his arms.

"You don't have to look away," Darren said. "I want us to be honest."

"I'm not dating," she murmured.

It was so like Darren to establish facts early on. That was one of the reasons he did so well in business. But what worked in managing a hospital didn't necessarily make for a comfortable personal situation.

Jill felt resentment raise its head. What right did he have to come into her life and ask those questions? Then she reminded herself that she had invited Darren into her life and he had to ask questions to know where he stood.

"I wouldn't blame you for going out," he said. "I dated for a while, too. I think that's what's made me see things about you I hadn't appreciated before."

"Like what?" She curled her legs up underneath her in the chair and waited to hear why he'd come and what he was looking for.

Darren proved better at asking direct questions than he was at fielding them. He lifted his shoulders in a shrug. "Oh, I don't know."

"What?" she persisted.

"That you're understanding and you know how to laugh. Some women are so serious. Or they're so empty-headed that they don't get a joke."

Jill waited, wanting more. He hadn't said anything about missing her. She wanted something from the heart.

"Anyway, I'm not dating anyone right now," Darren concluded. "I didn't think it was fair to come see you while I had someone on the back burner."

Jill thought about her weekend in the mountains with E.J.

Darren rose. "I just wanted to tell you where I stood before we started the weekend." He clapped his hands on his thighs. "Now, why don't we go eat and see what movies are playing in town?"

They went to a Mexican restaurant and afterward to an adventure film. The evening was pleasant and civilized. There were no sparks, but unlike her mother, Jill knew relationships were built on mutual interests and shared history and being at ease with each other. She wanted the physical feelings, too, but she could wait for those.

When they returned to her apartment, Darren didn't show any reluctance to sleep on the sofa bed.

In fact, he was agreeable about everything. The next day, he asked questions about her classes, and he met Mrs. Casey and he went with Jill out to the country to check on Xandralene and Fido. He seemed startled by Xandralene, but he was polite.

As if by unspoken agreement, Jill and Darren didn't talk about what had gone wrong with the marriage. They spent their time on more neutral topics. But Jill knew Darren was studying her as closely as she was studying him.

She knew he was measuring the woman she was now against the woman he remembered. She thought he liked what he saw, and that would have thrilled her two months ago. Now, she only felt uncertain.

REAL MEN DIDN'T SPY on the neighbors, E.J. told himself in disgust.

So what if the flashy red Mercedes that had been parked at Jill's on Friday night was still there Saturday?

It didn't take a brain surgeon to figure out it was Darren's car. The well-groomed man in the darkly conservative but stylish clothes that E.J. saw coming and going with Jill could only be Darren.

Big deal. So her ex-husband was here.

E.J. put plastic wrap over his uneaten lunch and shoved the sandwich into the refrigerator. He had come back from Asheville feeling more at peace about his knee, perhaps moving into the stage of acceptance that Jill had talked about. He had also backed away from her because he didn't believe he could provide the things she wanted. And he needed time to heal, instead of hiding from his problems in a relationship.

He had contemplated that briefly, but it wouldn't be fair to himself or to Jill to use her as a means of solace even if she would allow it. He needed to fix this himself.

Still, this ex guy was over there with Jill, and E.J. *had* been with her last weekend. It didn't seem right that she was with someone else.

He found himself staring out the window again.

E.J. looked down at his faded yellow T-shirt and white painter's pants with the knees rubbing out. He doubted Darren owned anything this old and ragged. He wondered how Darren would react if E.J. appeared at Jill's door.

Hell, why shouldn't he go over there? He shouldn't have to vanish just because she had a guest. E.J. wanted to meet Darren, and he couldn't think of one reason why he shouldn't.

Besides, he needed to return her casserole dish. Jill and Darren might decide to do some cooking.

E.J. picked up his cane and started out the door toward Jill's.

The fifty yards that separated his house from hers grew longer as he hobbled up her walk. He lost some of his resolve. He ought to go on back to his house like a sensible person.

He kept walking.

This was stupid.

Yet he moved toward her door as if some huge magnet were drawing him there.

The casserole dish thumped against his left leg. He leaned on the cane to support his injured right knee. Jill and Darren would both see how transparent this ruse was. Jill would know he'd wanted a look at her ex. Darren would think he was a moron.

But E.J. continued forward.

At the door, he stopped to catch his breath before knocking.

Jill answered. She was wearing a flowing Paisley dress. It was sleeveless and he could see the whole length of the arms that had once wrapped around him. She wore some new dangling earrings that drew attention to her earlobes. He had kissed those very spots.

He wondered if she remembered that and if the sensation still made her tingle.

"Oh, E.J., hi." Jill glanced uncertainly over her shoulder.

She didn't ask him in, but E.J. wasn't into formalities now. He was here, and he intended to see Darren. "I brought your dish back," he announced. "I'll just take it into the kitchen."

He moved straight toward her and Jill had no choice but to back away.

A decent guy would have left when he saw the reluctance on her face. But E.J. limped into the kitchen and nodded to the man sitting on the sofa in the adjoining living room. E.J. noticed the fresh white chrysanthemums in a vase and he smelled Jill's perfume.

He nodded to the visitor. "Hi, I'm E.J. Robbins."

"I'm Darren Howard." Darren rose and moved forward but he didn't extend his hand.

E.J. thrust out his own hand to prove he wasn't such a cripple he couldn't shake hands. Darren's hand felt soft, as if he hadn't done enough manual labor. E.J. looked for other things about him to dislike.

"E.J. lives next door," Jill volunteered. Her voice sounded strained.

"That's right." E.J. smiled at Darren and found a lot more things to dislike. Darren was too pretty and his clothes too well pressed and his shoes too shiny. Who could like a guy like that?

Jill could, he determined as he switched his gaze to her. She must like Darren or the man wouldn't be here. She'd gone to a lot of trouble with her appearance. The dress was new and she was wearing stuff on her cheeks that women use to add color. She didn't need more color, he thought in irritation. She had a beautiful complexion just as it was. She didn't have to try to impress or please Darren.

"Have you had a chance to get out and see Charlotte, Darren?" E.J. asked. Or had they spent their time together cozily necking on the sofa? Had Jill confided to Darren that she and E.J. had slept together?

If she had, Darren seemed blandly unconcerned. He just smiled one of those polished, professional smiles. Maybe he didn't consider a gimp any sort of threat.

"We're going to tour Latta Plantation," Darren said.

"The gallery crawl is nice, too." E.J. looked at Jill as he spoke. She had cried in his arms on the way back from the gallery crawl. Didn't that memory mean anything to her?

"Jill hasn't mentioned that," Darren said.

E.J. knew he ought to shut up and leave. He stayed. "It's a night the art galleries are open late."

"How interesting."

Jill busied herself plumping pillows in the chair.

Suddenly E.J. was filled with anger. They were standing here talking drivel and what he really wanted to know was whether Jill loved this guy. If she didn't, why couldn't she love him instead? Because E.J. was starting to think he was in love with her.

"Jill, do you want to go on this gallery crawl?" Darren asked.

"No." She sounded firm. She looked at E.J. and her eyes flashed irritation and warning. "It was nice of you to return the dish, E.J." She took it from him and set it on her kitchen counter.

E.J. knew it was time to go. A nosy neighbor with a bad excuse can only stay so long. But he had seen Darren and that had answered some questions.

Half the single women he knew would kill for Darren. He had a good job and good looks and he drove the right car. To land him would be to die and go to Yuppie heaven.

If that was what Jill wanted, more power to her. A used government car equipped for a disabled person probably didn't stack up too well.

"Catch you later, Jill," E.J. said.

"Yes," she snapped.

All the way home, he cursed himself for a fool.

JILL CLOSED THE DOOR and turned back to Darren with a perky smile, trying to pretend E.J.'s visit hadn't meant anything. Trying to pretend his penetrating looks and leading questions had been neighborly conversation. Why had he come? And why did she feel so rattled by his visit?

"He kept Fido when I first moved here," Jill explained. She polished her hands restlessly against the cotton skirt.

"That was nice."

"Yes."

Jill knew Darren had looked E.J. over and dismissed him. Darren didn't feel threatened by someone who dressed with casual disregard and whose hair wasn't clipped into a dress-for-success style.

What would Darren think if he knew she had clung to E.J. in the throes of passion? What would he think if he knew she still hadn't fully resolved her feelings for E.J.?

"Why don't we go for a walk?" she suggested. She needed to get out.

"Sure."

As they started down the block, her thoughts churned. She was mad at E.J. for intruding on her weekend and for forcing her to compare him to Darren. She was mad at Darren for being so agreeable. Why couldn't he have been this way when she'd needed him? She was mad at herself for feeling pulled in all directions—wanting the old and feeling afraid of the unknown.

"Not a bad neighborhood," Darren said. "Some of these older quadraplexes could be remodeled and rented for top dollar."

Jill hadn't thought of the charming old apartments in those terms. "I think they're nice the way they are."

"You're right, they are." He smiled at her. "Why don't we make a pizza tonight?"

Their homemade pizzas had always been a joint project. She knew he was trying to reestablish comfort between them. She had to try, too.

"With those awful jalapeños you put on it?" she asked.

"Hey, I like them."

She smiled back at him. "Maybe I'll let you put on jalapeños, but no onions."

E.J. would have made a retort, and she found herself waiting for one. Darren was silent, but she didn't object when he looped his arm affectionately through hers.

They had a good time that evening making the pizza. And he helped clean up the kitchen afterward. As they worked, they talked about people they both knew.

Things didn't get serious until Sunday afternoon, when it was almost time for Darren to go.

He sat down across from her at the oval kitchen table.

"I think we need to talk about why our marriage broke up," he said.

It wasn't fair to bring the subject up just before he left. It didn't give them time to probe and explore. She wondered if he was deliberately limiting the time for discussion. Then she realized she was being too critical. It was enough that they were talking.

"I felt I got shoved aside in your grief over the miscarriage," he said flatly.

She blinked. "Did you think I didn't care about you anymore?" It had never occurred to her that he would feel neglected. She wondered guiltily how much about him she had failed to see because she was so lost in her own emotions.

"You were pretty torn up, Jill. I didn't know what to think."

"Yes, I was." She tried to remember back to those dark days, but they weren't as clear as they'd been when she first moved to Charlotte. "I'm sorry if that left you adrift, Darren."

"And then you didn't get over it," he continued. "After a while I couldn't see a way to save the marriage. I know now I should have tried harder and maybe suggested counseling. But back then, I just felt angry and I didn't see any hope for us."

Jill didn't think he knew how his lack of support had pained her. But he'd said he felt deserted by her. Instead of dwelling on their weaknesses, they needed to look for the common ground they had once shared.

"What changed your mind about us?" she asked.

"I finally saw I still had feelings for you. I became more and more aware of that as I spent time with other women. It never felt the same with others."

His words touched her. Darren didn't talk easily about his emotions and she appreciated his effort to be honest with her.

"I had a good time this weekend," he said after a moment.

"I did, too." It hadn't been bliss, but it had given Jill cause to hope. It had also made her realize she might have been unfair to Darren and she owed him a chance.

"I don't know where we go from here," Darren said. "It's not like we're just starting to date. We've been married and we already know each other."

"We may not know each other as well as you think," Jill murmured. "I'm sure we've both changed over the past months."

"Maybe in minor ways, but the big things are the same."

Were they?

He glanced at his watch. "I'm going to have to go in a minute. Look, I'm not trying to be possessive, but I don't think we can work on a future if there's someone else in the picture. I'm not going to date. I hope you won't, either."

Darren was asking for a logical concession.

She wasn't really dating anyway, Jill told herself. She thought about E.J.'s solitary walks in the mountains and about their agreement to be friends. But the passion she and E.J. had shared still weighed on her mind.

Darren waited.

She could tell him she didn't want to try again and it would be over, but Darren was trying, and she knew he wanted it to be good again. How could she turn her back on that?

Jill cleared her throat. "I want to try with us again."

MRS. CASEY PICKED THE toddler's outfit off the top of the pile and placed it in the bin for children's clothing.

"Isn't it a lovely day, Ted?" she asked cheerfully.

He looked at her with that glazed expression he sometimes had. Grace had begun to fear there might be something wrong with his vision.

He shrugged bony shoulders. He was terribly thin for one so young. "It's all right."

"Ted, it's sweet of you to volunteer here," she began.

He blinked at her.

Yes, she was sure there was something wrong with his vision.

"But you really ought to get out and meet more people. I don't know any other young men who come every week to work half a day here. Even though it is very generous of you," she added quickly.

He laughed harshly.

Sometimes it was hard trying to talk with Ted.

Grace didn't give up, though. "Have you ever thought about ballroom dancing?" she asked.

"I don't have no time for that."

"Oh, we can always make time for things we enjoy," she assured him. "There's a very nice studio here in town."

She hated to be selfish, but she'd been promoting the Avanti studio to everyone she knew. She'd put up notices at her church, hoping that if the dance studio had more business, they would pay Rick more and he'd be able to stay there.

"Ted, that was a woman's jacket. You put it in the wrong bin."

"Sorry."

"That's quite all right," she said as he pulled it back out.

"It's the Avanti Dance Studio. Rick, the instructor there, is excellent. You can go one time for free."

"I think Rick is the fellow who was looking for you this morning."

Her head snapped up. "Rick was here?"

"Yeah. He left a message for you."

"Where is it!"

"Uh, I guess I've got it."

It took forever for him to dig into his jeans pocket while Grace waited anxiously. Finally he pulled out a wadded piece of paper and handed it to her.

She scanned it. "Oh, dear. He won't be able to practice tonight. Rick and I work on routines together. I'm helping teach right now," she explained. "When did he give you this?"

"He was leaving the building when I went out to have a smoke. He was getting in a car with some woman."

"A woman?"

"Yeah. Hot redhead."

"Pretty?" Grace pressed, hating herself for asking.

"I guess so."

"It could be a relative," she said.

"I don't think so. They looked real tight."

Now what did that mean? Ted had no way in the world of knowing who this woman was to Rick. Still, Grace felt uneasy. She began to work quickly.

"We really don't have time to stand around and chat, Ted. There are a lot of clothes to be sorted."

He lethargically pulled a pair of jeans off the stack.

"We're never going to get anywhere if you don't work faster than that."

He looked at her with that glazed expression again. Honestly, sometimes it was like he wasn't even there. Why should she listen to anything he said about Rick? Ted hadn't even remembered to give her the note when she first got here. He could definitely be wrong about the woman.

But she did intend to have a gentle talk with Rick about the loan. He hadn't yet repaid her any money, and he needed to start making some kind of payment.

That was only right. Once she explained that to him, of course, there wouldn't be any problem.

Meanwhile, her spirits were down and she chafed to get away.

CHAPTER FOURTEEN

JOE STUCK HIS HEAD into Darren's paneled office. "How did the weekend with Jill go?"

"Good. Real good." Darren leaned back in his soft leather chair and smiled expansively.

Joe ambled in and sat in the chair across from the large desk. "So you're getting back together?"

"I think so."

"I'll be glad to see Jill again. I like her."

"She's changed a little," Darren said. It wasn't just the new clothes. She was more confident, and that gave her a kind of sexiness he hadn't seen in her before. She hadn't been as wholeheartedly pleased to see him as he'd expected, but she would warm up.

"Is she ready to come back to little Simmerville from the big city?" Joe inquired, and shot a wad of paper into the wastebasket.

Darren laughed. "She has to be. Her only friends there are her elderly landlady, a weirdo and the man next door. He was a little strange." Why else had he come over and hung around?

"Sounds like quite a collection," Joe said.

Darren locked his hands behind his neck. "Yeah. Jill will be glad to get back here." She had more in common with the doctors' wives and female hospital executives than those Charlotte folk.

"Are you taking your house off the market?" Joe asked.

"Hmm."

Maybe that was the push Jill needed. Once she realized how serious he was, she was bound to get a lot more enthusiastic. He fished into his desk for the realtor's card.

"I think I'll call and get that taken care of right now," Darren said.

"Whoa, buddy. Don't you need to talk to Jill first?"

"No. I'll surprise her."

MONDAY, AS E.J. RETURNED from his first day at work, he saw Jill watering the flowers along her front walk.

He fought back the coward in him and approached her.

She must have heard his cane thumping. She looked up with a wary expression.

"Hi," he said.

"Hello."

There was no sense beating around the bush. "I'm sorry I acted like a schmuck when Darren was here."

She straightened.

He noticed she wasn't wearing gloves and there was actually dirt on her hands. He even saw a small smudge on the side of her nose.

"I don't know what got into me," he said. "Did you have a nice time?"

"Yes. Darren and I have agreed we want to try to work things out." She announced it with tense purpose, as if she'd been rehearsing the words.

He felt as if he'd been karate-kicked in the stomach. All his wise conclusions that there was no place in his life for Jill floundered in the face of her announcement.

Had she and Darren rekindled their passion over the weekend? E.J. felt hot jealousy at the thought.

But it didn't matter how he felt, he told himself. She wanted Darren.

Why wouldn't she? Hell, the guy was not only handsome and successful, he was whole. Darren didn't face a lifetime of therapy with no hope of recovery. Even though Darren hadn't been there for her when she needed him, Jill was willing to make allowances for him.

"Did you work today?" she asked in a clear bid to change the subject.

"Yeah." They had assigned him to a tiny cubicle where he was learning a computer program. The windowless room wasn't very cheery but he was determined to make the best of it.

"My writer's class starts this evening," E.J. said. That would let her know that he was busy in case she had any absurd thoughts that he was pining for her.

"It's from the continuing-education department of the junior college," he added. "I couldn't get into the fiction class, so I signed up for the investigative-reporting class."

"I'm sure you'll enjoy that."

She shook back her hair and he watched the dark curls spin. For a moment he allowed himself to regret that he wouldn't be touching that hair again.

"I will. I'm going to be busy from now on."

Tomorrow night E.J. would start his special exercise classes at the Y. If Jill wanted to stay stuck in her old life, that was fine with him. But he was getting his head screwed on straight and moving ahead.

"I'd better get ready for class," he said.

He thought she was looking at him as he walked away, but he didn't turn around and look back.

MRS. CASEY WORE A BLACK dress with her new shoes. The heels were high and she felt as if she was falling forward when she walked but the salesman had said they were fashionable.

Grace stepped inside the studio and looked around expectantly. The cruise tickets had come in the mail today and she was dying to tell Rick.

He was going to be so excited!

Grace looked at the dozen people already present but didn't see Rick. Maybe he was running late.

A tall, effeminate man she'd never seen before clapped his hands and told everyone to get into a circle. Why was he doing that? That was Rick's job. "I'm Alec. I'm your new instructor."

Their new instructor! Grace stood stunned while he explained the next step. What had happened to Rick? Then, when the other couples began to dance, she brushed past her waiting partner and headed for Alec. He was in the corner, fiddling with the tape deck.

"What happened to Rick?" she asked in a frantic whisper.

He must have been in a car wreck or hurt in a fire. Or maybe he'd been called away because of a family illness.

"Rick?" Alec looked up. "He quit. Just didn't show up one day, so they hired me."

"Why didn't he show up?" There must be a good reason. She tried not to think about the money he had borrowed. About the redhead. About a bad feeling growing in the pit of her stomach.

Alec lowered his voice. "The studio's owner went to see Rick. They had some nasty words. Rick told him to shove the job."

"Rick would never talk like that!"

Alec patted her shoulder. "Honey, that was the least of what he said. Got to go."

He moved to the center of the circle to clap his hands and began to teach another step.

Grace grabbed her purse and headed for the door. No wonder Rick had quit. These people were awful. Still, she wished he had let her know. He *had* brought a note to her workplace, she reminded herself. That proved he was considerate.

But a brooding thought lay coiled and ready to strike. Had Rick come looking for her because he wanted to borrow more money? Had he intended to leave the girlfriend in the car while he played her for a sucker?

Grace blocked the thought. It simply wasn't so.

She stumbled to her car and blindly fished for a tissue.

THE TEST WAS TOMORROW morning and Jill needed to raise her grade. But as she sat at the table with her book and notes spread out around her, she was too anxious to study. Her thoughts were pulled in too many different directions.

The knock at her door jerked her out of her reflections.

It was Mrs. Casey.

Jill opened the door. "Won't you come—"

"He's quit," Grace announced in a stricken voice.

"Who's quit?"

"Rick."

Jill was silent. Although her landlady was distraught, Jill thought it was for the best. Rick's leaving might mean heartbreak for Mrs. Casey now, but in the long run she was better off without this man.

"You don't understand. I went to see him after the lesson. Actually," she continued, garbling her words and moving her arms in quick, useless gestures, "I left before the lesson was over. I went to his house. I got the address from the phone book because he had never told me." She made another feeble movement of her hand.

"Come and sit down," Jill said gently. She led Mrs. Casey to the kitchen table and guided her into a chair.

Jill read the pain on the older woman's face and feared the story was about to get worse.

"Rick wasn't at his house but a woman was. A pretty, young person. He's living with a woman," she said, and looked hopelessly at Jill.

A storm of tears overtook Mrs. Casey.

Jill waited in supportive silence.

"I'm sorry," Grace finally said, and wiped her eyes with the tissue Jill offered.

"It's all right."

"The woman told me not to expect to get my money back." Grace looked at Jill with wide, hurt eyes. "She says Rick is a gambler. He was using my money to gamble."

Jill's heart sank. "You lent him money?"

"Yes. What a ridiculous old fool I was."

"You were lonely." Jill patted her hand.

Grace pulled three tickets from her purse and waved them pitifully. "I bought these. I thought we were going on a cruise together."

"I know it's a terrible disappointment, but you can turn them in and get your money back," Jill told her.

Grace shook her head. "No, I can't. They're nonrefundable. The cruise leaves next week and I can't get my money back."

"Oh, dear."

"Even if I could bear to go on the cruise, I have no one to go with me." She pressed her lips together against another onslaught of tears.

Jill thought rapidly. "My final is tomorrow. You and I will go."

"I don't want you to go just because you feel sorry for me."

"I want to go," Jill said.

"You do?" Grace asked in a trembling voice.

"Yes. It will be a treat for me." And it would help Mrs. Casey forget.

"I know it won't be the dream vacation I'd planned," Grace said, "but if I stay here, I'll only feel more lonely and upset."

"The tickets are paid for," Jill said. "We're going to use them."

"There's a third ticket," Mrs. Casey added uncertainly.

"It's a shame you won't be able to use every ticket, but you and I will go and have a great time."

The older woman nodded. "Yes. We will."

Jill knew Mrs. Casey's words were whistling-by-a-dark-graveyard bravado, but if that was what it took to help her get over Rick, more power to her.

"I hate to bring this up," Jill began, "but did you have Rick sign any papers before you lent him money?"

Grace looked away. "I know I should have, but it didn't seem right at the time."

Jill suppressed a sigh. "Then I don't think you have any legal recourse. You could talk to a lawyer, and you probably ought to, but I suspect your money is gone and there's no way you can sue to get it back.''

Grace's eyes misted over again. "How could he do this to me?"

"Some people don't have a conscience."

"I'm probably not the first woman he took advantage of," she said sadly. "And there will surely be others after me."

"Yes, I suspect so. But it's over, so try not to think about it too much." Jill smiled encouragement. "Let's concentrate on what a good trip we're going to have."

"Yes."

Jill knew Mrs. Casey was still hurt, but at least she had the cruise to occupy her thoughts. The trip would be a respite for *her*, too. It would be a time away from North Carolina and her ex-husband, and from a neighbor whose memory refused to fade.

Jill threw herself into studying for her test the next day.

As SHE GOT OUT OF her car after returning from the college, she saw Mrs. Casey.

"How did it go, dear?"

"Not so great." She knew she hadn't improved her grade. She would have been devastated by that a few weeks ago. Now it was a disappointment, nothing more. She didn't have to impress anyone with spectacular marks, and a *B* was perfectly respectable.

She knew Darren would be surprised if she told him that, but he would have to get used to the new Jill, the woman who was going to please herself more from now on, set her own priorities. He would have to learn that this would be a more equal partnership.

"YOU KNOW WHAT YOU ought to do?" Charlie asked as he sopped up gravy with his bread.

E.J. smiled wanly. "No. But I'll bet you're about to tell me." They were in some dive that only Charlie could have discovered. E.J. was glad to be here, though. He'd tried to keep busy the past few days, but even a casual date with Georgia hadn't kept him from feeling blue.

The waitress stopped to refill their teapot, and Charlie waited until she was gone.

"Take the nice woman up on the offer and go to the Caribbean with her."

"Jill's going." E.J. stacked the packets of sugar neatly in their tray.

"Is that supposed to be some sort of excuse for you not to go?" Charlie demanded. He made an annoyed swipe at the plate with his bread. "So what if Jill will be there? She was in the mountains, and I'm assuming the two of you didn't get into any trouble there."

"Quit leering, Charlie. And quit matchmaking."

"I happen to like Jill, but, hey, I'm not the one in your shoes. No one can throw you together if you don't want to be with her. Me, I had the impression you did want to be with her."

"That's in the past." It was surprising how much effort it was taking to keep Jill in the past. He found himself wandering to the back window to see if she was in her yard. And he found himself thinking about the sound of her laughter and the scent of her soap. Sappy stuff like that.

"Then how come I had to watch you moon around the whole four days we were in the mountains?" Charlie asked.

"I was thinking about my knee."

"Part of the time," Charlie conceded. "But the rest of the time you had something else on your mind."

E.J. leaned in closer. "Charlie, I'm going to tell you something because you've been a friend a long time and because, thank heavens, you're a little bit smarter than you look. I like Jill. Okay? But she's got other aspirations. She wants a man with a neat car and a good résumé."

"She tell you that?"

"Yes."

That took the wind out of Charlie's sails, but only temporarily. "Listen, a lot of times women say one thing and mean another."

"Pu-leez. She's not some high school tease. She's a sensible, grown woman. She knows what she wants." And she knew what she didn't want—which was him.

"You're turning into a wimp, E.J. There was a time when nothing would have stopped you from giving it a shot if you wanted something bad enough."

"Did you say a 'gimp' or a 'wimp'?"

"Very funny. Your banged-up knee isn't going to stand in the way of something you really want."

For the first time in many weeks, E.J. stared into the teeth of his longing and admitted he did want Jill. Bad. He wanted to hold her and laugh with her and sit at dinner with her. But he knew a man didn't always get what he wanted.

"I got over Lisa and I'll get over this," he said stoically.

"Lisa was taken from you. Jill, you're giving up."

E.J. hated it when he thought Charlie might be right. But what was he supposed to do?

ON SATURDAY MORNING, Jill and Mrs. Casey took a cab to the airport.

"E.J. is going to meet us at the terminal," Mrs. Casey said.

Jill whirled from looking out the window and stared at her. "To see us off?"

"No, dear. E.J. is coming with us."

She swallowed. "On the cruise ship?"

"Yes."

Several emotions battled for control. Joy. Horror. Uncertainty. Anger. Jill grabbed at that last one and demanded, "Why didn't you tell me?"

The cabbie looked back at them in his rearview mirror.

Mrs. Casey blinked. "Please don't shout. I'm sorry if I've upset you."

"You should have told me," Jill insisted. How could she avoid running into him on the ship? She'd made a promise to Darren to try to work things out. Being with E.J. was baiting a trap for herself.

"I would have told you, but E.J. asked me not to. Did I do something wrong?"

Jill struggled for composure and reminded herself Grace was taking this trip to forget Rick's betrayal. She couldn't cope with Jill's disapproval.

"I'm sorry if I shouted," Jill said contritely. "It's just that I'm surprised and, frankly, not pleased. My ex-husband and I are working to rebuild our marriage. E.J. could get in the way of that."

"I don't see how." Mrs. Casey still looked wounded. "He won't bother you, especially if he knows you don't want him to. E.J. is a gentleman."

"Then why is he doing this?"

"I don't know. Are you mad at E.J.?" Grace asked cautiously. "Don't you like him anymore?"

"Of course I like him." Jill felt a wave of anguish. She liked him very much. Too much? The weekend with Darren should have dispelled all doubts about E.J. But deep down she knew that it hadn't. Now she was being forced to come face-to-face with her feelings.

And she wasn't ready.

E.J. SAW JILL'S expression as she came down the aisle of the airplane toward him. She nodded stiffly to him as Mrs. Casey slid in between the two of them. Then Jill turned on her portable stereo and ignored him.

E.J. sat in his own seat and weighed the probabilities of his enjoying the cruise.

They didn't look promising.

JILL WAS ON THE AISLE and E.J. occupied the window seat. She was too far away to demand an explanation on a crowded plane, and too near to ignore him.

She willed herself to think about Darren and the conversation they'd had on the phone just last night. He had sounded sweet and charming, just like in the days when they were courting. He was busy planning his next visit and hinting at a wonderful surprise he had for her.

The only surprise she could think about was E.J.'s presence on this trip and the fact that he'd wanted it kept secret from her.

Jill didn't have a chance to ask him until they were aboard the ship half a day later.

It was late in the afternoon, and the sun spilled a golden path across the water when Jill found E.J. stretched out in a lounge chair with a notebook in one hand and a glass of beer in the other. He wore sunglasses, and his cane lay on the deck beside him.

Jill sat down next to him. "Why are you here?" she demanded without preamble.

He put the notebook aside, but his expression was concealed behind sunglasses.

"Grace asked me to come and I agreed."

Jill wasn't letting him off so easily. "Why?"

"Because I felt guilty about not steering her away from that bum. Tropical ports sounded good, too." E.J. removed the sunglasses and looked squarely at her—no evasions, no excuses. His eyes were bluer and deeper than the water surrounding them. "And you were going to be here."

She hesitated. Did that mean what she thought it meant?

"I wanted to be with you, Jill."

She wanted to maintain a buffer between them but the walls were crumbling. "I don't know what you mean."

"Yes, you do. Just when we were getting close, I found out I wasn't going to recover and I let it get to me."

She brushed back the hair the wind blew across her face and waited. Maybe it was the gentle rolling of the ship that made her want to put her head on his shoulder, or maybe it was the beauty of the fading day that brought a catch to her throat.

"I pulled back just when I should have pushed forward. I'm not saying that would have changed the outcome with you and Darren. Maybe nothing will. But I'm throwing my hat into the ring."

She wet her lips. "E.J., I—" Words tore through her mind but none of them were right. She couldn't tell him there was no hope, because there was. She was just beginning to realize how much.

He touched her arm and a sensation of warmth shimmered through her. She knew, then, that she had been wanting him to touch her for a long time.

"We never gave it a chance, Jill. Darren was always in the way. But we could have something if we tried, and we both know it."

She couldn't look away. His gaze held hers captive.

"When I first met you, you were a prissy thing from a small town who was shell-shocked from a bad divorce. You're still a little prissy, but you've got more comfortable with who you are. You started taking chances by making friends with people who were different from the ones you knew back home."

"What are you asking from me?" Jill knew she was going to scale walls to give it to him. She was running toward the future as surely as she'd tried to run backward to the past.

"I just want you to give it a chance, Jill. That's all."

It sounded simple. And right. But Jill felt as if she had been tethered to the same spot for so long, she wasn't sure she knew how to break free. It was time, though, to find a way.

"I want to, E.J." Her voice was a hoarse whisper. "But you have to give me time to think."

He smiled a slow, wraparound smile that disturbed her pulse and her breathing. "I'm not going to pressure you, Jill. The next move is yours."

Guilt interrupted her thoughts, and she was compelled to say, "I made a promise to Darren."

E.J.'s expression hardened. "Yeah, and he made one to you that said something about till death do you part. He didn't feel too bound by his promises."

"No, he didn't." And she wasn't going to make excuses for him anymore. Darren had had his chance with her and he'd failed her.

Just then, Grace appeared. Jill could have sobbed at her timing.

"There you two are," Grace said gaily. "It's time for dinner. I've signed us up for the early meals. I thought the food would be fresher then."

E.J. smiled and got slowly to his feet. Jill followed behind. Over dinner, E.J. played the charmer to Mrs. Casey's new circle of widowed bridge partners. Afterward, a shipboard chanteuse serenaded them. Then E.J. gallantly walked Mrs. Casey to her stateroom.

Jill returned to her room alone.

He'd said it was her move.

By midnight, the words had become a chant.

She no longer knew what was holding her back. Darren was offering her the chance for a life that had fit her well once. But the pull to be with E.J. was as strong as the tide. It was a physical need and an emotional need.

She couldn't think of one good reason why she was lying here alone, denying herself and E.J. what they both wanted.

She slipped out of the narrow bed and pulled on her Japanese silk robe. Barefoot, she walked out onto the deck.

The metal steps felt cool beneath her feet as she climbed to the next level. She heard the water splashing against the sides of the ship, and overhead the moon was a golden circle. While the cold ocean night licked through her flimsy wrapper, she made her way to E.J.'s cabin.

She tapped on the door. A moment later he opened it. She saw he was wearing only pajama bottoms.

Jill took a deep breath. "I thought you might be lonely."

"Do you want to talk?" he asked.

"No." She stepped inside and pulled the door closed behind her. She saw a bed that looked as rumpled from restlessness as her own. She saw his clothes left in a careless bundle on the floor. It wasn't the neat, folded-at-the-foot-of-the-bed care so typical of Darren, but it felt exactly right.

Jill reached for the wall switch and turned out the light. Only a soft beam of light came in through the porthole.

The undulation of the ship seemed more marked in the quiet darkness. Jill put her arms around E.J.

"Thank God," he said, and pulled her closer.

He kissed the top of her head and she snuggled closer against him. She felt the sense of sureness and rightness that had been lacking all weekend with Darren.

"Come here," he said huskily, and they stepped over the bundle of clothes to the bed. "You're cold. Let me see if I can help warm you."

She smiled and slid into the single bed.

"I was half-mad with jealousy, you know." He climbed in beside her and pulled her against him. "Why else did you think I made such a fool of myself by going to your apartment?"

She giggled and nuzzled against him. "I thought it was to return my casserole dish."

"Right," he muttered. "And you probably think you're here now to get a good night's sleep. Well, you're wrong."

"I hope so," she whispered huskily.

"Dead wrong," he said, before his mouth claimed hers. He dismissed the preliminaries. There were no soft, cajoling kisses. His first kiss was urgent with a passion too long repressed. He made a sound deep in his throat and buried his hands in her hair.

They clung together, body against body, mouth against mouth. She felt the magic of his tongue as it touched the interior of her mouth. Her whole body felt a delicious surge of aching and adrenaline.

She moved her fingertips up and down his spine, feeling the skin of his bare back. He groaned again and pulled away.

"If we're going to continue—and I strongly think we should—you're going to have to get out of that robe thing and I need to take these pajamas off."

"Yes."

He sat on the side of the bed and she felt a loss at even such a temporary parting. She heard the rustle of cellophane as she shrugged out of her silk wrapper and tossed it onto the floor.

"I brought these just in case," he said sheepishly.

Then he was back, hard and solid and offering her all the things she hadn't realized how much she yearned for. The tip of his tongue slipped into her mouth and she gave herself over to the kiss.

This was real. This was important.

All the other things that had once seemed necessary faded into a swirling fog in the back of her mind. She no longer wanted to return triumphant to Simmerville. She no longer wanted to find happiness in the only place where it had existed for her before.

She had a new source of joy, and he was here now, surrounding her, covering her and readying himself to become a part of her.

She grasped at a thread of reality. "Are you okay? I mean, your knee?"

"It'll be easier for me if we shift around a little here." He turned her slightly so that they were side by side.

"That better?" she asked.

"It's more than better," he said as he slowly ran his hand from her hips to her breasts. She felt every inch of his journey, and sighed.

Jill sighed again, deep in the valley of sensation and sensuality. She didn't ever want to move from here or stop feeling the electric pulses that made her whole body soft and pliant.

Then his mouth replaced his fingers and she was lifted to a whole new realm of excitement.

She almost cried out in protest when he abandoned her breasts and pulled her against him. The emotions that had been incubating so long burst into a fire storm.

They kissed like desperate survivors.

He moved closer to her. Closer. Then into her.

As their kiss escalated to a new frenzy, he moved against her. Jill was no longer able to separate emotions. Pleasure. Passion. A need for relief from the wanting inside her. A crazy sense of losing control, yet *wanting* to lose it.

Above all, there was the feeling of E.J. deep inside her, pushing her to greater heights. The she reached a plane of unimaginable pleasure, and her thoughts spilled together into a bright array of colors and sensations. She was on the edge of the universe, caught in a moment of pure ecstasy.

Slowly she subsided back to earth. The kaleidoscope faded into warm darkness and she was on the bed next to E.J. She felt content. Sated. Loved.

"I think you made a nice first move," E.J. said raggedly. "What are you going to do for an encore?"

"Just you wait and see," she answered. "Just you wait and see."

CHAPTER FIFTEEN

THE AIR THE NEXT DAY was surely no purer nor the sky any brighter. Yet it seemed so to Jill.

Everything was wonderful. Throughout the day, things kept getting better. Mrs. Casey's jokes were funnier. The captain's tales, when he joined their table at lunch, were fascinating. E.J.'s face was more dear and more handsome.

It was as if her vision had cleared when she made the decision that she wanted E.J. And a ship was made for romance. They strolled the decks and lounged over cocktails and gazed into each other's eyes.

It was a trauma to have to part so that E.J. could take a shower. Jill spent the time standing at the railing with Mrs. Casey, watching an island come into view.

"You don't seem to object to E.J. too much now," Grace said.

"No."

"You're looking at each other like a couple of love-birds."

"He's nice," Jill murmured.

He was more than that. He was kind and thoughtful and funny and sure of himself. His acceptance of his problem made him all the more dear to her.

"I think you've made a better choice than I did," Grace said ruefully, and looked off into the distance.

Jill bit her lip in guilt. In the midst of her excitement, she had lost sight of her landlady's heartache.

"I'm sorry, Grace. I guess I'm being selfish."

"No, you're not." Mrs. Casey tied her scarf more firmly against the sea breeze. "I want you to enjoy yourself. If E.J. is the man for you, I'm glad you found each other."

"But it must be hard for you to watch us while you're here alone."

"I'm lucky to be here alone. Oh, I'll admit I'm hurt by the way Rick treated me, but I could afford to lose the money. What if he finds someone as gullible as me who doesn't have the money to lose?"

"That could happen," Jill murmured.

Grace wrung her hands. "I wish there was something I could do to prevent it."

"There isn't, so you've got to stop worrying about it."

"I know."

Jill looked at her landlady and saw the face of a woman who had longed for happiness and had suffered for that wish. It wasn't fair, and Jill wished there was something she could do to change things.

On impulse, she hugged Mrs. Casey. "I think Rick was a fool."

"You're sweet to say that." Grace looked at Jill apologetically. "It makes me feel bad that I didn't let you keep Fido."

"Fido has a home with Xandralene. Don't worry about it."

"Maybe E.J. will let him come back, now that you two are on such good terms."

"We haven't thought that far ahead," Jill said.

It was true. Last night had been taken up with exploring each other's bodies while the ship rocked them. This morning, she slipped back to her own cabin before the others on board had cause for comment.

Jill's thoughts today had been on last night, and she sensed that E.J.'s had, too. The future hadn't come under discussion.

"Well, E.J. has never been the sort to rush into anything," Grace said. "He's dated lots of girls since Lisa died, but he's still single."

"Yes." Jill hadn't considered that E.J. might love her but still not be ready to commit. He'd said he was throwing his hat in the ring, she reminded herself. That meant something. She brushed aside Mrs. Casey's words, certain that she and E.J. had a future.

Now she must tell Darren that *they* did not.

"Is something wrong, dear?"

"I was thinking about my ex-husband," Jill confided slowly. "I'm going to have to explain that my plans for a reconciliation have changed."

"I'm sure he'll understand." Mrs. Casey patted Jill's hand and left.

Jill stayed where she was, letting the wind ruffle her hair as she leaned over the railing and watched the blue water. Darren would have to understand, but she hated to think about telling him. He'd tried hard to patch things up. It wasn't his fault that she wasn't the same woman she'd once been. Her needs had changed and Darren could no longer meet them.

To heck with him, Jill thought with a burst of defiance. She was here to enjoy herself. She was going to buy silly tourist trinkets at ports of call, soak up the sun and spend her nights with E.J.

There would be time enough to deal with Darren when she returned to Charlotte.

THIS CRUISE THING HAD come out of the blue, and Darren hadn't liked it one bit. Jill had explained she was going as a favor to her landlady. But during the whole week she was gone, she hadn't called him once. She hadn't even sent a postcard.

He was starting to lose patience with her. It was one thing for her to hang back about sleeping with him. It was another to play mind games with him. What else could you call this?

He bided his time until the Sunday night when she was due back from the cruise. It was late when he decided to call.

"Hello," she said brightly.

It must have been a good trip, because she sounded cheerful.

"Hi," he said.

"Oh. Hello, Darren."

"You don't sound real glad to hear from me," he said with blunt irritability.

"I wasn't expecting you to call."

"I called to see when we could get together again. Next weekend works for me."

"Darren, there's something I have to explain. You see—I hate having to say this over the phone—but I've changed my mind about us."

He couldn't believe what he was hearing. "What in the hell are you talking about? When I saw you two weeks ago, all systems were go." What could have happened to change things so fast?

He heard her inhale deeply, but before she could speak, he said, "We're on one minute and you go on a cruise and then it's all over. What gives?" he demanded.

"I was kidding myself about us," she answered in a small voice.

No, she wasn't, he was certain. He had become more and more sure he and Jill belonged together. Her sudden flip-flop was annoying, but it wasn't how she really felt.

"Jill, I don't know what's come over you, but I don't have time for all these games. If you're trying to get even with me because you think I broke up the marriage, you have to get over that. We can't work out any problems if you're still holding a grudge."

"I'm not holding a grudge," she said firmly

Of course she was. "I'm coming up next weekend. We need to talk in person."

"I—" She sighed. "Yes, maybe it's for the best."

"Good. I'll see you then."

He hung up, but his hand remained clenched over the receiver. Darren realized this was Jill's anger showing. She was paying him back for leaving her.

It made him mad, but it didn't mean they were through.

He'd already bought something expensive and showy to take to her. The marquis-cut emerald ring was going to go a long way toward softening her.

E.J. SAT IN HIS LITTLE cubicle at work and clamped the phone more tightly to his ear, as if by doing so he could make the words more real.

Dr. Findley was talking about an orthopedic surgeon who was doing cartilage replacement using tissue from donors. The transplants were new and experimental, but they showed promise. Dr. Findley was talking about the possibility of this working for E.J. He was talking about hope.

"I'm not promising anything," Dr. Findley said. "This is straight-off-the-drawing-board stuff."

"But there's a chance?" E.J. persisted.

"Yes. But you'd have to go to Chicago for the operation."

"I don't care where I have to go." *Timbuktu would be fine, thank you.*

"I flew to Chicago myself last week and observed an operation. It's impressive. Dr. Weinstein is one of the premier physicians in the country. I don't want to hold out false hope, and it's not for everyone, but I think it might work in your case."

"How soon can you get me in?"

"Since this is so new, not a lot of people have heard about it yet. I should be able to get you in quickly. I don't expect an answer from you now. Take some time to think about it."

"I've already thought about it," E.J. said. "Schedule me an appointment."

E.J. hung up and sat inside the bright blue walls of his office cubicle, allowing himself to believe that he could regain full use of his knee. That he could run and ride and do simple things like move from room to room without his cane.

Jill would be thrilled.

After six glorious days together, he had hated to see the cruise end. He hadn't said it aloud, but he half feared the enchantment would disappear once they arrived back in Charlotte. He had held off discussing the future because he hadn't wanted to break the spell.

He'd felt good until last night when she got off the phone with Darren. He'd watched her pace her little apartment in agitation. She said it was over between her and Darren, but Darren was coming to visit and she felt obligated to tell him in person.

E.J. wanted to believe her. But some cautious part of himself told him to wait and see how Jill acted when Darren arrived. E.J. was in love with her, but he had to make sure she loved him, too. He had to know it hadn't been just the temporary enchantment of the cruise that had swayed her.

He wouldn't know that until after she saw Darren.

"Lunchtime, E.J."

He glanced up at his co-worker.

"Want to go down to the snack bar with me?" Dale asked.

"No, thanks, I've got to run an errand."

"Where to?" Dale asked, with no apologies for prying.

"The Avanti Dance Studio."

Dale looked uncertainly at E.J.'s leg.

E.J. laughed. "I'm going to learn the tango."

Maybe he could after he went to Chicago. Meanwhile, he was going to the studio to pick up a publicity photo of Rick. The studio's disgruntled owner had been conned out of advance pay by the man. The owner had a stack of glossy photos of Rick, and he said E.J. was welcome to the ones he hadn't already scrawled obscenities on.

E.J.'s investigative-reporting class met after work. Although he'd signed up for the class only because he couldn't get into the fiction class, he was beginning to enjoy the digging around for facts. Maybe this was the kind of writing he should have been doing all along.

E.J. wished he could see Jill after his class. But he couldn't. He had no choice but to spend time with Roger; otherwise his plan wouldn't work.

JILL WAITED FOR E.J. with growing impatience. He'd been mysterious when he called to say he was meeting someone. Not that she suspected he was seeing another woman, but it was after ten o'clock and she wanted him here with her.

Now.

A knock sounded and she yanked the door open.

"You should look out the window first," E.J. lectured as he pulled her into his arms. "I could be a pervert."

"I hope you are," she whispered into his ear, and laughed in delight when he gave a low, sensual growl.

She drew him into the apartment, possessively keeping her arm around his as she guided him to the sofa. "It's late. I was getting worried."

"I was with Roger. It took a while because we had to spend the first half hour talking about what a cool stud he is and about how dumb women are."

Jill made a face. "I hope you didn't let him get away with that."

"I had to. I need a favor from him."

"What kind of favor could you need from Roger?" Jill thought she had a right to ask. After all, Roger had kept her from spending precious minutes with E.J. That alone was a punishable offense. Since the first night she and E.J. had been together on the ship, she had become obsessed with seeing him, touching him, loving him. It was as if she needed to make up for all that lost time.

"I'm working on an article for my investigative journalism course and I'm trying to convince Roger to get it on television."

"E.J., that's wonderful! What's the story about?"

He smiled. "It's a secret."

"I don't like secrets."

Chuckling, he dug into his pocket. "Here, I brought you a present."

That mollified her. "A picture. How sweet." She reached eagerly for it. "I'll frame it and—" She stared at it. "This isn't your picture. It looks like that sleaze, Rick."

"It is."

She threw it into the wastebasket.

E.J. laughed and wrapped an arm around her. "Never mind that. Let's talk about something more pleasant."

They didn't talk, though. They spent the next hour progressing from snuggling to deciding on a more comfortable location. They chose the bed. From there, things progressed delightfully.

Jill was still dazed and heady afterward when E.J. sat up in bed.

"I'm going to Chicago to have another operation," he announced.

She bolted up beside him. "When did you decide that?"

"Today. The doctor called me. He says a surgeon in Chicago is doing experimental work that looks promising."

"Experimental?" Jill felt she was standing on a cliff and it was eroding beneath her. She didn't want E.J. to take any unnecessary risks. "Experimental" sounded too iffy for the man she loved.

"Maybe you should wait until they've perfected it," she said.

"I can't wait. I'm too impatient. Besides," he added and pulled her into a hug, "I've got a good feeling about this."

Jill tried to stifle her fears. "You're not doing it for me, are you? Because if you are, I don't care about your knee."

"No. I don't think you do. At one time I thought you wouldn't consider someone who wasn't perfect. I don't think that anymore."

He stroked his hand down her back in a gesture so caring, her eyes misted.

"I'm doing it for me, Jill. I want to be active again. If there's a chance I can be, I want to try." He kissed the top of her head.

"Yes, but..." Her words trailed away. She ran her hands through his hair and wondered how she could object to something that was so important to him.

"When will you go?" she asked.

"They've tentatively scheduled me for three weeks from now."

She swallowed. It seemed so soon. E.J. would not only be far away from her, he would be helpless in a hospital.

"I'll go with you," she decided. Her new classes would have started by then, but that didn't matter. She intended to be with him to see him through this.

"I'd like that," he said.

Knowing she could be with him made Jill feel a little better, but she didn't like the thought of him going through surgery again, and she worried that he might be getting his hopes up for nothing.

Her thoughts were interrupted by the sound of someone pounding on the door.

"Who the heck is that?" E.J. asked.

Jill slid away from him and reached for her silk robe. "I can't imagine."

"Don't answer it without looking out," E.J. called after her.

She hurried to the door as the pounding continued, searching her mind for possibilities. Could Mrs. Casey have an emergency? What if it was Darren? That almost halted her. *Don't let it be Darren,* she prayed.

She peeked out and saw Xandralene standing there, Fido beside her.

Relieved, Jill threw open the door.

"Hi." Xandralene blew her long bangs out of her eyes and grinned. "I didn't, like, wake you up, did I?"

Fido barked and jumped on her. Jill rubbed his head.

"Did I wake you up?" the younger woman repeated.

Jill looked back at her. "Uh, not exactly."

"Good." Xandralene stuck a piece of gum into her mouth. "I'm sorry to show up on your doorstep like this, but we had a little problem out at the house."

"Oh?" Jill stood in the doorway without inviting Xandralene in. E.J.'s presence in the bedroom complicated things and she wasn't sure what to do.

"Yeah. It started with a little electrical problem. One of the guys thought he could fix it but, like, well, after the fire got started, see, the water pressure out there wasn't enough to really put out the flames, so—"

"Your house caught on fire!"

"Yeah, it kind of did."

"Was it serious?"

"Everybody got out okay. We saved a few things before the roof started to fall. There were still some walls standing when I, like, left."

Jill pulled Xandralene into the house.

"Were you inside trying to save things?" Jill ran a hand over Xandralene's shoulder to reassure herself that the younger woman was all right.

Fido pranced in behind them and flopped down in the middle of the rug.

"Yeah. When Izzy's kerchief caught fire, we, like, freaked and..."

Jill stared, dumbfounded. Someone's clothing had been in flames? It was a miracle Xandralene was alive!

"The fire department came real fast, but it was an old wood house. Anyway, we couldn't stay there tonight."

"I should say not," Jill said with feeling.

Xandralene shrugged, then added apologetically. "I didn't know where else to go, so I came here. Is that okay?"

"You did the right thing to come here. I'll get some sheets to make up the sofa bed."

"Great." Xandralene hesitated. "What should I do about Fido?"

"Put him in E.J.'s yard."

"Is that, like, okay? You two weren't hitting it off too good when I left. After Darren came, I didn't know if things got any better."

Jill glanced over her shoulder into the bedroom. She didn't want to get into a discussion now.

"I think it's fine to put Fido in E.J.'s yard," Jill told her.

"Yeah, well, okay."

As soon as Xandralene left with the dog, Jill rushed into the bedroom.

E.J. was sitting up in bed with his hands propped behind him. Jill glanced at the window. For one crazy moment, she wondered if E.J. could climb out the window. Then she realized she was being irrational. There was no way E.J. could sneak home and there was no need for it. Xandralene was a big girl. She would understand.

Jill pulled open the closet door and reached overhead for sheets. "Xandralene is staying here tonight."

"I heard."

"She doesn't know you're here."

"Our clothes are on the living room floor so it shouldn't take her too long to figure it out," E.J. said laconically.

Jill's hand flew to her mouth and she looked at him in horror. Then she rushed into the living room to gather up the telltale clothing.

Xandralene wandered in through the front door. "Do you mind if I, maybe, take a shower? I feel kind of grody and my hair smells like smoke."

"Go ahead," Jill said. "You know where the towels are."

"Yeah."

As Xandralene disappeared into the bathroom, Jill headed back into the bedroom.

"While she's busy, why don't—"

"We make mad, passionate love?" he finished.

The idea had an amazing appeal. With each new lovemaking, they became more in tune with each other, and the results were more exhilarating, more overpowering, more breath stopping.

She swallowed a lump of longing.

"I was going to say you could go back to your house." She thrust his clothes at him.

E.J. put his feet over the side of the bed. "I had a feeling you were going to say that," he grumbled.

"There'll be other times," she said regretfully.

He shrugged into his shirt. "I won't be able to see you until late tomorrow night."

"Why not?"

"More research," he said evasively, and kissed her determinedly before she could protest.

After that, Jill was too much of a rag doll to do more than say, "Get here as soon as you can."

"Always."

He kissed her again, then left her alone. She climbed into bed and tried to calm her body enough to go to sleep.

GRACE SORTED CLOTHES for the first half hour. She'd come in early because she didn't have anything else to do, and lately she'd felt particularly lonely at home.

She had too much time to think about Rick, too much time to weep over his betrayal and worry that he might do this to another lonely woman.

Someone shuffled over beside her and she looked up.

"Good morning, Ted."

He mumbled something that might have been a greeting. He looked thinner than ever today; his cheeks were positively gaunt.

"Are you eating well, Ted?" she asked.

"Uh, yeah."

"You know, Ted, I mentioned a few weeks ago that you might want to take dance lessons."

He looked at her with a vacant expression.

"At the Avanti studio," she added. "I hope you didn't sign up, because, frankly, I had a bad experience there."

"Oh, yeah?"

"One of their dance instructors turned out to be not very nice. Ted, that is a lady's nightgown that you put in the Children's bin."

Someone else strolled up. Grace recognized the man with the earphones who had spoken with Ted once before.

"You still here, man? When's your work release end?"

"Don't worry about it," Ted snarled.

"Just being friendly, man."

Grace watched as the other man moseyed away, his fingers clicking, his body gyrating.

"Ted, I don't like that young man. I think you were right not to be friendly with him. What is work release?" she inquired.

He stared at her.

"Never mind. Let's get back to sorting."

As they began pulling clothing out of the huge pile, Grace told Ted about the cruise and about E.J. and Jill. That had been a surprise.

"You see, Jill is a very orderly woman, very much a lady. E.J. is wonderful, but he's not worried about making a big show for anyone's benefit."

Ted didn't seem to be listening. Grace kept talking anyway. It made her happy to be here doing something useful. She was getting over her hurt and disillusionment, but the loneliness was still there.

"Do you know any nice older men to introduce me to, Ted?" she asked suddenly.

"There's this guy in charge of the treatment program they put me into. He's a priest, though, so I don't think he's looking for no woman." She looked away to cover her embarrassment. She hadn't really thought he would. She didn't want him to think she was desperate. But it would be nice to have someone who really cared for her the way E.J. seemed to care for Jill. She didn't know where to find a decent man.

The sad fact was, at her age, she probably never would.

It didn't occur to her until she got home to wonder what kind of treatment program Ted meant. Dear Lord, she hoped he didn't have cancer! Surely not. It might be some sort of treatment for an eating disorder. She'd seen talk shows about that. They were usually young girls, but Ted was awfully thin.

She made a mental note to take him one of her Mississippi Mud cakes the next time she worked. That would fatten him up and give her something to concentrate on instead of her loneliness.

LATE TUESDAY AFTERNOON, E.J. knocked on the door of the duplex. A gorgeous redhead opened the door.

"Is Rick Wilson here?" E.J. asked. He wondered why this woman's beauty didn't have the same effect on him as Jill's quiet radiance. At one time, E.J. would have been bowled over by the redhead.

"Who are you?" she asked.

She sounded like a woman used to screening Rick's callers for creditors and victims.

"I'm with WMMM news." It was half-true, E.J. reasoned. He had convinced Roger to do this story.

Roger stepped forward, flashing his newscaster's smile and showing deep dimples. "I'm Roger Richardson."

"Oh, yeah, I've seen you on television." She seemed impressed but still hesitant. "Could I tell Rick what this is about?"

Roger's smile got brighter. "We wanted to do a profile on him."

She glanced over their shoulders and seemed to notice the cameraman for the first time. "Is that thing running?"

Roger looked back. "You filming, Lyle?"

"Yeah."

The redhead started to shut the door. Roger stuck his foot in the door with impressive speed. E.J. thought he must have done that before. Often.

"Lyle, shut off the camera." To the woman, Roger said, "Ma'am, we only want to ask a few simple questions. We certainly aren't here to cause Rick any trouble."

E.J. was silent. They were here to cause Rick all the trouble they could, but saying so wasn't likely to gain them entrance. Mentioning Mrs. Casey's name wasn't going to get them through the door, either. E.J. stood back and let Rick handle things.

"I don't believe Rick would appreciate you interfering if he knew he had a chance to appear on television," Roger said persuasively.

She paused to consider that, and Roger pressed his advantage. "If he doesn't want to talk to us, naturally we'll leave. Why don't you go ask him?"

"Wait here."

She turned and went back inside.

A minute later Rick was at the door. He had a tanning-salon tan and an air of self-confidence that made E.J. want to punch him out.

"Mr. Wilson?"

"Yes."

Roger stuck out his hand. "Good to meet you. I'm Roger Richardson with WMMM."

"Yeah." Rick was tentative, but the pull of being on television had been more than he could resist. Rick flashed his own pretty-boy smile.

Keep smiling for the camera, you jerk, E.J. silently urged. He wanted to get as much footage as they could before Rick slammed the door in their faces. Then he was going back to the studio with Roger to make sure Roger didn't edit out everything except the redhead. After that, E.J. would finally be able to see Jill.

They hadn't discussed the question of where they would stay tonight, but with Xandralene at Jill's house, things were a bit tight. Why should he and Jill feel cramped when he had a whole empty house?

"I understand you were an instructor at the Avanti Dance Studio?" Roger said.

"Yes." Rick's smile flickered.

"There have been allegations you swindled an elderly lady out of a substantial sum of money."

"I don't know who told you that, but it's not true."

"We'd like to hear your side of this." Roger smiled to show he was Rick's friend.

Rick wasn't buying it. "I don't think I want to talk to you anymore."

"But I—"

This time, when Roger stuck his foot in the door, Rick kicked it out. Apparently Rick had as much experience with this sort of thing as Roger.

As the door slammed shut, E.J. turned to the newscaster. "Well?"

Roger chortled. "He was great. People love this on the news. Old Rick won't be able to borrow bus fare after this airs."

E.J. beamed. "When will it air?"

"Tomorrow, maybe."

"Great."

As they headed to the studio, E.J. couldn't wait to get back to Jill. She had become a drug for him. The more he was with her, the more he wanted to be with her.

He wasn't blind to the fact she was still a tidier person than he. But she was no longer obsessive about it the way she'd been when she moved in. She no longer had to be perfectly dressed before she left the house. She was freer, more fun, happier to be alive.

Jill had become so much a part of his life that he couldn't imagine a future without her.

Yet he knew he still had to get through the weekend and see her end her relationship with Darren before he could feel truly secure.

CHAPTER SIXTEEN

JILL STOOD AT E.J.'s kitchen window and watched Fido frolicking in the backyard. It was late Friday afternoon and Darren would be here soon.

She didn't look forward to the meeting, but she knew it was essential. Darren needed to know that it was over between them and that she wasn't going to change her mind. Because she had loved him once, she had to say her goodbyes in a civilized manner.

E.J. came up behind her. He slipped one arm around her and rested his weight on the cane.

"Do you mind Fido being in your backyard again?" she asked.

"Not on a temporary basis. But I know you'll find a home for him soon."

Did he mean that? She no longer wanted to give Fido up. She had missed him while he was living in the country with Xandralene.

Jill turned to look at him. "E.J.," she began carefully, "I was thinking about keeping Fido."

"Oh?"

She saw the amusement in his eyes and realized he was teasing her. Had he always looked this intoxicating when he smiled? Yes, he had, and she'd noticed it early on, she realized. The wonder of it was that she'd been able to convince herself for so long that he was wrong for her.

E.J. looked out the window. "Uh-oh, looks like Xandralene is still training him with the air-freshener."

Jill watched the black-haired woman bouncing around the deck with Fido bounding after her.

"What a pair," she said.

"Yeah."

She wished she could settle down in front of the television with E.J., but she needed to return home.

She sighed. "I guess I'd better go."

E.J. was silent.

"I'll be back later."

"Yeah."

She sensed he was troubled. "Look, you're not worried about Darren, are you?"

"I tell myself not to be and you tell me not to be, but I'll be glad as heck when it's over and he's gone."

She couldn't imagine what E.J. feared. She'd made it clear over the past two weeks where her heart lay. Neither of them had expressed their love in words, but they hadn't needed to. She was only holding back until she'd seen Darren, because it didn't seem right to say those words to E.J. until Darren knew that things had changed.

Jill leaned over and gave E.J. a peck on the cheek. "If you're very good, there'll be more later where that came from."

"I'll hold you to that."

But he wasn't smiling as she went out the door.

Jill wasn't overly concerned. She intended to put an enormous smile on his face in the very near future. First, though, she must say goodbye to her past.

THE RING HAD COST DARREN a mint. But it would be worth it to see the look on Jill's face. The emerald would match her eyes. The tiny diamonds flanking the big stone had been an extravagance, but Darren had sprung for them.

This would be like a second engagement and he wanted to do it right. He wanted Jill to know how serious he was, especially after she'd been so flaky on the phone the other night.

That wasn't like her, and once she returned to Simmerville, she'd get her head back together.

He pressed harder on the accelerator and passed a car poking along ahead of him. There was no time to waste. Tonight, after he and Jill went out for a nice dinner, he was going to explore some of this new sexiness he saw in her. It was time to push past a cordial relationship and cement things in that little bedroom of her crummy apartment. Then he'd get her out of there and back to a decent life.

E.J. DIDN'T USUALLY self-analyze, but he wondered if his fear of Darren had anything to do with losing Lisa so suddenly. Her death had made E.J. aware of how quickly things could change. Not that he thought Jill would defect to her ex, but fate had fooled him before.

Be cool, he told himself, and went in to turn on the television. It was almost six o'clock and he'd already told Grace to watch the news. He hadn't said why, though.

He clicked the remote, then immediately flipped it off. He shoved a hand through his hair.

Even though Jill hadn't invited him, he simply had to go over there. He couldn't handle just sitting over here, waiting. He saw Darren's car pull into the driveway. It looked even more intensely red today. It spoke of money and comfort and a lot of things E.J. couldn't offer.

So what? Jill didn't care.

But E.J. found himself opening his door anyway and heading down the walkway.

JILL TOOK A DEEP BREATH and opened her door. Darren beamed at her. She couldn't find an answering smile because she was too intent on saying what she had to say.

She wet her dry lips. "Come in."

He did.

She was getting ready to close the door when she saw E.J. coming up the walk.

Jill hesitated, then closed the door. What she had to say to Darren must be said privately.

"Darren, I—"

He folded her against him. "You look so good."

Jill couldn't imagine what was special about the mauve shirt and shorts. She hadn't even bothered to dress up for his visit.

A knock sounded.

Jill closed her eyes and pushed away from Darren.

"I have to get some things clear. I don't want to hurt you, but—"

The knock sounded again, more insistently this time.

Darren frowned at her. "Aren't you going to answer the door?"

"No," she said forcefully. She was going to kill E.J. She loved him but she was going to kill him.

He frowned. "What is going on with you?"

Jill forgot her nice, composed speech. "Darren, it's over," she blurted out. "I don't love you anymore."

"Since when?"

The knock came again.

She shook her head. "I don't know. It doesn't matter."

He moved toward her again. "Jill, I see the stress you're under, here. You're in this cramped apartment and you don't have any real friends. I know how hard it's been for you since we separated. Once we're back in Simmerville, we'll get you some counseling. That will help you calm down again."

"I'm not going back," she declared.

"Jill, you're being irrational. You've wanted to work things out for months. Now, within the space of a few weeks, you change your mind? I don't believe that."

Jill just shook her head again.

"Why don't you pack a few things and we'll go to Simmerville tonight," he said gently. "I hadn't realized how much this place was getting to you."

"Darren—"

He pulled a small box out of his pocket. "Before you say anything, I want you to have this."

He flipped the lid open and she stared at an expensive emerald. Her gaze went from the ring to him. He just didn't get it.

"Darren, it's not *things* I want. I wanted *you* once. I wanted your support and compassion, but I didn't get them. Now I've moved on. You have to, too."

His expression hardened. "I don't think you mean that. Let's go to Simmerville where we can think this through better." He put a hand on her arm.

"No, Darren."

He started walking her toward the door.

Startled, Jill stumbled along beside him. Darren pushed open the door. She tried to wrench away, but he tightened his grasp and pulled her down the sidewalk.

"What's going on?" E.J. shouted.

She looked up to see him standing at his gate.

"Let me go, Darren!"

But Darren was beyond listening to her. A cold fury showed on his face and his jaw jutted out defiantly. Jill realized he'd made up his mind that she would come to her senses once she was away from here. He didn't understand that it was here that she had finally come to see reason.

"She said to let her go."

Darren spared a glance for E.J., who was moving toward them. "Stay out of this, gimp."

Darren was being irrational and Jill knew E.J. couldn't help. It was up to her. She dug her heels into the ground, but Darren's strength was greater. He dragged her toward the car.

She heard E.J.'s cane scraping the sidewalk and heard Fido clopping along beside him. "No, E.J. Go away!" Darren could easily hurt him.

E.J. kept coming. Then she heard a *pssst* noise and saw E.J. spray something toward Darren. Suddenly Fido flung himself on Darren.

"What the—?" Darren released her so abruptly she almost fell backward. He turned and ran.

Fido chased Darren to the car, ripping at his pant leg and barking with glee.

Darren dived into the ritzy car and slammed the door. Fido stood on his hind legs and growled at Darren through the window.

Jill stared in disbelief.

Then she began to laugh.

DARREN GLARED AT THE mutt putting gashes in the flawless finish of his car, then at Jill. She had her arms around the man from next door and she seemed to be laughing and crying at the same time.

She was crazy. He was lucky he had found that out before he made a total mess of his life. And he still had the ring.

Cursing to himself, he stabbed his key into the ignition and drove off before the dog could do any more damage.

JILL LOOKED UP AT E.J. and wiped tears from her eyes.

"Herbal air-freshener?" she inquired when she could speak.

"Yes. Trail-mix scent."

"It seems to have done the trick."

"My bum knee has taught me I don't have to be stronger than the other guy, just smarter."

"I see."

E.J. looked at her with a warmth that made her body tingle. "I don't think Darren will be back," he said.

"No." Jill didn't want him back even if he brought all the jewels and status-symbol cars in the world. She wanted someone down-to-earth and real. That man was standing beside her.

"Since I ruined your chances with Darren, maybe you would consider marrying me?" E.J. asked, almost shyly.

The catch in her throat kept her from responding immediately. Then she questioned huskily, "Is that a proposal?"

"Yes."

"I accept."

She looked into his face and saw the incredible tenderness there. She leaned toward him, and their lips joined in a kiss of commitment.

Jill didn't even pull away when she heard someone rush up.

"What in the world is going on?" Mrs. Casey demanded. "I heard the dog barking and I looked out to see that poor man trapped in his car and the dog clawing at it."

Jill let go of E.J. There would be time enough later to complete their kiss.

"I would have come out that instant but I was watching television and just then they did a spot on Rick." Grace looked toward E.J. "You knew about it, didn't you? That's why you said to watch the news. It was wonderful!"

"A spot about Rick?" Jill demanded.

"Yes, telling how he takes advantage of widows," Grace said. "Oh, they kept saying 'alleged' and words like that, but you could see they thought he was a crook."

Jill turned to E.J. "Did you have anything to do with this?"

"I'm sure he did," Mrs. Casey replied. "But what about that poor man in the red car? Do you think he was hurt? I hate to say this, Jill, but that's why I didn't want to have a dog around to start with. They can be so dangerous. Did you see how he chased that man? I'm sure he ruined his nice trousers."

Jill put a hand over her mouth to stifle her laughter.

"Darren will be fine when he gets back to where he belongs," E.J. assured Grace.

"You're certain?" She looked from one to the other doubtfully.

"Yes, Grace."

"All right, then."

She went back into her house.

"Why don't we go inside and work out the details of our wedding?" Jill suggested. Laughter bubbled in her throat. She had ruined Darren's day, yet she had never been happier.

IT WAS A SIMPLE WEDDING.

They waited until after E.J.'s surgery. He still carried his cane, but he needed it less and less. Every day, Jill could see his strength returning in greater force. Every day she was more certain he would be able to do all the things he loved.

It was a nice feeling to watch him recovering.

The marriage took place in a little stone chapel near downtown Charlotte. It only seated a hundred people, but it was perfect for their intimate wedding.

Jill wore an ivory tea-length gown with lace on the collar and sleeves. E.J. wore a tux he'd rented for the occasion. It had to be back first thing Monday.

After the ceremony, they went to a women's-club building for the reception. Jill's mother eyed the Incredible Edibles caterers as if they were a terrorist group about to take over the reception with guns. Isaac wore a string tie and a clean white shirt. He brought a little group of musicians who played while Charlie examined the food uncertainly. Roger worked the room as if he were a politician seeking election.

The photographer had just finished taking pictures of Jill when her grandmother came up beside her. She tugged at her white gloves and pursed her lips. "Is there something wrong with the young lady serving the cake?"

"No, Grandmother."

"I consider red satin inappropriate attire for a wedding."

Jill smiled indulgently. "Xandralene looks good in red."

Her grandmother sniffed. "At the very least, I don't think she should hand out cards for her new palm-reading service while she serves the cake."

"Is she?" Jill giggled.

Her grandmother's chin lifted, but she didn't say anything further, apparently having despaired of making Jill see reason.

Around the room, a few people danced to the down-home music. Others watched or chatted in the background. Jill looked across the room at E.J. He seemed to beckon her with his eyes, and that was good enough for her. She started to head toward him, but halfway there, Grace intercepted her.

"Maybe we could go powder our noses, dear," she suggested, and patted her newly permed hair.

"Of course, Grace."

"Tell me about Isaac," Mrs. Casey said before they'd even reached the ladies' room.

"He's a nice man."

"He took a break from playing music and danced a waltz with me. He's not a great dancer like Rick," Grace confided, as she pulled a compact out of her purse, "but he has a certain homespun charm."

Jill looked at the sparkle in her former landlady's eyes. "Do you like him?"

"Yes. I wanted to make sure you think it's all right to take him up on his offer to teach me how to play the spoons."

Jill smiled. "I think that's a wonderful idea."

"Good. I might even see if he'd like to play putt-putt golf sometime. I'm not bragging, but I am rather good at it."

"I'll bet you are."

Grace put her compact away. "We can't keep the gentlemen waiting."

They made their way back out to join the others, and Jill looked up to see E.J. approaching. He pulled her into his arms.

"Let's go somewhere private," he said in a tone that made her want to purr.

"Yes, let's." Jill was more than ready to slip away with him and begin their life together.

They said their goodbyes amid a round of kisses and hugs, then darted out to E.J.'s old blue car.

Fido waited in the back seat, ready to accompany them on their honeymoon and protect them from anyone unfortunate enough to favor the scent of herbal air-freshener.

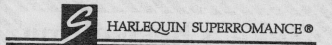
HARLEQUIN SUPERROMANCE ®

COMING NEXT MONTH

#618 MEG & THE MYSTERY MAN • Elise Title (*Class of '78*)
Meg Delgado goes undercover as a wealthy socialite on the
cruise ship Galileo. Her mission: to catch a thief. Her suspect:
Noah Danforth, who's got the looks, the charm and the wit of a
Cary Grant. But if Meg isn't who she seems to be, neither is Noah.
And together they discover that deception and disguise lead to
danger...and to romance!

#619 THE COWBOY'S LOVER • Ada Steward
Lexi Conley kidnaps rodeo cowboy Jake Thorn because she
needs him to manage her family's ranch while her father's in the
hospital. It doesn't help that Jake, her sister's ex-husband, may be
the father of Lexi's adopted son—or that he's still the only man
she's ever loved.

#620 SAFEKEEPING • Peg Sutherland (*Women Who Dare*)
An unexpected snowstorm traps Quinn Santori and her two young
companions in an isolated mountain cabin. A cabin that's already
inhabited—by a man toting a gun. They make an odd foursome—
Quinn, the two little girls in her charge and ex-con Whit Sloane.
And chances are their number will increase to five before the snow
melts. *Quinn's about to have a baby!*

#621 THE LOCKET • Brenna Todd
Transported back through time, Erin Sawyer is mistaken for her
double, the adulterous Della Munro, whose husband is a powerful
and dangerous man. But Erin finds herself attracted to his partner,
Waite MacKinnon, a man whose compelling eyes have been
haunting her dreams for what seems like forever.

AVAILABLE NOW:

Take 4 bestselling love stories FREE

Plus get a FREE surprise gift!

HARLEQUIN SUPERROMANCE®

WOMEN WHO DARE
They take chances, make changes
and follow their hearts

#620 SAFEKEEPING by Peg Sutherland

The last thing Quinn Santore expects when she plans a fall
afternoon with her two young companions is to be trapped by a
snowstorm in an isolated mountain cabin. Especially a cabin
already inhabited...by a man toting a gun. They make an odd
foursome: Quinn, the two little girls in her charge and ex-con
Whit Sloane. And chances are their number will increase to
five before the snow melts. Quinn's about to have a baby!

Author Peg Sutherland weaves an emotional tale of excitement,
intrigue, danger and romance.

Watch for SAFEKEEPING by Peg Sutherland

AVAILABLE IN NOVEMBER, WHEREVER
HARLEQUIN BOOKS ARE SOLD.

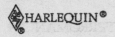 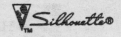

The movie event of the season can be the reading event of the year!

Lights… The lights go on in October when CBS presents Harlequin/Silhouette Sunday Matinee Movies. These four movies are based on bestselling Harlequin and Silhouette novels.

Camera… As the cameras roll, be the first to read the original novels the movies are based on!

Action… Through this offer, you can have these books sent directly to you! Just fill in the order form below and you could be reading the books…before the movie!

48288-4	Treacherous Beauties by Cheryl Emerson $3.99 U.S./$4.50 CAN.	☐
83305-9	Fantasy Man by Sharon Green $3.99 U.S./$4.50 CAN.	☐
48289-2	A Change of Place by Tracy Sinclair $3.99 U.S./$4.50CAN.	☐
83306-7	Another Woman by Margot Dalton $3.99 U.S./$4.50 CAN.	☐

TOTAL AMOUNT	$
POSTAGE & HANDLING	$
($1.00 for one book, 50¢ for each additional)	
APPLICABLE TAXES*	$ _____
TOTAL PAYABLE	$ _____
(check or money order—please do not send cash)	

To order, complete this form and send it, along with a check or money order for the total above, payable to Harlequin Books, to: **In the U.S.:** 3010 Walden Avenue, P.O. Box 9047, Buffalo, NY 14269-9047; **In Canada:** P.O. Box 613, Fort Erie, Ontario, L2A 5X3.

Name: _____

Address: _____ City: _____

State/Prov.: _____ Zip/Postal Code: _____

*New York residents remit applicable sales taxes.
 Canadian residents remit applicable GST and provincial taxes.   CBSPR

"HOORAY FOR HOLLYWOOD" SWEEPSTAKES

HERE'S HOW THE SWEEPSTAKES WORKS

OFFICIAL RULES — NO PURCHASE NECESSARY

To enter, complete an Official Entry Form or hand print on a 3" x 5" card the words "HOORAY FOR HOLLYWOOD", your name and address and mail your entry in the pre-addressed envelope (if provided) or to: "Hooray for Hollywood" Sweepstakes, P.O. Box 9076, Buffalo, NY 14269-9076 or "Hooray for Hollywood" Sweepstakes, P.O. Box 637, Fort Erie, Ontario L2A 5X3. Entries must be sent via First Class Mail and be received no later than 12/31/94. No liability is assumed for lost, late or misdirected mail.

Winners will be selected in random drawings to be conducted no later than January 31, 1995 from all eligible entries received.

Grand Prize: A 7-day/6-night trip for 2 to Los Angeles, CA including round trip air transportation from commercial airport nearest winner's residence, accommodations at the Regent Beverly Wilshire Hotel, free rental car, and $1,000 spending money. (Approximate prize value which will vary dependent upon winner's residence: $5,400.00 U.S.); 500 Second Prizes: A pair of "Hollywood Star" sunglasses (prize value: $9.95 U.S. each). Winner selection is under the supervision of D.L. Blair, Inc., an independent judging organization, whose decisions are final. Grand Prize travelers must sign and return a release of liability prior to traveling. Trip must be taken by 2/1/96 and is subject to airline schedules and accommodations availability.

Sweepstakes offer is open to residents of the U.S. (except Puerto Rico) and Canada who are 18 years of age or older, except employees and immediate family members of Harlequin Enterprises, Ltd., its affiliates, subsidiaries, and all agencies, entities or persons connected with the use, marketing or conduct of this sweepstakes. All federal, state, provincial, municipal and local laws apply. Offer void wherever prohibited by law. Taxes and/or duties are the sole responsibility of the winners. Any litigation within the province of Quebec respecting the conduct and awarding of prizes may be submitted to the Regie des loteries et courses du Quebec. All prizes will be awarded; winners will be notified by mail. No substitution of prizes are permitted. Odds of winning are dependent upon the number of eligible entries received.

Potential grand prize winner must sign and return an Affidavit of Eligibility within 30 days of notification. In the event of non-compliance within this time period, prize may be awarded to an alternate winner. Prize notification returned as undeliverable may result in the awarding of prize to an alternate winner. By acceptance of their prize, winners consent to use of their names, photographs, or likenesses for purpose of advertising, trade and promotion on behalf of Harlequin Enterprises, Ltd., without further compensation unless prohibited by law. A Canadian winner must correctly answer an arithmetical skill-testing question in order to be awarded the prize.

For a list of winners (available after 2/28/95), send a separate stamped, self-addressed envelope to: Hooray for Hollywood Sweepstakes 3252 Winners, P.O. Box 4200, Blair, NE 68009.

CBSRLS

OFFICIAL ENTRY COUPON

"Hooray for Hollywood"
SWEEPSTAKES!

Yes, I'd love to win the Grand Prize — a vacation in Hollywood — or one of 500 pairs of "sunglasses of the stars"! Please enter me in the sweepstakes!

This entry must be received by December 31, 1994.
Winners will be notified by January 31, 1995.

Name _____

Address _____ Apt. _____

City _____

State/Prov. _____ Zip/Postal Code _____

Daytime phone number _____
(area code)

Mail all entries to: Hooray for Hollywood Sweepstakes,
P.O. Box 9076, Buffalo, NY 14269-9076.
In Canada, mail to: Hooray for Hollywood Sweepstakes,
P.O. Box 637, Fort Erie, ON L2A 5X3.

KCH

OFFICIAL ENTRY COUPON

"Hooray for Hollywood"
SWEEPSTAKES!

Yes, I'd love to win the Grand Prize — a vacation in Hollywood — or one of 500 pairs of "sunglasses of the stars"! Please enter me in the sweepstakes!

This entry must be received by December 31, 1994.
Winners will be notified by January 31, 1995.

Name _____

Address _____ Apt. _____

City _____

State/Prov. _____ Zip/Postal Code _____

Daytime phone number _____
(area code)

Mail all entries to: Hooray for Hollywood Sweepstakes,
P.O. Box 9076, Buffalo, NY 14269-9076.
In Canada, mail to: Hooray for Hollywood Sweepstakes,
P.O. Box 637, Fort Erie, ON L2A 5X3.

KCH